DOG

GIRL

GABI JUSTICE

Swoon
ROMANCE

Trade Paperback ISBN: 978-1-951710-05-7
ePub ISBN: 978-1-951710-06-4
Mobipocket ISBN: 978-1-951710-07-1

Published by Swoon Romance, Raleigh, NC 27609
Cover design: Danielle Doolittle

Praise for *Dog Girl*

"Fast-paced and poignant, *Dog Girl* expertly conveys the anxieties of high school, the thrill of a first love, and how dogs transform our hearts in all the best ways. Kendall is the underdog you'll love rooting for." — Cheyanne Young, YA author of *The Last Wish of Sasha Cade* and *The Breakup Support Group*

"Gabi has built vivid, complex relationships that are real and heartwarming. *Dog Girl* starts with a thrilling rescue that thrusts you into the story and has you rooting for Kendall from page one. Gabi seamlessly weaves tough topics like anxiety, death, and animal abuse, with light-hearted, laugh-out-loud, coming-of-age romantic comedy." — Jaimie Engle, MG and YA author of *Metal Mouth* and *Dreadlands*

"A great YA for those who love romance, dogs, and a bit of mystery." — Katie Kaleski YA author of *You, Me, and Letting Go* and *Bookstores, Crushes, and Mortal Enemies*

For my furry babies that filled our home with love and laughter, and kept my skin babies safe and warm.

DOG

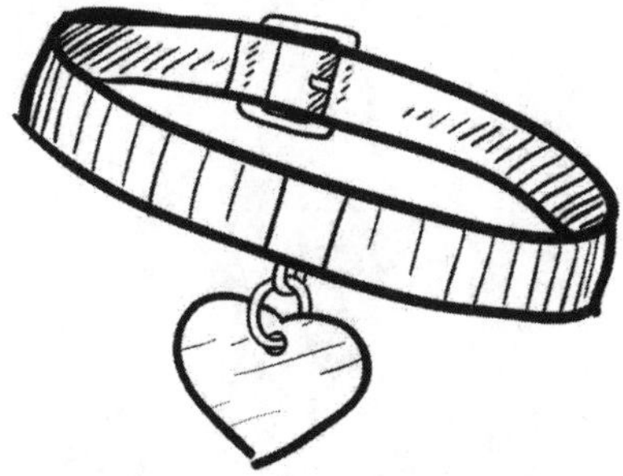

GIRL

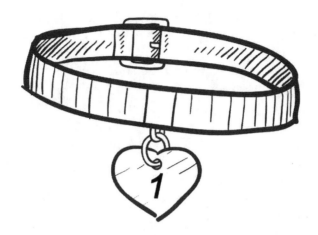

The pit bull watches me pull the utility cutters from my bag. She thrashes and barks. Foam oozes from her pink and gray lips. She's not rabid, just in shock. Glassy eyes open wide and dart from me to Rock to the equipment. It's the equipment that frightens her the most. The cutters are shiny and sharp. Abused dogs don't like the hardware.

My gut plummets.

"Kendall," Rock says.

"I know." I set down the cutters. Right now, her trust is most important.

"Now!" I shout.

Rock brings the snare down around her neck, securing my safety.

Let's see if I can work the knot loose without the cutters.

I take in her beauty. She's a blue. Precise diamonds tattoo her ankles. White fur paints her chest like the perfectly imperfect strokes of an abstract painting. Red blood smudges her gray coat and stains the rope that binds her to the railroad tracks.

The rails pulsate, and the air rumbles. I wince. I shouldn't be worrying, I should only be acting, but of course, I freeze like a newbie.

Get your shit together, Kendall! This isn't your first rescue. So what if Mom's not here.

"You okay, Peanut?" Rock's deep, rich voice falls over me like a hug of encouragement.

My hands steady, but my insides quiver.

The dog's lip curls, exposing fierce teeth. It's a warning. Rock has a good hold, but pits are powerful, and her adrenaline is pumping. One false move and she could jerk free.

I work the knot wrapped around her front paw. Someone with strong hands secured this. With all my force, I can only loosen the interlock a millimeter. The prickly rope cuts and splinters. Hurtful fibers slip under my fingernails. I should have gloves on. Rookie move.

In my head, Mom's voice scolds, *Stop being a baby.*

The pit twitches.

Have I pinched her? No.

It must be the tremble of the rails. She's smart and realizes the train is close. Too close. I tug and tug and tug until the first knot gives. But she remains bound at her hind ankle.

A maroon stain sneaks across her. She's fading. Oh my God! Is that a bullet wound? It looks minor, but I need a tourniquet. But the knot. The train. The blood. I can't do it all.

The train's single headlight emerges as it rounds the bend several football fields away. The pit starts shaking again, and I can't blame her. My heart pounds in my chest, and the tears, layering under my eyelids, burn. Her body squirms. She's still fighting.

Fight, Kendall. Fight!

The train is way too close. I need more time. The wind stirs. Gritty granules of dirt lash my cheeks. The whistle screams murder. The shriek scrapes and claws at my eardrums. It's a death sentence.

I work and work the knot. So much blood. I reach for the cutters, and she thrashes again. Rock struggles to keep her down.

"Shh. It's okay. Okay," I coo.

Not okay! I need those cutters. The train is way too close. The angry face of the mechanical beast roars at me louder than Rock's hollering. What's he saying?

The cutters! I have to use cutters.

"Pretty Blue, please don't freak out." In one fluid movement, I grab them and slice the rope in half, then shove her away from the tracks as the train barrels past.

Rock whisks the pit far away from danger.

I stumble, hands and feet digging into the ground for traction. Finding my balance, I stand upright and watch in awe as the train cars clatter by. Tornadoes of dust swirl around us. Blood and sweat and earth taint the breeze.

I did it.

Rock muzzles and wraps the dog, then carries her to the cage in the back of the truck.

Exhaustion, thrills, shakes all travel from my head to my toes as I trail behind Rock's enormous shadow.

I did it!

The middle-aged woman in a housedress stares at us. I need to approach her. Usually, I'd be the one consoling her while Mom did the heroic work. Today, I have to do both, since Mom got stuck in downtown Miami traffic.

I swallow away the biting dryness in my throat. "Hello, ma'am, I'm Kendall from Delray Dog Rescue. You called us, right?"

"Yes. Oh my goodness. I couldn't believe it when I saw her there. It's just awful." The lady's voice trembles. She takes a steadying breath. "Thank you. She would've died." Her brow creases, several horizontal lines crisscrossing the diagonal ones, making her face a road map of worry. Her hands grip together, turning her fingers blue.

"She's lucky you found her." I unfold her hands, taking one in mine.

She gladly squeezes my hand and the lines on her face smooth.

"Will she be okay?" She hesitates. "Will she live?"

"I've seen many dogs recover one hundred percent. She'll be fine. Don't worry. We'll find the right home where she'll feel safe and live a normal life." I've given this speech so many times that it's embedded in my gray matter.

The lady reaches out a hand to touch the squares of the dog crate. "You're a strong girl."

Wrapped in the bloodstained blanket, all adrenaline drained, the dog beholds the lady as if to say, *Thank you.*

Then the well breaks, and tears gush out. Trembling, the lady wipes her face and tries to hold in her sobs, but it's hopeless.

I hand her a clipboard with paper and pen. "I need your address and phone number."

She scribbles her information as best as she can and hands it back.

"Thank you. The police will be contacting you."

She nods, still too overwhelmed to talk.

The truck's tires are rolling when I jump in and pull the door shut. Rock speeds away. I'll see that lady again at the rescue center. These two are destined to be together. The paper she signed reads, "Julia Shapovalov," and she lives in an apartment complex close to here.

Before she disappears into the distance, I wave to Ms. Shapovalov and smile.

She smiles back, stands taller, and waves rapidly. She saved a dog's life today.

"See you soon," I whisper. My heartbeat sends the warmth of satisfaction into my blood. It's a steady beat now, all anticipation gone.

A boy points an iPhone at me. He stands on the grass near the tracks with his BMX bike between his legs. He looks familiar.

Spencer Conard's little brother? I squint for better focus. It must be him. What's that little ass doing here?

T he truck pulls into the animal hospital. Rock rushes the pit bull inside. The five-thirty alarm on my phone buzzes, reminding me how late it is. Typically, I'd be done with chores by now, or at least almost done, and heading into the house for a shower. God, I need a shower.

I could follow Rock. I'm definitely concerned about that sweet dog, but my part in this rescue is over.

You're so far behind. The anxiety stirs.

Inhale. Exhale. It's okay.

I hurry along the sandy path between the vet and the rescue center. Gotta get back on schedule. Three rambunctious, disobedient dogs need training, and the wolf-rescue flyers for Spring Festival are still not finished. Plus Algebra II homework. There's no way. Not enough time. My breathing quickens.

Calm down. Slow inhale. Exhale. A few deep breaths, and the rapid-fire breathing reduces to a controllable smolder.

I pass the length of the yard and close in on the barn, when Cruz nearly knocks me over. "Cruz!"

Mid-jog, he says, "Sorry. Damn bus was late. Just got here."

"Where's Mom?"

"Don't know." He gives me a small wave, but no smile. "Gotta go do work."

That's weird. Cruz never misses an opportunity to talk, especially when it comes to rescues. He loves to hear the stories. He's desperate to go on calls, but he's only been here a month, and so far, none of us are very impressed with his abilities.

I didn't expect Mom to be gone this long. And she never explained why the Miami agent wanted to see her.

The phone alarm shrieks again, snapping me back to panic mode. I rush into the barn.

My boy, Rascal, spots me. His tail whips in quick circles, and his paws drum the ground. The unconditional love soothes me. He smiles. I grin back. I love him so much.

"Let's go, boy." I lead him to the training area.

Rascal, being his usual stubborn self, won't crawl through the agility tunnel, so I enter the tube on my hands and knees, creep halfway, then turn around. He pokes his head in and growl-mumbles.

"Get in here. I don't have time for this." My fist pounds the ground.

"Arrooh," he answers.

I laugh. "Come on, boy."

He tilts his head, backs away, inches forward, tilts his head again, and talks in his hilarious dog howl.

"You can do it." At the sound of my high pitch, he perks up and touches the tube with his front paw but doesn't enter. "Tease." I pound the floor with my fists again, shake my head, and whip my stringy brown hair around. That gets him. He races inside, trampling me with dirty paws in an attempt to ram his way past.

"Rascal!" I'm shoved up against the wall of the tube.

We're squished side by side. Wet, slobbery kisses drench my face. His deafening bark rings my ear. Lick, bark, lick, bark, as if this is a fun game we're playing. He nudges me with his slimy, wet nose and eventually squeezes past, scratching and tickling. With difficulty I turn and follow. I'm sure from the outside it looks like some freakish anaconda digesting a gator.

"Ouwa! Rascal!" One of his nails snags my skin.

He whips around to face me. I brace for another impact. Instead, he opens his mouth in a tongue-dangling, bull terrier smile, so I can't stay mad at him. He's adorable with that long nose, pink tongue, and goofy spotted face. He has muscles so dense he can drag a person without a problem.

"Rascal!" I cover my nose as the foul odor of his fart encircles me. "Rude!"

No remorse. He simply turns back around and saunters out the other end to chase anything that moves.

I crawl to the opening, stick my head out, and gulp in the fresh air.

A guy leans over the fence. An extremely cute guy. He's grinning wide, laughing. How stupid I must look, bested by a fifty-pound bull terrier. My cheeks burn. Oh my God, is my face bright red? I'm a tomato-red idiot rolling around in a tube with a dog. Wonderful!

"That looks fun." His piercing blue eyes mock me.

"Very." I'm still stuck in the tube. I start to ask him if he's a Saint Paul's guy. He looks like a preppy asshole. They're all the same—fauxhawk haircut with spiked blond tips, clean sporty clothes because he probably doesn't sweat, and a superiority complex. However, the amount of embarrassment zooming through my body will not allow proper functioning of speech right now.

I rush to stand, tripping over my feet, and brush the dirt off my clothes in an attempt to look somewhat presentable. It's not working. In fact, it's worse. Large mud stains smudge my shirt. The old, faded Spider-Man shirt! All the air leaves my lungs. No wonder everyone thinks I'm weird.

He's even more gorgeous close-up. A flawless face, a bad-boy grin with boy-next-door dimples, and those blond tips are actually from the sun, not the salon.

God, I sound like one of Vicky's stupid *Cosmo* magazine articles. Listicle: "Top Five Things on the Hot Meter."

But honestly, he's probably an Instagram model. I can't help but gawk with a huge smile plastered across my face. I might as well have a neon sign flashing: *Seventeen-year-old virgin, approach with caution. She might attack.*

I snap out of it and force myself to act professionally. It's strangely difficult to get my mouth to cooperate and stay straight.

"May I help you?"

"Yes. I need community service hours for school, and I'd like to help out here."

Even his voice is smooth.

"Have you ever been convicted of a crime?" I ask.

"Huh? No." He laughs, the kind of choke-laugh that gets stuck in the back of your throat when someone has just said something ridiculous.

"Then you can't work here." I turn my back on him. Those perfect cheekbones are too much. If I don't look at him, then maybe my heart will stop doing circus acts.

"I can go to the Walgreens and shoplift a pack of gum if that's the prerequisite to volunteer here," he says.

My lips defiantly curl upward at his joke. Cute, articulate, and funny. I'm screwed.

Just keep your uncooperative face toward Rascal. Remember, he's a Saint Paul Boy, and they're all spoiled, entitled tools.

I struggle to ignore whatever this is that's happening inside my body, and gather my facial expression into a proper attitude of indifference. I spin around and face him. "I'm afraid that even if you so generously shoplifted on the rescue's behalf, we still would *not* have a position available for you."

Rascal takes advantage of my distraction and digs a giant hole in the dirt.

"No, Rascal!" I grab the leash and clip it to his collar, then he jolts. His brute force pulls my legs out from under me, and I face-plant in the mud. He drags me a few inches before I can get to my knees and wrestle him back into obedience.

Suddenly Saint Paul Boy's hands clamp under my sweaty armpits, pulling me to my feet.

"What are you doing?"

"You're welcome." He removes his hands.

"No! You never jump the fence. Rascal could've attacked you, and we'd get sued." He's in my personal space. I'm nearly as tall as him, and it takes all my nerve not to look away, to stand my ground, to inhale his hypnotic cologne.

Why didn't I take that shower?

But he just snickers and gestures to Rascal. "Him?"

He's still too close. Maybe his olfactory glands don't work? That's a possibility, right?

"Rascal doesn't look vicious at all." Cute Saint Paul Boy cocks one luscious eyebrow.

Rascal sits next to us with his tongue flopping out and gooey slobber bouncing all over the place, that goofy grin lighting up his expression.

"It's obvious you know nothing about dogs." I turn to Rascal and deflate. *Come on, you're a bully breed. Do something to support my argument! Growl? Just a little growl. How about a rumble?*

I yank Rascal, which I shouldn't, and immediately regret it. My social helplessness isn't his fault. I lead him over to the ramps, hoping that will normalize this situation. Saint Paul Boy doesn't move and continues to stare at me. The mud dries on my cheek. It itches and reeks of dog poop. If I could, I'd curl up in the corner and die.

Why is he still here? Don't look at him. Keep working.

My eyes never leave Rascal as he masters the first ramp and ascends the second.

"You're bleeding," Saint Paul Boy says.

"What?" I glance down and see a smear of blood on my arm. It's from earlier. It must be the pit bull's blood. "I'm fine." I rub it, but it's dried onto my skin and won't wipe off.

Saint Paul Boy offers a bandana handkerchief.

What is this, the fifties? "Uh. No, thank you."

"Hello. May I help you?" Shane appears out of nowhere. Rascal didn't even notice her, but he does now. He barks and tugs the leash. My stepmom is his favorite.

She eyeballs me, concerned I've allowed a stranger into the dog pit. Mom would be livid, but Shane gets worried, not mad.

"Yes, you may." He politely extends his hand over the fence.

She shakes it generously. They exchange greetings that I can't hear over Rascal's barking. I give up and let go of the leash so he'll shut up.

"I need community service hours for my senior year. It's a graduation requirement. I love dogs and was hoping I could help out." His dazzling blue orbs slide in my direction.

He wouldn't last a day here. We don't need him. I'm sure Shane is going to say no.

"Yes," she says.

What? Yes! Why is she doing this?

"We could use a strong boy like you. Corvette just left us, and he was about your build. No medical conditions, right? You can lift heavy bags?"

Ah. That's it. Cruz is late, I was gone, and nothing got done, so she needs someone to unload the Science Diet truck.

"Sure." He shrugs.

As if he's ever done manual labor. Ha!

"Great. Come with me," Shane says.

His eyes widen in surprise.

I snort. Those neat, sporty clothes are going to get so filthy.

"Now?" he asks Shane, but looks at me for assistance.

I smirk and glance down at the pristine whiteness of his shorts. Overwhelming satisfaction fills my chest, and I suppress the giggles.

"Yes, of course." Her chin lowers, and her brows rise.

"Great, let's go." His voice remains smoothly confident, but the slack in his smirk reveals the effect of Shane's challenge.

He follows in her wake. He's tall, six feet or more, and thin but definitely strong, carrying those broad shoulders proudly. Long, lean, tan legs with powerful quads and calves. And that butt. Wow!

He turns around and busts me checking out his ass. His lips return to a full smirk. It's a gut punch.

Frantic anger strikes like a bolt of thrilling—but painful—electricity. I can't stop the critical voice inside my head. *He saw you checking him out! You're an idiot! Good job, Kendall. You deserve that dog girl label. Actually, you've stepped it up to dirty, red-faced, weird dog girl. Why in a million years did you think you were capable of interacting with a guy like that?*

I should've been busy training Rascal and totally ignoring Saint Paul Boy.

Rascal's exuberant face bounces as he pants, oblivious to my internal death.

"Traitor!" I growl. "You're as dumb as a stump."

To this he bows his head.

My heart breaks. I bend down and give him a generous scratching on his sternum. "I'm sorry, boy." The tightness in my chest fades as I watch Rascal's tongue hang and flap with joyful satisfaction. "You're way cuter than he is."

I risk a peek over my shoulder. Saint Paul Boy is carrying one of the giant dog-food bags off the truck, and he's looking over here.

What's behind me? I turn around. Nothing's there.

I turn back and catch his eyes on me. Now he's smiling. This isn't good! The web of anxiety stretches and shudders.

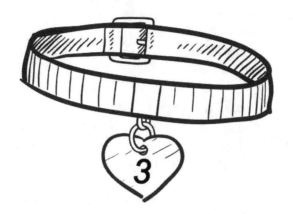

About twenty balled-up pieces of paper lie next to the Spider-Man trash can three feet from my bed. My best friend would be appalled.
You're killing the trees. And you suck at basketball, she'd say.
I snap a photo of the crime scene and send it to her.
She responds immediately, and I laugh at her funny Bitmoji.

    Vicky: Stop mrdring trees n u need a
    new trashcan.
    Me: Ha! I do

Remnants of eight-year-old me dot the room. Spider-Man trash can, one poster of Black Widow and two of Thor, along with several Marvel comics stacked on top of the dresser. I still read those.

    Vicky: Go 2 Bed!
    Me: k Night V!
    Vicky: Goodnight :)

I hold up the flyer. It's finally perfect, with a tug-at-your-heartstrings photo of the timber wolf, Dragon. His eyes are big and round and precious. Just enough desperation but not too much. I don't want to come across as pathetic, even though I am. At this point, kissing feet for money is a valid option.

My glass jar overflows with dollar bills, but it only adds up to $137.14. That may be enough for a one-way plane ticket to Puerto Rico, but it's not enough for two tickets and not enough for the three-hour shuttle ride.

I bow my head and moan, "Why does it have to be so hard?" But I plod on and review the flyer one last time.

> *Timber wolf abandoned in Mayaguez, Puerto Rico. Domesticated. Needs a home. Please donate to the Delray Dog Rescue before it's too late to save his life. Any amount will go a long way! Thank you for your support!*

My phone chimes. It's an email from Daniel, the assistant at the shelter holding Dragon. He's sent a nice get-well-soon note. I read it and can't hate myself more. I've dropped to a new depth of deplorable. He doesn't deserve my lies.

On this week's menu of excuses—the flu. He thinks I'm suffering from a fever of 103 degrees. His sweet email might just make me sick to my stomach. I can't believe I've given him another made-up reason for not being on that plane to Mayaguez, the one I promised I'd be on five months ago. Five months of lies. I mean, really, what kind of person does that? I've dug a hole so deep that not even a prairie dog could claw its way out.

Peter Parker, the personification of my anxiety, a coping mechanism my therapist mentioned and one I twisted to a whole new level of distortion, spins his nasty webbing inside of me. Guilt and self-loathing combined with exhaustion are the perfect storm for him—my friendly neighborhood inner demon. More proof that I'm fricking weird.

Forcing my way out of this self-inflicted pity party, I snatch the flyer and head to the office inside the barn to print off copies. The machine spits out one after the other.

Is this going to work? Will I finally make enough money to get Dragon?

Dragon's face swims in my thoughts. I can't let them euthanize him. His precious little life can't go to waste because some asshole deserted him on an island. I don't care how many dog biscuits I have to bake and sell, how many times I need to solicit money from strangers, or how often my panic attacks skim the surface of my outer calm. I'll do it! I'll fight to keep Peter contained inside the glass vivarium overwhelming my chest. Use every penny I can scrounge up. That wolf is going to come home.

The copier chokes out the last flyer, then makes a strange noise that sounds dangerously bad. Shane will kill me if I've broken it, but I don't have the strength to deal with this right now. I'm so tired, and it's so late.

Most nights I sleep in the barn. It can be warm, but tonight the sea breeze flows through. The east-to-west design was intended to carry the air right through the middle to keep the horses comfortable. Now dog kennels line the walls. Two beanbags sit toward the back, my designated corner, where I keep my books and a photo of Dad.

I stand at the edge of the squishy mounds, close my eyes, and let go. Weightlessness rushes through me. It only lasts seconds, but it's ecstatic, or as close as I'm ever going to get to ecstasy. My thrills come from free-falling into beanbag chairs. So sad.

The rhythm of the breathing dogs relaxes me. My eyelids shut, but my mind races from Dragon's plight to the train speeding toward Rock and me over and over again. Spencer Conard's little brother on his fancy bike loops my thoughts too. Why was he taking pictures of us? He's so creepy. I'm cold and disturbed and jerk awake. It's been six years since I slept without nightmares.

Little Lucy whimpers. I need to check on her soon, but right now I don't want to move. I want to keep staring out the back window above the door at the ten stars that light the blackness. One must be an airplane. If I concentrate, I believe it's moving. It glides ever so slowly across the vast inky space. It makes me feel small in my tiny corner of the world, the place where I talk to Dad. He's out there, somewhere in that great dark abyss.

"Crazy day today. We got a new rescue, and it was bad, Dad. Real bad."

He grimaces, and I shiver.

"Third shot dog in two months. And Mom hasn't said yet, but I think she found something awful in Miami today."

He nods as if he's sitting on the beanbag next to me with a pensive expression and his legs crossed. All college professor–looking.

"I named her Trax. Clever, huh?"

His approving smile morphs into a sly grin. He wants to talk about Saint Paul Boy.

My eyes roll automatically. I don't want to talk about this. As horrible as the pit's rescue was, I'd rather talk about that. But he persists, so I cave.

"Yeah! So what?"

He gives me that look. The look only parents can give, like you're paper-thin.

"Okay, okay. We have a new guy, and he's cute. Too cute. I can't act normal around him, or as close to normal as is possible for me."

His voice comes through, *Good. You need more human friends.*

I argue, as always. "These are my friends. Little Lucy, Rascal, Duke, and all the others who will come and go. Four-leggers are most trustworthy, Dad."

I can almost hear his laugh. Almost.

"Plus, Jimmy and Vicky are humans!"

He smiles so reassuringly that I need to keep explaining. How he does that, I don't know. He's always been able to get me to babble on and release all my secrets.

"I don't feel the need to have more friends. It's quality over quantity. Isn't that what you use to say?"

Used to.

The tears don't reach my eyes, but they're always ready to report for duty like obedient guard dogs. Their twinge creeps as far as my throat, but I swallow them away. It's been six years. Six years of insomnia. Six years of talking to a photo. But I haven't forgotten his laugh, his sayings, his everything.

I study his face in the crumpled four-by-six photo nailed to the wooden wall, taken a day before the car accident. The characteristics of my face have grown and spread into his. I'm lucky that he was good-looking. He was beautiful for a man, and I am handsome for a young lady. At least, that's what people tell me. I'm sure I'll like getting old with his face. It's strange, though, to watch my face morph with age, and yet his will remain the same, faintly lined, lightly tanned, and deeply striking. Mom says that's why she's with a woman now: no other man on the planet could match the beauty of Dad inside and out. Maybe she's joking, but I'm not sure.

Mom has told me their love story several times, but I never tire of it. At sixteen, she fell madly in love with this bad boy about to go to jail. According to her, he hung with a loser crowd and did stupid shit. When he got out two years later, he swept her off her feet. They foolishly got pregnant, as Mom says, then adds some take-back comment like, *You weren't an accident honey*, or *You were born out of passion and love*, or *Being pregnant with you was the best time of my life.*

14

My usual response is, *Whatever, Mom, I get that being pregnant at nineteen is not ideal.*

Then we laugh, and she tells me how they bought the property from some guy named Uncle Bill, who is of no relation to us. He'd sold the remaining two horses on his ranch and wanted to retire to Wisconsin. So with me strapped to Mom's chest or Dad's back, they turned the barn into a dog rescue. A place for second chances.

The story is beyond romantic, and I can't fade the smile that sneaks across my face whenever I relive it in my head. It's the reason I have to work so hard. The reason making friends means nothing. I don't need friends. I need this place. The dogs and the parolees need this place too.

My fingers trail across the photograph. "Miss you." I have his determination, his pride, and his sense of obligation to save dogs.

Lucy whimpers again and stirs me from my smudgy thoughts. I clamber out of the beanbag sinkhole and release the latch on the metal gate. It clatters. Mom has impressive silent opening skills, but I don't, and Little Lucy lifts up her head, wet nose in the air, eyes mostly closed. She sniffs on instinct, but she knows it's me. I pick her up and bring her to my perch and plunge back into the cushy lumps.

We snuggle. This infuriates Mom. She's told me over and over, "I can't find a home for a dog that requires human contact to sleep. You're ruining Lucy's chances for adoption." But I've done this for six years, and my special scared pups always find a home. I think I need them more than they need me. The person who drifts to a dog like Lucy needs a dog like Lucy more than he or she realizes. Like me, that person has a snag. It's a rip deep inside that only the pure innocence of a dog can mend.

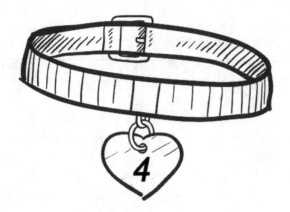

I conquer four whole periods of social awkwardness at Atlantic High and make it to the lunch table without incident.

One point for Kendall, zero for Peter!

I'm first to the table, and the fear builds. It's unreasonable, but it's there brewing in the pit of my stomach—the irrational idea that my only two friends won't show up for lunch.

    Me: WTF Hurry!

One. Two. Three. Four. Five. Six. Seven. Eight. Nine. Ten. I count. Mixing the corn in with the mashed potatoes, I glance at my blank phone face. Eleven. Twelve. Thirteen. Fourteen. Fifteen. The corn and mashed potatoes now look like soupy vomit. The phone screen remains black. My fingers pick another scab as the anxious feeling rakes my skin from the inside. Sixteen. Seventeen. Eighteen. Nineteen. Twenty. I throw down my fork in surrender.

No! The stable part of my brain pulls it together, insisting I count some more. Twenty-one. Twenty-two. Twenty-three. Twenty-four. Twenty-five. I'm tired of counting. Maybe I should watch YouTube or something. Every neurotic cell in my body begs to leave the cafeteria—the twisting in my stomach hurts—but then their wonderful faces bob through the door.

I laugh out loud. She actually wore those pants. Last night she'd sent me a Snapchat to get my approval. Not really. My fashion sense is dismal. The pants are cherry red, and they match her frames. She's half hot mess and half geek, and the only person in this school that could pull it off without consequence.

Jimmy rolls in next to her. He's almost taller than her, even in his wheelchair. His 'Fro growth adds two inches.

Now that they're here, I can breathe without pain.

Lunch anxiety has contributed to my record number of ditch days. But I've gotten better at dealing with it. I've counted as high as one hundred, when before I'd bolt at twenty. Vicky taught me this trick. She says it's the only thing that stopped her from ripping apart the faces of her schoolmates, but it wasn't enough to prevent her from getting kicked out of Saint Paul's Academy. I have anxiety, and she has anger management issues, the marvelous by-products of death and divorce.

"Here, Kens." Jimmy tosses his phone across the cafeteria table. "I think Lucy will come into the yard if you play this. I almost had her. She liked the horn melody, and she loved the birdsong, so I centered the mix around those two elements just for her. Download it."

"Awesome, Jimmy, thanks." We're working together to bring music into the dog rescue kennel. It's incredible how music can affect the dogs, good and bad. And I need to improve Lucy's confidence. A dog that won't go into the yard will never get adopted.

"What's all this?" Vicky points to the stack of bright-yellow flyers on the table.

"They're for the Spring Festival tonight." I say the words out loud, making it real, making it impossible to back out.

Vicky's jaw drops. "You're actually doing it?"

I nod.

"Good for you, Kens!" Jimmy says through the massive amount of food in his mouth.

"Yeah, I'm proud." Vicky claps my shoulder.

"Thanks. You guys have to come too." My fingers are crossed under the table. The thought of standing behind a booth while the entire school and their parents parade by makes me dizzy.

"I'm there no matter what." Vicky's determination hardens her soft face. "Besides, you need the car."

"I do." I sigh with relief.

"Is Cat ever going to get that car fixed?" Jimmy asks.

I shrug. It's a beat-up Toyota Corolla from the Stone Age that needs new brake pads, and something's wrong with the fuel pump, so it sits behind my house waiting for money to rain from the sky.

"I'll be there anyway." Jimmy gives the thumbs-up.

"Of course you will, Mr. Popularity. You'll be at the Drama Club booth, the Honor Society booth, the MADD booth … and what else?" She counts on her fingers.

"The Down with Disabilities booth. Duh!" Jimmy smirks, then turns to me. "I'll come see you."

"Thanks." I'm offering myself up on a silver platter for all the haters at school to ridicule me even more than they already do. There's probably no way in hell that I'd actually go through with this if they'd said no.

Maybe I would've. For the dog's sake. For my home's sake. For Dad.

"Oh my God, I almost forgot to tell you guys." I relay all the horrific details of yesterday's rescue. They're both amazed at the story, but they're not surprised. I've told them a million incredible rescue stories. My negativity infected Vicky a long time ago, but Jimmy is still delightfully hopeful in the human race's kindness.

We finish our food, and Vicky's mood shifts, which is a tangible thing like a dementor's frost or a ghost's chill. "I won't be in school tomorrow. Are you going to be okay?" She specifically directs this question at me, her unstable friend.

"Sure, I'll be fine." I smile, but my lunch begins to curdle inside my digestive tract. "Jimmy, you'll be here, right?"

"Yup." He pats his hair, confirming it's still puffy.

"Where will you be tomorrow?" I ask.

"Court. That bitch Sarah, remember?" Vicky scoffs, then bites into her fried chicken breast vampire-style.

"Oh yeah," Jimmy and I both say.

"I didn't break her nose. It was an excuse for her to get a nose job. I may just hit it again so her parents can waste more money on her ratchet face. She's ugly on the inside. Can't fix that with a scalpel."

"Try to be nice. I can't go weeks with just Jimmy."

"Hey." Jimmy is mock offended.

"You want me to call you with my feminine issues?"

"Every day. All day." Jimmy's flippant attitude makes me uneasy.

There's a good chance she'll be sent away to a rehab center, and he'll be left to pick up my diagnosable insane pieces. The thought of not seeing her, not being able to call her for advice or share stories with her, breaks my heart. With my bad luck, I'll likely lose my best friend tomorrow.

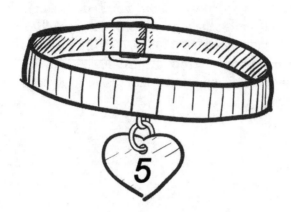

After school Jimmy rolls his wheelchair, and I walk next to him. He comes over every Tuesday for what we jokingly refer to as Eighth Period: Music Appreciation for Dogs. I used to drive us home when my car worked. Vicky would drive us, but she has drum lessons on Tuesdays, so we're stuck strolling in the Florida heat.

Before we're out of the school's parking lot, Jimmy says, "You need to check your phone."

"Why?"

"Just do it."

"Okay." Panic swells as I dig my phone out of my backpack.

Peter unfurls his silk webbing from the top of my head to the bottom of my feet.

Jimmy has a dog-who-just-peed-on-the-rug look on his face. He knows I rarely check my phone, since I never post on social media and my two friends see me in person every day.

It's gonna be some pathetic old photo of you from the second-grade yearbook like last time.

My ex-BFF from PDD—pre-Dad's death—posted the photo, and the entire school shared it. I felt as if all of Florida saw the image of me picking my nose, only I wasn't actually picking my nose. It was a photo of show-and-tell when I was seven years old. Susan Rodriguez had brought in an old clock that had a cute character that popped up every hour. The focus of the photo

20

is on her, and she looks adorable in a blue dress and perfectly curled hair. I'm in the background in a Spider-Man T-shirt smudged with chocolate, not paying attention, with my hand near my face, and the angle makes it appear as if I'm picking my nose. Of course, at seven, I didn't care, but at sixteen, it was devastating. Plus, my ex-BFF wrote as the caption: *Can't believe I was ever friends with Dog Girl! Yuck!* And the label stuck.

I power up the screen. My heart tangles in the imagined sticky silk. The light-headedness kicks in. I halt mid-step.

Jimmy stops midroll. "See?"

My screen has notification after notification after notification. So many I have to scroll. I *never* have to scroll! I'm the antonym for popular.

"Why, Jimmy?" There's tender fear in my tone.

"It's not bad, Kens. Honest."

Relief surges. Peter and his webs start to dissolve.

I relax my fingers too much and drop my phone. It lands on the asphalt, facedown. The glass breaks. "Shit!"

"Sorry, Kens. My bad. I should've explained. I know how you are."

"It's okay." I pick up my phone and brush off the tiny glass particles. A droplet of blood pools on my thumb, and I suck it clean. "It still works."

"It's my fault. I'll get it fixed this weekend," Jimmy says.

I smile at his sincerity. He has this patch of muted freckles just underneath his left eye. Vicky and I like to take photos of him in black and white because then the freckles pop out like they've been drawn on with invisible ink. On the downside, you can't see his hazel eyes and nutmeg skin.

"Don't be dumb. I dropped it. I'll get it fixed. So what's going on anyway?" I resume walking.

"You know Spencer Conard's little brother?" he asks.

"Yes." The word draws out as dread creeps up the back of my neck.

"He took a video of the rescue you were telling us about at lunch."

His remark tickles something in the back of my brain. "Oh God. Did he, like, do something perverted with it?"

"No. He just posted it this morning. It's pretty terrifying, Kens." He does a one-eighty, clearly excited, rolls backward, then whips forward.

I laugh, impressed. "I told you. The train came within inches of me."

"I know what you said, but seeing it play out. Wow! And I'm not the only one that feels this way."

"Obviously." I press the broken screen of notification bubbles. "Two thousand and fifty shares!"

"Check Twitter."

"I don't tweet."

He tilts his head and snarls.

"What?" I shrug.

"Social studies." He stresses every syllable.

"Yeah." I roll my eyes. Mr. Young claims opening a Twitter account for the class is a hundred percent voluntary, but everyone knows he makes the students who don't have one do a ton of extra work.

"You've been retweeted thousands of times too, and it's all over Snapchat. You might even be a GIF."

I walk on in silence, unsure of what this means. It's a video of what we do all the time. Save dogs. But for some reason, it feels unnatural. This is confirmed when we reach my dirt driveway. Four television news vans block the entrance to the barn.

I zigzag, and Jimmy maneuvers the wheelchair around the crammed vehicles to find the center of a paparazzi attack. A mob of aggressive journalists bombards Mom, Shane, and Saint Paul Boy.

Mom's rough voice shouts, warding them off. "I've told you everything. She isn't here! Do I need to call the cops?"

No one's listening. Everyone's still yelling questions and moving in for the kill, like a scene from a zombie apocalypse movie.

Mom's face could actually be on fire. Sparks seem to fly from the top of her head. We lock eyes, and the fierceness in them tells me she's fending off these zombies on my account. They came here looking for the girl in the viral video. I freeze in my hiding spot.

I guess Saint Paul Boy sees Mom's severity too, because he eases between her and the press. "For one, Kendall isn't here. For two, she's a minor, so don't think you can stalk her without permission. For three, we've told you everything. You've got your story, now please exit the property."

The zombies drone on, talking over one another. The words "train," "miracle," "killer," and "hero" are tossed around.

"Listen, that's all Mrs. Shepherd knows. Anything more you'll have to get from the police or the vet," Saint Paul Boy yells.

"We need a photo," one journalist calls out.

"Okay." Saint Paul Boy turns and whispers to Shane, who nods.

This is too much. This is nuts.

"Who's the new guy?" Jimmy asks.

"Honestly, I don't know." I don't even know his name.

"Does he work here?" Jimmy's talking as if there isn't a herd of zombies about to discover us.

I wide-eye him and touch my lips with my finger. "He's here for his senior community service hours."

"Oh. He doesn't go to *our* school," he whispers.

"No. Saint Paul's."

Mom catches my attention again. I shake my head. Don't look over here! One of those zombies will catch my scent and track me down. Vivid images of the Walking Dead eating my brains out consume my mind. Finally, I get the message Mom's trying to convey with head spasms. *Get out of here!*

"Come on." I grab Jimmy's wheelchair. He hates to be pushed. He clasps the wheels, resisting my assistance, but I ignore him. It's crucial that I get away from all the craziness. Mutant Peter starts to stir awake again. Who knows what I'd do or say in front of those zombies with cameras? It'd be pitiful.

Once out of the commotion, I let out the breath I hadn't realized I was holding hostage.

"If I wanted a roller-coaster ride, I'd go to Disney World." His hazel eyes turn indignant.

"Sorry." I step away from his chair and try to keep the tremble out of my voice—and Peter locked in his glass vivarium. Breathing is still difficult. The thought of all those cameras and people has made me a train wreck.

My three-thirty alarm shrieks. I jump and hyperventilate, nearly shattering the glass, letting Peter escape.

Jimmy snatches the phone and shuts off the alarm.

"It's time for Lucy's lessons." My words float on puffs of breath, barely audible.

Jimmy nods. "Stay here. I'll get Lucy?"

"Okay," I sigh. "Thanks."

Luckily, Saint Paul Boy has everyone preoccupied at the opposite end of the barn. Jimmy can sneak Lucy out of her stall and into the yard without notice.

My nerves begin to calm, and Jimmy starts the music. We're back on schedule. This is good. Structure and schedules keep my anxiety in check.

The music plays, and Jimmy was correct. It soothes Lucy. We sit in the chairs just as an adopter would and watch her discover that there's nothing scary about the fenced-in area.

"I hope V does well in court tomorrow," I say.

"Yeah. If she doesn't speak, she'll be fine." He tosses a stick for Lucy to fetch.

"Who's this?" A voice from behind startles me.

I turn to ogle Saint Paul Boy. "The pup or the guy?" I ask, even though it's clear Saint Paul Boy is talking about the puppy.

A hint of embarrassment washes over Saint Paul Boy. I've wounded him. Interesting. But I hate it when people bypass Jimmy. A six-foot-two, athletically built, handsome biracial guy shouldn't be overlooked just because he's in a wheelchair.

"Both," Saint Paul Boy recovers, then turns back on me. "Please introduce me?"

Needles of panic poke and prod my chest. How can I introduce him when I don't know his name? Why can't he just introduce himself? He's doing this on purpose.

"Jimmy, this is Saint Paul Boy. Saint Paul Boy, this is Jimmy Morrison, and this is Little Lucy." I smirk and nod.

"Nice to meet you both." Saint Paul Boy still doesn't offer his real name. "Jim Morrison?" Saint Paul Boy smiles.

"Yeah, I know. Most people don't make the connection, especially when I played football, but my parents love sixties music. Are you into old music?" Jimmy asks.

The name Jim Morrison sounds familiar, but I can't remember him clearly enough to engage in the conversation. I don't want to look like a fool again, so I keep my mouth shut and hope Saint Paul Boy won't call me out.

"I'm into poetry," Saint Paul Boy says.

What? I don't even read poetry, and I read a lot. Novels. Comics. Poetry? His glance zips to me.

Crap! Did he just read my thoughts?

Words spill from Jimmy's mouth in a bizarre tone. *"'You feel your strength in the experience of pain.'"*

"Good one," Saint Paul Boy says. "I can see how that would've meant a lot to you."

"Yeah, after my accident I recited it over and over again."

Saint Paul Boy uses that same round voice. *"Expose yourself to your deepest fear; after that, fear has no power.'"*

Have I been transported to some freaky poetry bar where people sit in dark places and get stoned or sip espresso?

"Sweet." Jimmy rocks his head and shoulders, apparently enjoying this break in the schedule way more than I am.

"Am I supposed to snap my fingers now, or are we going to get to work sometime soon? I still have to get ready for Spring Festival."

"Sorry, Kens." Jimmy nods.

I lower my gaze, trying to hide my pulsating nerves.

Jimmy knows my compulsions, but Saint Paul Boy doesn't, and he won't.

"We're quoting Jim Morrison." Saint Paul Boy leans into my space, eager lines crossing his forehead.

"Yeah, I got it. I don't need a poetry lesson." I tear my eyes from the ground and force them to stare into his. It's a mistake. They're like cool blue swimming pools that I sink to the bottom of. The small amount of air left in my lungs spats out, "Why are you here anyway?"

"Your mother wants you in the office," he says.

"Why?"

"My orders were to come get you, nothing more." He swipes his thick wave of hair, and the point flops to the left.

He's got great hair. God! He lured me in again. Fricking man siren.

"I have Music Appreciation with Little Lucy. She needs me." I gesture in the general direction of my adorable beagle-mixed mutt. I twirl around, expecting to see her cowering in my shadow. Instead, her paws pad excitedly around the yard, scrambling to catch lizards. I'm both proud and pissed at her. Weeks I've been working on her confidence. Weeks. And she picks now to be independently stable.

"She seems fine." Jimmy shrugs.

I glare at him.

He begins to stutter. "Maybe she's not."

"The dog's fine. Your mom needs you." Saint Paul Boy walks over to Lucy. He picks her up and nuzzles her face.

"Lucy, not *the dog*."

I storm off, leaving Saint Paul Boy with my little girl and my best friend. They continue to recite poems. Saint Paul Boy's taking over my space, my friends, my life. This whole incident is ruining my schedule. Peter tries to spin trouble again, but I fight it.

Deep breaths, Kendall. Deep breaths.

After walking a few yards, I turn around to spy on them, hoping they're quiet and bored without me. No. They're engaged in deep conversation and seem to have a lot in common. How is this possible? It goes against all my personal experience with Saint Paul's Academy rich kids, but then again, Jimmy befriends everyone with his easygoing attitude.

As I walk through the barn to the office, I spot Mom. Her usual bitch face is different. This face would even scare Vicky.

"Kendall." Mom grabs my arm and pulls me into a huddle with Shane. "We've sent all but one television station away. This one is getting a photo of Trax. You need to skip school tomorrow."

"Gladly, but I'm already on probation. You'll have to call the school."

"I will. It's a family emergency," she says.

"What?"

"Trax is national news. We got a call from *Good Morning America*. They want to highlight us and our work."

"Really?" I'm not sure how I feel about this. Shivers run up my spine. Do I have to do an interview?

"Out of all of us, you and Ryan look the most presentable."

"Who?" I ask.

"Ryan, the kid volunteering for school." Mom shrugs with bewilderment. Does she think we're friends?

Shane glances hard at Mom. "Of course, we're not hiding who we truly are."

"Why would we do that, honey?" Mom's sarcasm escalates. "We're a couple of fine, upstanding queers raising our daughter among a bunch of felons. I'm sure we'll get invited to *Dr. Phil* next!"

"There's a happy medium, Cat." As usual, Shane has a different opinion.

Mom snorts a laugh. "I'm not exactly television ready."

Mom is rough-looking, but you can see the once-pretty girl underneath. Grief, manual labor, and too much direct Florida sunshine have taken their toll on her good looks. Then there's her go-to outfit: braless in a black tank top, camouflage pants, and lace-up field boots topped off with sweaty bleach-blond hair knotted in a bun. And let's not forget about her inked-up arms. I laugh at the image of her on a national morning talk show. She has a point. Ryan is the most marketable.

Mom continues, "Digit can't speak without an f-word—plus, he's covered in gang tats. Squid babbles. Cruz just got here. There's Rock, who of course we'll spotlight … later. He's too … large."

"Rock's fine." Redness dusts Shane's pale complexion as her frustration mounts.

Mom sighs heavily. "Okay, but Ryan looks most professional."

"But Ryan's newer than Cruz." Shane's eyes bug out of her head.

"Maybe, but he's already proved more reliable. He handled this mess better than we did." Mom swipes a hand through the air.

Shane doesn't argue.

"Where's Ryan?" Mom asks.

Again, like he's my responsibility. I shake my head. "Talking with Jimmy."

"Alright, Kendall, you and Rock will take the reporter to the veterinary hospital," Shane says. "Let him take pictures of Trax. I've already answered all of his questions, so don't let him pry any more information. The police are still investigating, and I don't want us to reveal certain facts."

"What facts?" I ask.

"Location, name of good Samaritan, type of bullets, that sort of thing." Shane has the look and tone of an over attentive kindergarten teacher.

"But it's all already out there." I shrug.

"Where?" Shane's plump cheeks squeeze as she bites down on them.

"On video."

"What video?" Mom barks.

"The one that Spencer Conard's brother took and posted on YouTube."

"What?" Mom and Shane both ask.

"Yeah. I'm sure that's how all these reporters knew about it."

"No!" Mom's eyes squint to intense slits.

"It's all over Instagram, Twitter, Snapchat—"

"And God knows what else." Mom sighs.

"What exactly is on the video?" Shane is the calming force in our family. Without her Mom and I would be a wreck.

"I'll show you." I whip out my busted phone. Mom gives me an *Again, Kendall? What happened?* look. I shake my head and press play.

Mom throws up her hands. "So the location and details of the rescue are out there for the whole goddamn world to see. That's just great!"

"Well, nothing we can do about it, but we want them to catch this jerk, so you tell them 'no comment.' The press has enough information. Okay?" Shane pats my arm.

"Sure. But why can't the guy just walk over there by himself? Let Dr. Ferrera handle it."

"Because this kind of publicity can bring us donations, and Lord knows we need the money," Shane says with a heavy sigh.

Mom hasn't bought herself a new pair of field boots in two years. And when the feed truck delivers, Shane gives the driver two credit cards instead of one while she crosses her fingers behind her back like a child. The growing number of lines across Mom's forehead. My car still not fixed. All these little things add up, and they equal we're broke and struggling to stay in business, struggling to keep our home.

"With extra funds we may be able to rescue that timber wolf in Mayaguez after all." Shane's amber eyes beam.

That's the key phrase. She knows I want that wolf so badly. Five months of begging Mom may now be worth it. My feet are ready to jump for joy, but I hide my elation, since this is another touchy subject between Mom and Shane.

I leave them and join Rock. We escort the reporter and his cameraman across the parking lot to the path that runs along the field and leads to the impressive veterinary hospital next door.

I get a funny look from the reporter. My smile is too wide. But I might save the timber wolf. I might get my car back. All that extra money would mean major improvements around here for the dogs and my moms.

"M-ma s-su," the reporter stutters, before saying, "I'm drawing a blank. What did you say was the name of the woman that found Trax?"

"She didn't." Rock glowers, ending all future probing.

I stop smiling. Rock's not mad at me, but his angry expression can put the fear of retribution in anyone. He's a massive man, bald-headed, with fierce black eyes, tree trunks for legs, and the biggest heart, which he shares with very few people. He doesn't trust easily, and the reporter is a stranger.

I've known Rock for as long as I can remember, and he would take a bullet for me. He's already saved me from a vicious attack by a rottie. He got bitten up pretty bad, and Mom shot the rottie. It ranks up there as one of my top ten worst days ever. I owe my life to Rock.

The photos are brief, and I stay behind as Rock leads the man out of the building. I sit on the floor next to Trax. The area around her wound is orange from iodine and shaved. Her eyes cloud from sedatives. I pet her gently behind her ears and kiss her forehead. She's too drugged to acknowledge my touch, but I stroke her anyway. My heart aches for her, and my rage strengthens with every breath. This evil is personal. And it's shoving my fragile composure into the spotlight of *Good Morning America*.

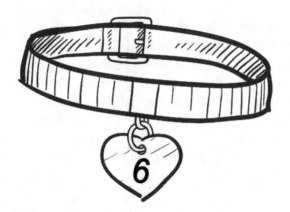

6

Somehow a booth with a tablecloth makes begging for money legit, but I still feel like an idiot standing here. Spring Festival booths line Atlantic Avenue for shoppers to peruse. All the booths are student-driven, from teenage entrepreneurs to organizations with a teenage market. My booth falls into the nonprofit/activist category. I'm raising awareness and hopefully a lot of cash.

"That makes me so angry." Vicky refers to the woman with the four-thousand-dollar Prada bag over her shoulder who didn't put a quarter in my jar.

Vicky snatches a handful of flyers and steps in front of the booth. She aggressively attracts people over, and now I'm forced to talk to several strangers. I stammer and stutter the explanation of how their donation will not only save Dragon but help support the rescue center, which in turn helps the community by getting stray dogs off the streets. A few dollar bills or quarters drop into my jar. The small amount isn't going to cut it.

Peter's noose of silk strangles my voice. I try to loosen the hold, to release the anxiety that makes it impossible to talk. As time goes on, it does slacken, and my sales pitch improves. I wrangle a few five, ten, and even twenty-dollar bills out of their wallets. It still seems like a measly pile. I need hundreds of dollars to save Dragon from being euthanized and thousands to stop the imminent foreclosure of my home. It's like climbing up a down escalator all the way to heaven.

An hour passes in a flash. Jimmy stops by briefly to say hi, and Vicky hands out almost all of my flyers.

Electric-blue manicured nails snag the last copy. A blaring light and camera shine in my face.

"Hello, Kendall. I'm Johanna Wells from the hit YouTube show *Get Out and Off Your Ass*." The girl with the loud nail polish shoves her hand at me for an introduction. I've watched her show before. Jimmy constantly plays clips. The guys love her because she's hot, and the girls love her because she's cool. She's funny, witty, foul, and very popular.

I extend my hand, and she shakes it vigorously. Peter's stranglehold returns, and I have no voice to say hello until Vicky nudges me.

"I'm Kendall."

Johanna smiles but says nothing, just continues to hold the camera contraption in my face. She nods, then taps me with her foot.

Frozen and feeling ridiculous, I nod back at her and force a smile.

"What do you do, Kendall?" she prompts.

From somewhere I muster the courage to converse about my cause. "My family owns Delray Dog Rescue, and we're raising money tonight to save a wolf from being euthanized. The money will also go toward the many dogs at the rescue struggling to find loving homes."

A crowd has formed around us. Luckily, the bright light from her camera deforms all the faces into black shadows—except one. Ryan's. He smirks. He's mouthing words I don't understand, but he's attempting to help me. She shifts the light again, and he vanishes. The light is all I can see now. It's like talking to an alien spacecraft. *Take me to your leader!*

"I saw the clip of Trax's rescue. Fucking wow!" Johanna's assistant holds up an iPad and plays the video for her crowd of followers. "Isn't she a brave, badass bitch, everyone?" She incites the crowd, and they respond by clapping, hooting, and whistling ear-piercing whistles.

This girl is incredible. She can't be much older than me. She's tiny, but she's taken charge of the entire Spring Festival. She's the brave, badass bitch, not me.

I step in front of my booth for a closer shot with her. She squeezes me like we're best friends. With the camera outstretched and pointed at our heads, she says, "You all better donate. Save Kendall's dogs. We all love dogs. Now send them your fucking money!"

She's about to shut off the camera when I burst out, "Delray Dog Rescue—225 Hallow Lane. Your money will go a long way in getting strays off the streets and abused puppies out of the hands of horrible abusers. Thank you."

Camera off. Lights off. I'm plunged into blinding darkness, dotted with little halos. The crowd rushes the booth and drops loads of money into the jar. Vicky does an excellent job, smiling and gathering up the cash, shoving it into her bag before anyone has the chance to steal it or take it back.

Johanna clutches my shoulder again. "Great job. Way to spark up in the end there. I was a little worried at the beginning. Stage fright. Everyone has it. But it's no big deal, right?"

"Sure." I nod, but actually I'm not sure what I've just said or done. It all happened so fast. Survival instinct took over. Greed, maybe. I need all these people to donate so I can keep my rescue, keep Dragon alive, keep Dad's dream alive.

"You're doing a great service, helping these dogs. When I heard about Trax and heard you'd be here tonight, I had to come fucking see you. We have to put an end to this shit. I mean. Really! What sick fuck can harm an animal? And you're doing something about it. Good for you. Here's my card." She says it all in one breath.

She's like a tornado, and I'm still whirling from her words and actions.

"When will this be on your channel?" Vicky takes the business card and examines it.

"Now. That was live," Johanna says.

"Cool." Vicky smiles.

"Bye, bitches," Johanna shouts, and struts away.

I'm still in a state of shock and turn to face Vicky. I think my jaw scrapes the ground. "Did that just happen?"

"It did." Vicky grins wider than a supervillain.

"Live! Oh my God, what did I say?" Burning panic rushes through my blood. Sweat gushes from the top of my head, drenching my hairline. "Ryan!" I scan the crowd, but he's not there.

"Relax, K. You barely said anything. Johanna talked enough for all of us. But you got your point across and the name of the rescue center. You did good!"

I huff a laugh. The sweat chills, and so does my pounding heart. Tonight is over, and I accomplished my goal to raise money and get through the night without making a complete idiot out of myself. The feeling of accomplishment is satisfying and something I never thought I could achieve.

I glance over at Vicky. "*We* did good, V."

"Yep." She's busy organizing the money and folding the tablecloth. "I gotta get home."

"Me too. The morning show is coming tomorrow." The words bite. Peter's fangs slip deep under my skin.

You could barely get through a quick YouTube blurb—how are you going to sit through an entire morning talk show interview?

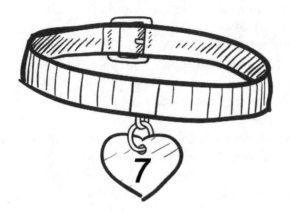

7

Lucy springs to her feet, pushing me off my beanbag. Her wake-up call is usually more pleasant than this. Groggily, I sit up and rub the back of my neck. Lucy jumps and wags her tail, and it takes me seconds to see why she's so enthused. Saint Paul Boy stands over us.

"Good morning." He smiles.

Lucy is way more excited to see him than I am.

"What are you doing here?" I'm too groggy to figure out if I'm mad or embarrassed that he's caught me sleeping in the barn.

"You're not happy to see me?" A hint of mischief laces his words.

I stand, but before I can speak, an icy shiver rips through my body, making me acutely aware of the fact that I'm braless. I cross my arms to cover the nips. His impish grin sends a warm flush through my face. I prepare for a typical guy comment, but instead he takes off his jacket and pulls it across my shoulders. He tucks the soft fabric of the Ralph Lauren hoodie snuggly around my neck. It's warm and smells incredible, sweet citrus combined with something spicy, something I've smelled when spraying the fancy bottles that sit atop the Nordstrom counter. His body is close to mine. We match in height, and I realize I have morning breath.

I twist away. "Thank you."

"Come on. You need to get ready. We're scheduled for the *Good Morning America* interview in an hour." He puts Lucy in her kennel and starts to walk.

I fall in step next to him. "You don't have school today?" It's a dumb question. Obviously he doesn't have school. He's here, isn't he? But I'm trying to fill the empty silence as we stroll over to the house.

"Well ... ah ... my—"

"I get it. Mom gave you a note so you could skip."

He cocks an eyebrow. "Looks like I picked the right place to do my community service hours."

"Yeah." It's weird, because it feels as if he's worked at the rescue center for a lot longer than a day and a half. "You know, this is so not normal for us. I'm not sure why Trax is creating such a buzz. I mean ... I know why ... it's just that we've rescued a lot of dogs that have been shot before. I mean ... well, I guess ... tying a dog to the train tracks is creative."

"When something goes viral, it's like a bullet. You can't stop it." He opens the front door of my house for me.

Once again, his courtesy feels strangely rewarding. I smile at him, then shy away from his stare. I don't like this. I'm not timid. An anxious mess, yes, but shy? Not really. What's the matter with me?

Inside the house, giant, beaming lights shine on the worn-out couch, exposing years of yellowish-brown stains. A woman positions a very large, intricate camera, and a man sets makeup on a table. Another man holds a clipboard and looks important. He's talking with Mom and Shane.

I stand awkwardly next to Ryan in the front entrance, overly aware of my arms. They've become heavy baggage, and I fumble to put my hands in the pockets of Ryan's hoodie. He looks well-slept and tidy; I feel tired and ragged. He smells delicious; I smell like dog and dirt.

"Thanks." I whip off Ryan's cozy jacket and thrust it at him, then race up the stairs to my bathroom and hop in the shower. Perfume. Mascara. I pick up the hair volumizer that Vicky gave me and wipe off the dust. I flip the pressurized container upside down and press. "Whoa!" I'm not sure how much of this glop to use, but I'm certain a handful of foam overflowing in dollops would be too much. Half plops into my sink, and the other half spreads through my hair.

Why am I doing all of this? Not for Ryan. I shake my head, reassuring myself. I need to look professional and pretty to represent the rescue center. It's a big deal. It's national news coverage. The face in the mirror staring back at me grimaces.

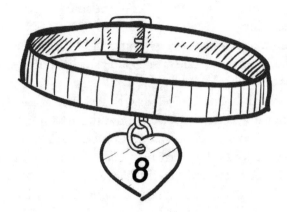

B right lights blaze on my face. They're bigger and scarier than Johanna's. It's like having the sun's hot ball of glowing gases in my living room.

River, a medium-sized American pit bull who we found shot and nearly drowned in a reservoir near Spanish River Boulevard, sits on my lap. She's recovered tremendously and now lives with Mr. and Mrs. Jensen in Boynton Beach. Mrs. Jensen sits next to me, sandwiching me between her and Ryan. The sofa sags under her weight, pulling me down into her mushiness.

I scoot out of the crater she's formed and inch closer to Ryan, which creates another situation possibly more uncomfortable than the first.

He doesn't move away.

My thigh stops a millimeter from his.

He's still there, not moving.

The atoms ricochet between us like some sort of electric force field. It's both thrilling and nauseating. All I can think about is chemistry class and negatively charged electrons.

His head tilts in my direction. He whispers so only I can hear, "I saw you last night. I would've come to say hi, but my friend had to leave."

"Oh." My voice cracks.

Oh my God, get it together, Kendall! Peter shifts, wobbling the vivarium I've contained him in.

The attractive interviewer bares her teeth. She leans in and asks if I'm ready.

"Yes," I say.

"Great." She winks.

Hand signals are made. People rush but stand still at the same time. Then a hush falls over the room. A man holds up his hand and counts down.

The interviewer looks at her notes, then up at me. "What was it like to see the train barreling toward you and the pit bull?"

Ryan adjusts his weight. The millimeter buffer of space decreases to zero. He doesn't seem to notice our touching skin, but I do. The sensation of my hips and legs touching his hips and legs erases all logic.

Kendall, she's looking at you. Answer the question! Peter bangs the glass.

"What? Oh, yes. Yes, it was awful."

Slick sweat forms between my leg and his. I inch backward, but the microphone contraption jabs my bony spine. I jolt forward and startle the interviewer.

"Huh, sorry." I chuckle nervously.

She asks another question. "Were you ever concerned you might die saving the dog?"

She hasn't blinked once. She's like a robot—a voluptuous, stunningly beautiful fake person with giant hungry eyes that don't blink.

Answer the question, Kendall! Peter jabs inside my chest.

"Uh, yeah … yeah … of course."

Ryan peels his leg off mine. Sweat droplets drip. He's trying to get away from the human puddle. I shouldn't have worn shorts.

River's paws slip on my perspiring thighs. The poor dog is sliding off my lap. I death grip her. *No way, buddy! You're my security blanket.*

The robot's eyes shift to River, and I can breathe again. In a flash her stare zooms back on me. "Tell me about River and how you rescued her."

"River was shot."

She's still looking at me. I glance around and see everyone is looking at me. *Say something. Anything.*

"She almost drowned. It was terrible. On Spanish River. Ha! Get it? River." *Are you mental? What was that?* But I can't take it back. All I can do is refuse to say anything else. I'm making a complete fool of myself. I won't say another word, and Crazy Robot Lady can't force me.

Ryan places a hand on my shoulder and speaks. His mouth moves, but the words are a muffled, distant echo. His eyes are warm and soft as they take me in. His glance slides from me to Robot Lady to River to Mom. There's laughter, and I turn to see Mrs. Jensen's enormous chest heaving with laughter. She's telling the story that I failed to tell. Then all the attention shifts to Mom and Shane. Mom looks drab in all black next to the colorful flowers on Shane's dress. They chat for a very short time.

Then it's over. Everyone stands up and stretches. I'm alone on the sofa. Even River has jumped to the floor. I'm a melted Frosty the Snowman. Blackness edges my peripheral vision as Peter's venom slowly spreads through my blood. It's fuzzy, and then …

The living room slowly comes back into focus. Shane's familiar round cheeks hover above. Mom's mop of blond hair flops over Shane's shoulder.

"Sweetie." Shane gently shakes me.

"Here's the soda." Ryan hands her a glass.

"Sit up." Shane pulls me up. "Slowly."

I nod.

"Drink this." She puts the lip of the glass up to my mouth.

I sip. The sugar takes immediate effect. The falling feeling disappears as the tingle of sweet, fizzy bubbles cascades down my throat.

"Is that better?" Shane asks.

I nod. "Thanks. I'm okay." I nod some more.

"Okay." Shane rises from the couch and walks over to talk with the crew.

Mom pats me on the head like a dog and half smiles. Her forehead wrinkles tensely. She's in the in-between, the upside-down, teetering on affection or aloofness. Our years of therapy together taught us nothing. I still scare her. Then laughter blurts out of me, and this breaks the tension. She laughs back and tousles my hair.

"I'm not a dog, Mom."

"Are you sure, Kendall?"

"Yeah."

She smiles fully and retreats to stand next to Shane.

Ryan flops down on the sofa. "Bad case of stage fright, huh?"

I huff. "I guess so."

"Maybe you need to eat."

"Yeah, I think that's a good idea."

He gets up and grabs two doughnuts off the craft services table. "Red velvet or maple bacon?"

"Maple bacon."

He hands it to me. It's enormous, as round as a personal pizza.

"Thanks." It's heaven in one bite.

"You're welcome."

When he grins, two dimples slice down his cheeks. It is the most incredible thing ever. Concave skin has never looked hotter.

"Do you think it's big enough?" His mouth stretches wide, and his eyes bug out. He takes a significant bite but barely reduces the size of the monstrous doughnut.

I laugh and, for the first time this morning, feel genuine.

As we sit on the couch eating doughnuts, they play the interview. It's more like a horror movie. I should've stayed asleep with Lucy in the dirt. I hardly say two words, and the lady is clearly disappointed. She wanted me to be the hero and expand in great detail about the train and the rescue. My mouth gapes open stupidly, and I look like a deer in headlights. I'm going to be the laughingstock at school tomorrow. My bloodless-white skin shines under the bright lights, and the eyeliner the makeup artist added to my mascara creates black circles under my eyes. My hair looks three times darker on camera, and the volumizer didn't work. My hair flattens and separates into stringy strands as usual. I look like an emo in desperate need of a bath.

Ryan's a natural. He glows and says all the right things. River, of course, steals the show with her adorableness. Mrs. Jensen is a hit and so funny. The spliced-in photos of Trax pull at the heartstrings, and the interview with Mom and Shane is professional and informative.

When it ends, Ryan turns to me. "You were great."

I choke on the last bite of doughnut. Did he not just watch the same segment as I did? I swallow. "I looked like Bellatrix!"

"Who?" he asks.

"The Death Eater from Harry Potter."

He chuckles. "No you didn't."

The *Good Morning America* crew packs up and leaves while another news van pulls into the driveway. Chewed doughnut crawls up my esophagus, threatening to spew all over Ryan, Exorcist style.

I can't do another one. No way! I bolt out the door, heading to the barn. I grab my bike and watch the production crew haul their equipment into the house. Money or no money, I'm out of here.

The pedals spin, and the handlebars steer directly toward Vicky's. But she's in court, so I ride around aimlessly.

You left Mom and Shane! You crumbled under pressure! You looked like a fricking witch on camera! Do something useful and find the jerks that hurt Trax. They're the reason you're in the spotlight now. It's their fault. Peter's hiss haunts me as he toys with my digesting doughnut.

The pedals whiz under my push. Sweat slides down my face and dribbles from my elbow creases. Finally, the physical exhaustion has freed my mind of all the nasty, insecure thoughts. The mission is clear. Three dogs shot within miles of each other is no coincidence.

The train tracks lie still and silent, but this is definitely the spot where they hummed and trembled and nearly killed Trax. My bike falls to the ground as I hop off and walk the line. There has to be a clue here, something that would put the criminals behind bars for a very long time. I traipse a far distance but see nothing, not even a footprint.

You're wasting your time. Let the police find them. Peter returns, spewing insecurities.

"Jeez! Make up your mind."

I turn back toward my bike, scanning the area I've covered. Wooden railroad ties; steel rails; patches of weed-filled grass; rocks, dirt, and sand mixed with broken seashells. Everything's calm, even the wind. It's all completely normal.

It's hot, a spring heat wave, probably eighty-five degrees. My bare arms burn from the direct sunshine. I smell whiffs of the ocean and fresh-cut grass, but there's also a sour stench that's unique to this place. I stroll back. This time I walk the edge of the bushes, not the tracks, but there's nothing out of the ordinary.

I bike straight to Vicky's house. She's still not home, so I wait on her doorstep till midafternoon, when her car rolls up. Her mom invites me inside, and I don't dare ask how it went with the attorneys.

Vicky drags me to her room and shuts the door.

Together we sit on her bed in silence, squeezing each other's hands.

After a few seconds of reflection, Vicky starts to talk about her case. "I have to serve six weeks in some sort of rehabilitation center for disturbed youths. It was that or a permanent record and a huge fine. Mom chose BTR."

"BTR?" My chin juts out.

"Behavioral Therapy Ranch." Vicky exaggerates an eye roll.

"BTR like better?" I frown.

"Yeah, and they have some lame jingle about how I'll be better after. Can you believe it?"

I snicker.

"It's no big deal." Vicky pushes back and leans against the headboard.

A massive black hole opens up in my universe, and it sucks my best friend out of my life at a time when I need her the most. "It bites, V."

"Yeah, but I'll be fine." She slides the bridge of her glasses into place.

She wore her classic black Ray-Ban frames today. I guess she figured the studious look would work best in court. She has every style frame in a rainbow of colors. Her blue retro Clubmasters are her favorite. That's the funny thing about V; she looks like a trendy geek, not a tough girl. But anyone that makes the mistake of testing her bad mood gets a quick lesson in *don't judge a book by its cover.*

"Don't they know she's a troll, and she swung at you first?" I ask.

"Nobody backed my story, and since I'm a loser with prior anger issues, and she's a goddamn princess … " The weight of her predicament drags her eyes down.

I need to cheer her up. Heck, I need to cheer myself up. "Can you believe that Saint Paul's jerk is working at the rescue?"

"Is he hot?" she asks.

"Yes, which makes it worse."

"How?"

"Because I'm a freak show carnival act that talks to my dead dad. I have an invisible friend!"

"No. You have a name for your anxiety. There's a difference." She sits forward.

"It's an imaginary disturbing spider demon."

She sighs and reaches for my hand.

I clutch it. The tears build and snotty sadness clogs my throat. I blink and swallow. Everything, except the sorrow, clears. "I can't have a panic attack in front of an Abercrombie model with an amazing ass!"

"Ooh. Tell me about his ass." She scoots closer.

At least she's smiling, even if it's at my expense. "Yes, and I was checking it out, then he turned around. I died!"

Vicky bursts into laughter, and so do I. My joy quickly flips to angst.

"I'm gonna miss you, V." I grab a pillow and hold on to it tightly.

"Me too."

"I was doing so well, and now this guy, and all this TV stuff." The tears return. I squeeze the pillow harder to keep them inside.

She strokes my arm. "He's not going to find out about Peter and your anxiety. Trust me."

I sigh and shake my head. Shame is a void that threatens to grow with all these new and terrifying events in my life.

"He won't."

"But what if I lose it?" I blink away the tears.

"You won't. You haven't in a long time."

"I'm not so sure, V. With you gone and all this weird viral video craziness. I had *Good Morning America* in my house today! That's fricking nuts!"

Vicky's eyes stare into me, but she's quiet until she looses a long sigh.

"You're the only one that knows," I say.

"Your moms know."

"That's not the same."

She nods and grabs her own pillow to clutch. "So tell me more. What's his name?"

"Ryan."

"Ryan." Her eyes crinkle. "I don't remember any Ryans when I was there. What's his last name?"

"I don't know." I shrug.

"Let's get my yearbook." Tossing her pillow aside, she rushes to her shelf and pulls out last year's yearbook. "Saint Paul's Academy" is stamped in gleaming gold on the front. She had gone there for her freshman year, my sophomore year since I'm a year older. She flips through the juniors' photos, pointing to each guy.

I shake my head and more fervently hug the pillow.

She slaps the book shut. "I don't think your guy went to Saint Paul's last year."

"He had to." Curiosity explodes inside me. What do I really know about this mystery guy?

"What does he look like? Tan? Dark hair or blond?"

"He's tan. Brownish-blond hair that comes to a point." My hands try to charade a fauxhawk. "And blue eyes. Looks athletic. And he's actually nice."

"What? No way!"

"He is. He held the door open for me." I grip the pillow again.

Her mouth falls open.

"And he offered me his jacket so I wouldn't be embarrassed."

"Embarrassed about what?"

I roll my eyes. "Nipple awareness."

"Get the eff out!"

"It was first thing in the morning. I was cold."

"Jesus, K!"

"But that wasn't the worst of it. I was sleeping in the barn with Lucy. Bad hair, morning breath, and all."

She giggles. "You poor thing."

A smile creeps across my face as my anxiousness lifts.

"And Cat likes him?" she asks.

"Yes—and Shane and Jimmy!"

"That's a miracle. Better snatch him up." She swipes the pillow from me and hugs it.

"I'm not snatching anyone."

"Fine. Keep him around for six weeks so I can have him." She kisses the pillow, leaving a giant red lipstick stain, and laughs.

I don't laugh. Six weeks!

"I guess I'm leaving you in good hands." She hands me the stained pillow. My eyes close.

"I am." She sits up straight, beaming enthusiasm. "I'll come back, and you'll have finally kissed a guy."

"Or be in a straitjacket."

"Stop it!" She leaps off the bed and begins to change out of her court clothes.

"Well, it's true. Remember Corey?"

From inside her closet, she says, "Yes, exactly my point. That kid was in love with you."

"And I nearly flunked tenth grade skipping classes to get away from him." The memory pushes me over. I fall onto the bed and stare up at the ceiling. It's covered with tiny holes because she used to vent by throwing darts.

"Lucky for you, Ryan doesn't go to your school."

"Yeah, he just works at the one place I can't get away from." My body sinks into the mattress. It might be creating a valley. Somehow I've accomplished my goal of making her feel better—with the consequence of making myself feel worse.

"K, just be yourself. You're funny and nice and … and what the hell is up with your makeup this morning?"

"Oh my God." I roll over and bury my head in the comforter. "I knew it was bad."

"Bad—it's horrendous!" She laughs.

"Thanks a lot."

"Sorry, K, just being honest." She pulls on a sequined cardigan. Her idea of casual.

"Ryan said I looked good."

"Well, Ryan's really polite." She laughs some more. "See, he's a keeper."

"I look like an emo, don't I?"

"Kinda. More like Snow White on meth."

"Oh, nice. Kill me now."

"You don't look like that usually."

"I don't know! How did it look on TV?" I ask.

"I taped it. Let's see." Vicky hops off the bed, grabs the remote, clicks to the recorded episode, and we watch. She turns to me, mouth gaping, eyebrows cinched. "He is cute."

"What about me?"

"I'd stay off Snapchat, 'Gram, and Twitter." She wraps her arms around me. "But if anyone messes with you, I'll deal with them."

"You'll be gone." My weak voice is a reverberation of my despair. "When do you have to go?"

She hesitates, then mutters, "Tomorrow."

"Tomorrow!" The sweat bursts out of my armpits like ice shards.

I can't barricade the tears any longer. They burst out. Tomorrow is too soon. My tears trigger hers, and then we're both hugging and sobbing.

44

It's a long, sad bike ride home. When I finally arrive, it's quiet, just as I like it. No hideous news vans. Digit works Rascal on the agility course. That's my job.

"Sorry, Digit." I wander past the yard to the pathway that leads to the vet.

"No problem, kiddo." Digit waves a boney, white hand with inked knuckles that spell F-E-A-R-D. "Hey, where you goin'?"

"Dr. Ferrera. Why?"

"Cat say to tell her when you back."

"Please, don't tell her."

Digit lowers and shakes his head, mumbling a string of curse words under his breath.

I sigh. He's afraid to lie to Mom. "Just give me, like, ten minutes."

His head bounces up. "Deal."

My feet pick up speed, and my heart pounds heavily. I did text her to let her know that I was safe and at Vicky's. She responded, "Okay," followed by the mad face emoji. I texted back that she had her perfect and eloquent Ryan to fill the void. It's not fair to use him. I truly am grateful that he's here to deal with all of this.

I rush into the veterinary hospital, desperate to ask Dr. Ferrera about Trax's progress. But the vet has left for the day. I lean over her desk to write a note telling her I stopped by, when Ryan abruptly sits on the desktop.

I jump a foot high. "Really!" Jerk!

"I could've used you today. The interviewer had a lot of questions about this place that, naturally, I didn't know."

"Sorry." I finish writing my note and walk to see Trax.

Ryan jumps off the desk and follows me to Trax's cage. "She had a rough day."

She's sound asleep and pitifully weak.

"What happened?" I ask. "She looks horrible."

"She had a seizure."

"What?" I snap. "That's it. No more TV shit."

"Yeah, I guess a local station called to do a follow-up, and your mom said no because of the seizure. They'll just have to make do with what they already have or what comes over the wire service."

"Poor girl." I kneel and lean my forehead on her cage. My heart rips and aches for her.

"We need to set up a website. I told Cat I'd be here tomorrow to help her get started."

"Really?"

He keeps using the word "we." This isn't his home or his rescue center.

"Well, I've got practice. See you tomorrow." He strolls out of the room.

My mouth opens to ask him what he's practicing, but I don't speak. Where does he go when he's not here? I stare at the door he walked out of. So many questions, but only the smell of citrus and clove. Suddenly I'm very alone.

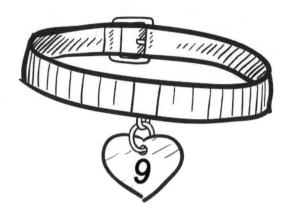

9

"Tomorrow. Tomorrow. I hate you, tomorrow," I sing to my bedroom ceiling. My bed clung to me last night. It cradled my massive misery. I couldn't even find the strength to walk to the barn. Lucy probably cried all night without me.

If I could afford to skip school today, I would. School without Vicky will suck. We haven't spent more than a few days apart since I was thirteen.

Four years ago the barista at Starbucks switched our drink orders, and I had to chase down this girl with two Minnie Mouse–ear buns on top of her head to get my Mocha Frappuccino back. I looked at the Sharpie scribble on the cup, then up at Vicky's face, and asked if her name was Katniss Everdeen. She burst into laughter. I hadn't read or seen *The Hunger Games* and had no clue.

It ended up we were walking in the same direction, and we started talking. First, she told me all about her favorite movie. Next, she explained how she'd be able to kill someone if she really had to if she was in *the games*. At the time, her obsession with the dystopian world bordered on delusional. That was the era of her hugely round gold frames that overwhelmed her small face. I remember how they fascinated me on that day.

"What are you looking at? Do I have a booger?" she had asked.

"No. Your glasses are so big and gold," I had replied.

"You wanna come over and watch *The Hunger Games* with me?"

I was apprehensive, considering her murderous comments, but said yes anyway, and that'd been the best day I'd had in two years. We talked about our schools. We attended different middle schools but had a lot of the same issues. She was twelve, and I was thirteen. Her dad had just left them, and mine had died two years before. She told me all of her personal baggage, even though I barely knew her. I just listened in awe.

"Fifty-eight … fifty-nine … sixty!" The girls at the other table turn to look at me. I have no strength for a controversial staring contest and bow my head. Jimmy rolls up to the table, and relief flushes through me, followed by annoyance.

"Is it too much to ask for you to be on time?"

"Sorry, K."

"It's fine. I'm sorry too. It's just … "

"I know."

We examine the lumps of our lunch in silence. Vicky's chair sits empty.

"They call this pizza!" Jimmy slaps his tray.

"How do you screw up pizza?"

He laughs. "Right?" His head bounces in a continuous nod. "Surprised you're here today."

"If I thought I wouldn't fail eleventh grade, then I'd definitely be home under my covers."

He's still nodding, staring at the empty chair.

"Yes. I saw it." I answer his unasked question.

"It's just Elaine being Elaine. Ignore her."

Elaine Winters, my ex-BFF, the one and only horrible girl that shared my humiliating nose-picking photo on social media last year, tweeted *#GMA #funny #dirtydoggirl needs a bath and a makeup lesson. https://www. google.com/amp/s/abcnews.go.com/amp/-GMA/News/pittbull-rescue-train-FL/ story%=610348.* And if that wasn't bad enough, she captured a still frame of me with my eyes half-shut and my mouth wide open.

I exhale, wishing he was Vicky, but he's not. "I know, but it's not just her. One hundred and sixty comments and still counting." I raise my phone. The numbers by all the icons multiply continually.

"Ouch."

My fingers swipe the phone face. "Here's a good one. *Trashy, heroin-addict-looking, Skeletor, dirty Dog Girl.* From some boy in Wisconsin."

"Harsh!" He takes my phone. His eyes ping-pong as he scrolls. "Here's someone that likes your tattoo."

The paw print tattoo on my ankle next to the date of Dad's death got a cameo on the morning interview.

He scrolls some more. "And here … a guy … He's good-looking." He looks up and smirks, then down at the phone to read—*Kendall u r beautiful. DM me. Let's do it doggie style.*

"Oh. No. My bad." He hands the phone back to me like it's a smelly sock.

I cringe. My lips mash together so I don't scream. Jimmy doesn't want to deal with this stuff for weeks! I can't. I just can't deal.

"I'm sorry." Jimmy's eyes swell with pity.

We sit in mortified quiet: me playing with the crust on my pizza and Jimmy shoving more food into his already-full mouth.

I sink back into the chair and push away the tray of half-eaten lunch. A million microscopic pinpricks spread across my chest and up my neck. The manifestation of my anxiety itches, and I scratch wildly. I stand up. The fiery itch invades my entire body from the inside out.

"Where are you going?" Jimmy asks.

"I don't feel good. Don't eat that pizza."

Jimmy spits out a glob of cheese.

We bring our lunch trays up and dispose of the garbage. Jimmy goes to class. I go to the bathroom.

I shut the stall door. *Dog Girl is so weird* is written on the back of it in ink. I just sit there reading it over and over again, scratching my neck raw, and waiting for the lunchroom to clear.

I fought all morning to stay strong, not let Vicky's absence or the social media tornado bring me down, but I've reached my limit. People I don't even know hate me. The razor edge I walk along daily has sharpened. A few deep breaths fade the angst enough to risk exiting the bathroom and race off campus.

I linger in the driveway. My stomach still threatens to blow half-digested pizza. Do I go into the house and rest or go into the barn and work? Work. Stay busy, keep my mind on dog poop and dog training and …

A hand slaps my shoulder. I jump and take a swing.

And Ryan … No! No, no, no, no, no!

My fist barely misses his nose. Once again he's managed to sneak up on me in complete silence. Maybe I need my hearing checked, or perhaps I'm just used to canine sounds and not human ones.

"Whoa! Nice forehand swing." He laughs.

His playful smile makes his face so cute and friendly. It makes me question the small amount of time I've actually known him.

"You're out of school early."

"And you're not in school why?" I ask.

"We've been working on the website. Thirty thousand dollars has already been deposited. It's unbelievable." His contagious excitement leaps onto me.

"Thirty thousand! Are you kidding me?" I stop walking. My backpack suddenly gains forty pounds and slides off my shoulder.

"Let me take that." He reaches for it, but I hold on tightly. Releasing the bag feels like I'm giving him more than just books.

We stand together in an awkward, silent tug-of-war until I let the backpack go. "Are you sure it's thirty thousand dollars?"

"On my honor." He holds up his right hand.

"Do you know what this means?" I ask.

"That the rescue is almost out of debt." He hoists my backpack over his shoulder.

"Yes, of course." My head swims with happiness, but I can't think. Everything I worry about on the daily explodes. Shards of my life's debris hit me, but the pain is a satisfying release. "This means … " Is the rescue center really saved?

"What? What does it mean?" he asks.

I shake my head, not realizing what I'm saying out loud or what I'm thinking inside. "It also means I can go to Puerto Rico and get the timber wolf."

"Cool. But we don't deal with wolves," he says.

There's that word again, *we*. "*We* deal with canines. It's a Canis lycaon. I've been stalling the Mayaguez shelter for weeks, claiming we're on our way, while trying to raise money for the travel expenses."

"That's why you were at Spring Festival."

"Yeah. Mayaguez is about a three-hour drive from San Juan."

"I know where it is," he says.

Ha! I doubt it. Mayaguez is no resort area. From what I've gathered through my research, it's a rural area except for the university. It definitely isn't a top travel destination for rich playboys.

"Really?" I halt and cross my arms.

"I know you want to save this wolf." He continues walking into the barn with my backpack.

I move to catch up.

"But this rescue needs a lot of updating. We have animals *here* that can really use that money."

We!

"Dragon."

"What?" he asks.

"Dragon. The wolf's name is Dragon. He's only twenty months old. I'm his only chance."

"Do you know how much Trax is costing your mom?" he says.

What's with the authoritative tone? He isn't Dad, he isn't anything to me, and there is no *we*. Plus, I know more than he does how badly we need the money.

"You don't go to Saint Paul's." The words blurt out all in one breath. I yank my backpack from him and set it down in my corner next to the beanbags. I'm instantly thirsty, with a nasty case of cotton mouth. I grab my usual giant plastic cup and fill it with water from the cooler. The old cup has Spider-Man on it, something that never bothered me before, but now I might as well be holding my inner demon incarnate.

"Yeah, so?" he says.

"I thought you went to Saint Paul's."

"You actually never asked me." A coy grin plays on his lips.

He's right. But that's not the point.

His smile sharpens. "Do you even know my name?"

"Yes, it's Ryan." I give him a satisfied smirk and take a drink. My hands wrap around Spider-Man's image as if covering it up will hide the Peter Parker thrashing inside me.

"Ryan what?" He steps into my personal space, and the only thing between us is the ridiculously large red cup of water.

"Ryan ... " I hesitate, hoping he'll release a hint or mouth the words.

His lips lock. However, they do seem to be getting closer. My heart flutters as my eyes focus on his temptingly full bottom lip. His sweet breath renders me speechless. I can't even breathe. Then I glance upward. His blue eyes dance, teasing me. I'm such a fool.

A half inch away from my face, he says, "Kast. Ryan Kast, and I'm homeschooled."

I taste his candy breath as it floats on the air, then gasp as my chest blooms ice cold. I've tilted the cup and drenched my shirt.

"Now look what you've made me do." I push past him and march out of the barn, throwing Spider-Man into the nearest garbage can. If only I could throw Peter away that easily.

I feel his eyes on my back. It's wonderful and horrible. I throw up my fist and extend my middle finger as I stomp up the wheelchair ramp. The wood creaks loudly in protest.

He laughs.

Don't look back. Don't! I turn around and glare.

"Check out the web page while you're inside," he shouts.

I don't answer, but I will go check it out to see where people—strange, caring people—trustingly give us money. The screen door slams behind me.

"Why are you home?" Shane asks as I storm farther into the house.

"I got sick. Food poisoning from what the cafeteria claims is pizza. I just vomited, and now I have to change my shirt." It's an impressive on-the-spot lie, and I'm proud of it. I always think more clearly when I'm pissed off. Not sure what that says about me. "Can you send an email to the school, please?"

"You just left? You didn't tell anyone?"

"I hurled all over myself! Then I rinsed my shirt off with water. I wasn't going to parade around the school like a wet T-shirt contestant. I already have no friends."

Silverware scrapes the ceramic plates. The chewing of baked chicken echoes loudly inside my head. In desperate need of entertainment, I stare at every scratch and dent in the wooden tabletop, recalling each occurrence.

I haven't spoken a word, because I'm not sure if Shane ratted me out. By Mom's intensity, she has, but I'll keep quiet until I'm sure. I've brought all my grades up, and until today, I hadn't skipped a class period in over three months.

Mom puts her fork down with purpose, then looks at me. It feels as if she's reading my thoughts. I brace for the lecture, for the disappointment in her tone.

"Kendall, has anyone been bullying you?"

My shoulders bolt back in shock, pushing me upright. "No."

Shane shifts in her chair, her telltale sign that she wants to explain further. "We know you were on some sort of YouTube show, and there's been a lot of ... tweets?" She furrows her brow.

I nod, assuring her that the terminology is correct. Both my parents are social media inept. She smiles proudly for getting it right.

"Long story short. I know some of those tweets haven't been kind. I don't want you to suffer because I'm with Shane. If anyone makes fun of you for that, you need to tell me." Mom's stern voice and severe face hint at her level of frustration.

Most people don't understand our family dynamic at all. I've cried myself to sleep many nights because of some insensitive remarks about my mom being in a relationship with a woman. I didn't even understand it at first. But now, I can't imagine our life without Shane.

"Mom, you're overexaggerating. It's not even about that."

The deep-set lines across Mom's forehead soften. Shane recedes. The relief leaves their bodies like ghosts. Maybe someone has said something horrible to them or worse.

I need the truth. "Has someone threatened you?" South Florida is a blend of über-liberals and right-wing crazies. People who smother our alternative lifestyle with fake love or viciously tear it apart. Neither side understands.

"No," Mom answers a heartbeat too late.

She's lying.

Shane fidgets clumsily with her cup. "It's just that there's a lot of media coverage of Trax, and now of us, not just as a rescue center but as a family, and we want to make sure you're okay with it."

"I'm fine. We need it."

"No, we don't," Mom barks.

That's just like her. Always act strong, stand tough. Just like after Dad died. She had to make everything okay, better than okay, better than it was before. For a long time, I thought I was weak to be sad, to mourn. I pushed it all down until it manifested itself as Peter.

"You said this will bring in money, so I'll deal with it."

Mom nods. Worry is written all over her face, fear that I'll relapse into the troubled little girl that wouldn't leave her bedroom. The girl she couldn't handle. The girl she sent to a therapist.

"You have to deal with a lot of shit to get to the diamonds." I repeat one of Dad's favorite sayings to break the tension.

It works.

Mom laughs.

Shane smiles. "If it gets too much for you, please tell us."

"Of course. I promise I'm okay."

"We have another problem." Mom's face stiffens again. "You can get the wolf week after next, but we can't go with you." Her eyes dart to Shane. They've been stealing glances at each other throughout dinner.

Mom won't repeat our last mistake and ship an animal sight unseen. I had found a dog from Arkansas on the internet and relentlessly begged to save him. He barely made the trip alive. I'll never forget seeing a dog like that—terrified, in pain, open sores, practically dead. So if I want Dragon, I have to go and get him and, apparently, go by myself.

"Okay. I can do it. I'll go." I've forced my voice to be sturdy and strong as my heart pounds and Peter spits sticky threads, readying to suffocate me.

"I know you can. I'm proud of you. You've proved you're more than capable, but I can't let you go by yourself," Mom says.

"Who's going? Rock? Digit? Are they allowed to leave Florida?"

"There's another option. Ryan's going to Cabo Rojo next Saturday. You can go with him," Mom says.

WTF! Is this actually happening right now?

"I'm not going with him," I say.

"Kendall, you have anxiety attacks sitting alone at lunch," Mom says.

"I *used* to, not anymore. I haven't freaked out in school since … " *Today, but she doesn't need to know that.* "Since last year." I sneer smugly with false confidence.

Shane clears her throat.

Shut up, Shane! Peter rattles his container.

She doesn't say anything.

The fire sparks at my feet, and the heat inches upward. It takes all of my willpower to sit here and prove them wrong. Prove to myself that I can overcome Peter. I need to. I'm Dragon's ticket out. "Why the hell is he going?"

"Language," Shane scolds.

I grab on to the chair and grip so hard that my butt indents the cushion. *Don't bolt! Stay and convince them you don't need an escort.*

"I won't have my daughter traveling on an airplane for the first time by herself."

"But me going with some random guy is okay?"

"He's not a random boy, and his coach will already be there. So there's an adult to supervise." Mom rubs her temples in annoyance.

"A week is too long. I should leave tomorrow or over the weekend so I won't miss school." The lies spill from my tongue. I'm not brave enough to hop on a plane tomorrow. I need prep time. Time to raid Dr. Ferrera's medicine cabinet for tranquilizers.

"I've already confirmed it with Daniel. And it's over your spring break, so no school will be missed. It's perfect timing."

Mom has an answer for everything. I reach to Shane for another option. Anything! But she just grins a little and pats my hand. I pull it back and clasp the chair tighter this time. I grunt gutturally to make sure they understand just how awful of a situation they've put me in.

"So I'm tagging along on some sort of fancy spring break for rich kids? That's just fucking great!"

"Language!" Shane's scolding holds more weight this time.

"No!" Mom's eyes narrow.

Maybe she sees my facade of courage. A forced smile stretches across my teeth, but the attempt fails miserably.

"There's an international tennis tournament in Cabo Rojo, and Ryan's playing in it. He's actually a very good tennis player. Full scholarship to Northwestern next year. He's booked to leave next Saturday. Seats are still available on his flight. If you feel you're ready for this," Mom explains.

"It's your choice," Shane adds.

"Choice? What choice do I have? I can't leave Dragon to die. Why can't one of you, or Rock, take me? It's just a couple days."

Mom and Shane steal a glance again.

"We need Rock here." Shane pulls the ends of her short black hair around her soft jawline.

"Why?" I practically squeal the word.

"We just do." Mom's words are loud and final.

Since she's declared the conversation over, my death grip on the chair releases. I'm no longer in danger of losing it in front of them and totally proving their point, totally letting Peter detonate. I've come too far to go back. This is my choice, and I'll make it. I lean back and cross my arms, wondering how to manage Peter and fly on an airplane for the first time. All the while sitting next to Ryan. Perfect, gorgeous Ryan.

"I'm sorry, Kendall. There's too much going on right now. The bank, bills, the vet. We've got a sicko out there shooting dogs, and I need to help find him. It's just not a good time." Mom stiffens with each trial she lists. Her rugged clothes and sun-toughened skin are thin layers that don't completely cover her vulnerability. Regret and sorrow cloud her eyes as she stares into mine, but it only lasts a second, then she looks away.

I have Dad's eyes. She can never bear to look into them for more than a few seconds.

"Fine." I lean back farther in my chair, the baked chicken aroma beginning to rot in my nostrils. This whole idea stinks. They're not telling me everything. "Did you check all of this out? How do you know Ryan is telling the truth?" Unspoken accusations lace my tone, and the ignited flame behind Mom's eyes proves they don't go unnoticed.

"Of course I did. Ryan showed me the tennis website that lists the tournament with his name on the list of participants. I also spoke with his mother." Mom forcefully snatches her empty plate and glass and leaves the table in disgust. "You actually think I'd send you to Puerto Rico without due diligence?"

I shake my head, then murmur, "Glad to hear he has a mother."

This earns me a hostile fix from Shane.

The dishes land hard on the counter, and before Mom goes upstairs, she asks, "Remember that Humane Society Charity Gala your father and I went to on the beach?"

"No," I say.

"Well, Ryan's parents hosted that entire event and raised a lot of money. They're good people, Kendall." She marches up the stairs to the bedroom.

I rack my brain and can blurrily remember a night when Mom and Dad got dressed up to go out, and Rock babysat. I must've been five years old. I'm sure Mom does know a lot about him and his family. She's probably asked a lot of questions. I, on the other hand, hadn't asked him any questions. And that's going to change.

Shane rises, gathers our dishes, and carries them to the sink. I remain stuck in the chair, frozen until my phone alarm buzzes. Time for homework. I pull it out of my pocket and shut it off.

"Let me know soon what you decide. There's only a few seats left on the plane," Shane says over the sound of running water.

"Alright."

"By this Saturday?"

"Night. Saturday night."

"Fine, but the sooner, the better."

I press Vicky's name on my phone. It rings and rings until her voice mail picks up. It's the default greeting, not even her voice. End call.

In less than forty-eight hours, I will pardon Dragon or sentence him to death. *Some choice!* Peter wraps my heart in his threads of silk and crushes it.

The decision balances on each toss of the ball, like wishing on daisy petals—he likes me, he likes me not. Go to Puerto Rico with Ryan, don't go to Puerto Rico with Ryan. Dragon lives, Dragon dies. Mom's pissed because the price of the plane ticket went up this morning, but my forty-eight-hour deadline officially ends at 8:00 p.m. I can't rush my choice, because once she purchases my ticket, that's it, no turning back.

I pick up the spit-laden yellow ball, toss it into the air, and strike it hard with the tennis racket on its decline. *He likes you not. You don't go to Puerto Rico with Ryan. Dragon dies.* The ball sails through the air, and Duke has already shot across the yard to retrieve it on the bounce.

"Nice stroke."

I snap around to see Ryan walking toward us. Duke sees him too and beelines to him. The regal long-haired German shepherd, the epitome of grace in strength, gallops across the field.

"Hey, Duke." Ryan pats the black diamond on the crown of Duke's head, then scratches his back. Duke wiggles uncontrollably, the ball still in his mouth. "That's an old Head."

"What?" I ask.

"The racket."

"Oh, yeah. It was Dad's. I use it to play fetch."

"Cool. I have some old rackets in my garage. I'll bring them over."

"Okay, but I'll just use this one."

He lowers his eyes. "Oh, of course."

Idiot! He was being kind. Say something nice. "But can you fix this?" I point to the busted string.

His eyes brighten. "Yes. I can restring it tonight if you don't mind me taking it home."

I do mind. I don't like it out of my sight. "Sure. Thanks."

"Weather's looking bad." He looks up at the sky and shuffles his feet.

Wow, that's how boring I am. He's resulted to talking about the weather. Think, Kendall. Think! But I have nothing to add to this miserable conversation.

"Can I?" He reaches out his hand.

"Sure." I give him the racket.

He tosses the ball and swings. Duke darts toward the fence. The ball soars farther than I've ever sent it.

He shuffles some more, and soon, I'm shuffling too. We don't speak. We just watch Duke as Ryan sends two more tennis balls flying to the back fence. Then a bolt of lightning splinters through the dark clouds, leaving a glowing neon trail. The three of us run for cover, but not before a sheet of rain swipes us.

"Why am I always getting wet around you?" The words erupt from my mouth before I can stop them, and I cringe. I hope he doesn't think that's my ridiculous attempt at flirting. Why can't I talk when he's around?

"But this isn't my fault." His eyes shyly slant in my direction. He nudges the side of my leg with the racket.

Could this actually be flirting? With me?

"Oh, so you admit the spilled water cup was your fault?"

"Ha, ha! Isn't it always the guy's fault?" He sets the racket down and runs his fingers through his hair. Golden streaks shine from the dampness.

"Wow! That's sexist." I stare at his beautiful hair.

He throws up his hands. "I give up with you."

"What's that supposed to mean?"

He wanders over to my corner of the barn and plops down on a beanbag. "It means ... you ... I don't know. I feel like you think I'm a tool."

I lower my head and lumber to the other beanbag. My knees sink into the cushy balled furniture, then my butt drops to my heels. I shrug and shake my head.

"So that's a yes or a no?"

"No. You're not a tool. I'm not good with people. I have two friends." I slowly unfurl two fingers. "That's it. And as of Thursday, I have nine thousand–something followers, of which nine thousand and one are haters. They're following me so they can watch me make a huge ass out of myself on TV."

"You too? My Twitter followers tripled."

I smile. "I don't even tweet. I opened the account for social studies class. I'm just waiting for Mr. Young to realize he has his very own social media project sitting in the second row. It won't be long before the class starts critically analyzing the development of me—the social disorder."

He laughs. It's a raspy, manly laugh that makes him seem a lot older. "I've gotten three prom proposals and some special photos."

"Special how?"

He hesitates. "Girls half-dressed or not dressed." His eyebrows rise.

"Oh." I nod. "I don't have fans like that. I have evil trolls."

"That bad, huh?" Another swipe of the hair.

Engrossed in hair awe, all sensibility kidnapped, I say, "I have my own hashtag."

"Really? What is it?" He perks up.

Why would you say that? Peter twirls strings of entrapment.

What's he gonna think when I tell him what it is? I close my eyes, shove Peter aside, and find the courage. "Hashtag dirtydoggirl, or doggirl for short."

"Well, then." He whips out his phone, snaps a selfie of him hugging Duke, then types.

"What are you doing?" I ask.

He turns the phone so that I can see the photo. To my surprise I'm in the shot too. It looks as if we're huddled together.

> @RyanKast—Staying dry with my friend Kendall. Hope this rain ends so we can continue training Duke. #doggirl #doglife #fun

Peter rattles the vivarium enclosing my chest. One more idiotic tweet and Peter's going to shatter the glass. He'll scamper around terrorizing me, and I'll never be able to trap him again.

"Trust me; you can turn this around and use it to your advantage."

"I know we just met, but in case you haven't noticed, I'm not a bright-sunshiny-day kind of person."

"Well, I'm optimistic."

I huff a laugh, but Peter shrinks, and my chest loosens. Maybe Ryan's positivity rubbed off on me. It's actually nice sitting next to him and Duke, watching the rain pour down outside. Maybe Puerto Rico with him won't be so bad after all.

"Is that your dad?" He points to the picture pinned to the wall.

"Yeah."

"Cool."

I smile.

"Lots of books. Have you read them all?"

"Yep."

He leans back, stretching out like an alluring cat, and runs a finger over the spines. "I read this one, very depressing."

"Yeah, well, suicide generally is," I say.

"Yeah, it was deep."

"Since you're homeschooled, do you get to pick the books to read?" I ask.

"No, I have to follow a curriculum."

"Oh."

"There's a lot of NCAA guidelines." He picks up a comic book.

I'd forgotten about the stack of comics on the shelf. God, I'm such a dork. "Mom said you're going to Northwestern."

"Yeah."

"Are you excited?" My voice spikes, hoping he'll move on from the childish comic book pile.

"I was." He draws in a long breath and looks out at the rain. "I really like working here. Way more than I expected to." He turns his head back in my direction and smiles, flashing heart-melting dimples. He holds up one of my *The Amazing Spider-Man* comic books. "So is he your favorite?"

"No."

His eyes pop. "But the cup, the shirt, and these ... "

"I know." I start to tell him that Spider-Man is my least favorite, but he might ask why. Then what do I say—that his demon alter ego, Peter

Parker, dwells inside me? That the special treat of reading comics with Dad at bedtime morphed into a compulsive obsession after he died? That I chose Peter because I felt trapped in a web? "He used to be. Who's your favorite?"

"I just know them from the movies." He shrugs. "I guess, Thor."

I nod and smile. "Thor's pretty awesome."

"There's a few people I'd like to pummel with that possessed hammer." A lopsided sneer lifts one side of his face as darkness shadows his intense blues.

I'm out-of-my-mind intrigued.

"Me too." A girlish giggle slips out, instantly inflicting me with self-consciousness.

He peers into me, and I fear what he sees there. Are Peter's eight beady eyes staring back at him? Must end this, say something to make this weird moment go away, but all rational thought has blown away with the storm. Plus, whatever comes out of my mouth will probably only drive him away, and I like sitting here with him.

Eventually, he asks, "Where do you want to go to college?"

"Me?" I choke a laugh.

"What?"

"I'm not exactly an A student. Not sure I'd get into college."

"So you plan to keep doing what you're doing?"

"What's wrong with *keep doing what I'm doing?*"

"Nothing, I love this place. I didn't mean to—"

I don't want to talk anymore. I start to stand, but he has his hand on my leg. I hadn't even felt his touch on my skin, but now that I see it there, it's the only thing I can feel. It's a hot iron skillet slapped on my bare skin. My brain fails me again, because it won't tell my body what to do, like some sort of neural traffic jam. I should stand and get back to work. The rain slows, and I need to exercise the other dogs, but paralysis prevents it. Why is he so touchy-feely?

With the effects of his touch still swirling around inside me, I finally manage to form a coherent thought. "I've missed a lot of school. I'm barely getting by."

"Why'd you miss so many days?"

"My dad." Surprisingly, I admit this. His hand hasn't moved, and my knee is starting to sweat.

I jump to my feet and look down at him still lounging on the beanbag like the incredibly good-looking Thor. "The rain's clearing."

"Yeah." He stands next to me. "Lucy looks petrified."

The tidal wave of emotions I've just experienced plummets into the pit of my stomach. I'd forgotten what thunder does to Lucy. I rush to her stall, thrust open the gate, and swoop her into my arms.

"Is she okay?" His blue eyes are pools of concern.

I'm drowning in his presence. "She'll be fine. I usually put a ThunderShirt on her."

"What's that?"

"It wraps around her body and comforts her."

"Aren't all dogs scared of thunder?"

I nod. "Pretty much. I can't really remember a dog that liked the thunder, but for Lucy it's terrifying."

Again, he gets super close, smelling of citrus spice and cherries. He scratches behind Lucy's ear as she snuggles against my chest. I lock my stare on Lucy, to avoid gawking at him. I swallow, hoping to regain some sort of normalcy in my blood flow. Can I handle this while trapped inside a metal cylinder flying through the air?

He steps back. "I guess I should go help Cat."

My mutinous eyes forget our agreement and drift up to look directly into his. Having my body react against my brain is really annoying. First, it won't act; then, it acts too much! *Face, do not betray me. Don't frown or smile, just do nothing.* He can leave. I don't care. But my eyes don't obey. They wilt.

"We're linking the website to a Facebook page," he says.

"Facebook?"

"Yeah. I can't believe the rescue has survived this long without a website or Facebook. Can I get your number?"

"My what?"

He laughs that deep rasp again. "Your cell number."

"Sure." I relay the digits as he types them into his phone.

"Got it. Do you mind if I text you? We can coordinate about the trip."

"I'm not for sure going yet."

"I hope you do." His voice is tender, how I imagine velvet would sound.

"Uh-huh." My voice cracks, and I swallow as my cheeks burn with fear that he heard it.

He walks out, and my gaze falls to his butt. It's Thor-worthy. Catching the slip, I turn away. He's not going to bust me again.

Dad's racket leans against the wall. Ryan forgot to take it. I put Lucy down and pick it up. We mosey outside. The grass is wet. Water puddles in the dirt. Steam rises as the sun's heat returns. I love the after-storm effects.

Duke brings me a ball.

"Last one, boy." I send another slobbery, yellow orb sailing into the field. The final daisy petal—*He likes you. You go to Puerto Rico with Ryan. We save Dragon.*

The third-period bell rings, and Mr. Young rises from his desk. His eyes are like darts, and I'm the bull's-eye.

"Miss Shepherd," he says.

I nod.

"Remember, you have to speak up in my class."

I resist the urge to roll my eyes. "Yes, Mr. Young."

"It's come to my attention that the Twitter account you started for your class project has grown by one thousand percent. Impressive!"

I nod again.

He tilts his head, clearly irritated.

"Yes, sir."

"And today there's been a lot of activity regarding your hashtag."

"There has?"

"Yes, how are you handling it?"

By ignoring it! Why did you make me open this stupid Twitter account in the first place? I should say. "I'm handling it okay. It's strange."

"I bet it is. Class, take out your phones and go to @Kendogsrescues. You should all be following her, as I've instructed you all to follow and actively participate in others' accounts. Look at the latest Tweet she is tagged in. It seems Miss Shepherd has a few—" he hesitates "—trolls. That's the slang used to describe people that post or comment negatively in order to incite controversy or be provocative."

My heart plummets. What the eff?

My back slides down the chair, and I wish I could crawl under my desk and die. Instead, I'm forced to read the latest mentions. I've been avoiding this miserable account. Choosing to focus on other social studies projects and figuring I'd get around to checking my account soon enough. I couldn't cope with thousands of strangers dabbling in my life.

I see the tweet Ryan posted. It's not bad, but the comments are. The first comment is from @eLaineW, Elaine's username. She must stalk my hashtag daily. Doesn't she have anything better to do?

> @eLaineW—She doesn't even know it's a pity date. #loser #clueless #dirtydoggirl #hotguy.

On further inspection of the photo, I see that my face does beam at him like an obsessed groupie. But is that pity in his eyes? I had thought it but never wanted to admit it.

> @RUcrazy—That pitiful face! OMG! He's so not into her. #dirtydoggirl

God. All weekend I dreamed of him, of the possibility of us.

You're such an idiot. Peter taps his way into my consciousness.

Mr. Young strolls up and down the aisles. "Miss Shepherd is experiencing a viral phenomenon due to the rescue of a pit bull that was shot and tied to the railroad tracks. This act has catapulted her into the spotlight of public opinion. People she doesn't know are now emotionally attached to her, but is she emotionally attached to them?" He stops in front of my desk and hesitates. "Well, Miss Shepherd, are you feeling an emotional connection to your new followers?"

"No."

He turns away and continues talking.

Thank. God. This isn't Psychology 101. Peter and I would give Mr. Young a hard-on.

"I've tracked the negative to positive ratio of @Kendogsrescues activity, and it's clearly filled with both. I'm sure the negative tweets have forced Miss

Shepherd to disconnect emotionally from this form of social media."

You think? And the fact that I don't know most of these people, at all! My eyes squeeze shut, begging for it to stop.

"But can we, as human beings, truly disconnect our feelings when it comes to these social media sites?"

Corey, two rows to my right, raises his hand.

"What do you want to add, Mr. Williams?" Mr. Young asks.

"She could turn off her phone."

"But that's a physical reaction, not an emotional one. Focusing on this particular tweet, count how many positive replies versus negative replies. Don't count the likes or retweets, as we'd be implying our own opinions as to whether or not a like is positive and a retweet is negative. We have no way of proving that, but replies carry some evidence to sway it to the positive or negative side." Mr. Young stops talking as everyone delves into my timeline.

I freeze. I'm staring at my phone, the tweet and photo, but I can't bring my fingers to scroll down or click on any replies. I'm hyperaware of everything happening to me right now, like an out-of-body experience. My mind drifts to darkness as panic builds slowly from my gut, winding through my serpentine intestines, scaling the steep incline of my lungs, sticking to the back of my throat. Both icy shivers and hot bolts run through my blood. Sweat beads on the back of my neck. Each droplet that springs to life feels like a piece of Peter oozing out. He pierces through the delicate skin of my underarms. A life-sized spider forms from sweat and sloshes around the classroom, exposing all my insecurities.

I grab the bottle of water on my desk and gulp it to force the panic down, to stop giving Peter life.

I focus on breathing and count. One. Two. Three. Four. Five. Six. Seven. Eight. Nine. Ten. Eleven. Twelve … Twenty-one. Muffled sounds of students relaying sentences to Mr. Young as the chalk scrapes against the board. Twenty-two. Twenty-three. Twenty-four. Twenty-five … .Fifty-five.

"So that's the assignment, class," Mr. Young announces loudly.

Mr. Young claps, snapping me out of my counting trance. Everyone else packs up, getting ready to leave the classroom, but I stare at the chalkboard. Eighty-four negative replies to only nine positive ones. Wow! I begin scrolling.

@abby_bae—He's a fame whore and she's

```
just a whore #dirtydoggirldoesitdoggystyle
```

Jeez! Abby's a really nice girl. I click on her profile. She lives in Pennsylvania. Why would a girl five states away even care about this?

```
    @TomSlayer—She needs that cute dog to
get any boy to talk to her #loserville
    @Jenlovestennis—@RyanKast I see you've
lowered your standards!
    @ELaineW Replying to @Jenlovestennis—
You know him?
    @Jenlovestennis Replying to @ELaineW—
Yes. Very VERY well!!
    @ELaineW Replying to @Jenlovestennis—
Warn him. She's raised by criminals.
    @Jenlovestennis     Replying     to     @
ELaineW—She's     hideous.     Get     a     clue
#wayoutofherleague
    @ELaineW Replying to @Jenlovestennis—
And she smells like dog shit all the
time. #dogshitgirl
```

Then another reply pops up. I stop reading Elaine and Jen's conversation. I doubt it gets any nicer.

```
    @dancermandy—They make a cute couple.
Way to go Dog Girl. #beautiful
```

Amanda sits in the front row. She smiles. Amanda is one of the most popular girls in the eleventh grade. She's also one of the kindest people in our school. She's captain of the Dancing Devillers for the basketball team and very involved in student government.

I smile back in appreciation, then the bell rings.

"Remember, tweet your positive response at the time slot I've given you. Let's see if we can influence social media," Mr. Young shouts over the rustling of backpacks and chattering students.

Class is over. There's no giant sweat monster. That's good. I'm the last to cram my stuff into my backpack and leave.

Mr. Young gently places a hand on my arm before I step into the hall. "Kendall, if you ever feel overwhelmed by your viral predicament, I'm here for you. Feel free to knock on my door anytime. I think that pit bull rescue was fascinating and heroic. You should be very proud of the good service you do for this community. Don't let social media affect you negatively. And maybe, as a class, we can help spread more positivity."

"Okay. Thanks, Mr. Young."

At least Mr. Young tries to make learning interesting. He's actually one of my favorites despite today's disaster. He never punishes my absences with extra work or passive-aggressive comments. He has an old-man hippie vibe. Last week he wore a Coachella T-shirt.

"Whether we like it or not, social media will be a part of our lives, and my goal is to teach all my students to navigate through it in a way that is helpful and safe, not hurtful." His eyes express genuine heartfelt concern.

I huff a fake reassuring laugh. "It's all good, Mr. Young. I'm fine."

After the class from hell, there's the hallway of gawking classmates, so I put my head down and text Jimmy.

Me: U better b early 2 lunch!
Jimmy: Sure thing, Kens

I read Amanda's reply once more and admit that her kind words do help, but I turn off my phone nonetheless.

One hundred and twenty hours until school ends and spring break begins, and I don't have to see any of these people for an entire week!

Only 120 hours, Kendall! … Until you're trapped on an island with a guy that's #wayoutofyourleague. More Peter sweat bubbles break through my skin layers. Thousands of them. All with little hairy legs that scratch. The itch is unbearable.

The rescue call comes in around four thirty. A man has trapped two feral pit bull puppies inside his warehouse and needs someone to come and take them away. Not a hard job. The only problem is no one's here to go with me except Ryan.

All week I've successfully avoided awkward alone time with him. When Jimmy's around, it's fine. The three of us hang out, and there's always plenty to talk about, but Jimmy's not here today. I could wait. Shane, Mom, and Rock should be back soon. But the man on the phone sounded frustrated.

Cruz walks by. For a split second, I consider asking him instead of Ryan, but that's a stupid idea. Cruz never shuts up. I'd probably punch him before we got to the location. And he's not that competent. He's always late and on his phone. He's got some sort of side job that distracts him. Rock's nearly fired him twice.

I search out Ryan. "You get to go on your first rescue today."

Ryan stops filling the water bowls. "Okay."

I snatch the keys to the van and open the back to double-check that everything needed is there. Before Ryan's out of the barn, I say, "Grab a rope."

He returns with it and hops in the passenger side.

I hand him my phone. "You're the navigator. I've already entered the address in my maps. And I won't need help until we're close. Not sure where Reed Road is."

"Got it." He secures the seat belt.

The van is old, and nothing works, including the radio, so we fall into silence for miles.

Ryan clears his throat and licks his lips.

I roll my eyes.

He sighs loudly.

"What?" My fingers clamp the steering wheel.

"I just wanted to say I'm sorry about Jennifer." His voice wavers.

"Who?"

"@Jenlovestennis." He swallows.

I should've guessed. The word "tennis" is right there, screaming at me. "Yeah. I don't think she likes me."

His husky laugh catapults him out of boydom and into manhood. "She's my ex."

"Oh." I glance at him and nod.

"Who's Elaine?" he asks, his voice returning to charming smoothness.

"My ex."

The quizzical look that takes over his face is priceless. So I go with it and don't say another word.

"Well. Must've been a bad breakup, because her comments are messed up."

"Oh. It was awful." I fake sad eyes and furrow my brow, but my smile deceives me. Finally, I laugh. "I'm not gay. It was a best friend breakup a long time ago."

He nods but says nothing.

"It was my fault. I guess. Dad had just died, and I was no longer interested in gossiping about boys or picking out lip gloss. I'm sure if you asked her, she'd say I ignored her, that I was mean, but really, she didn't try. I was dealing with people telling me, *Your dad's in a better place. He's at Peace.* Or the best one was, *Everything happens for a reason.*" It still hurts. I swallow the choke of tears.

"How old were you?"

"Eleven."

"That's tough." He doesn't say it, but the apology hangs in the air.

That's another one of those absurd things about death. *I'm so sorry.* Elaine kept saying it over and over and over. I'd reply, *Why are you sorry? It wasn't your fault. Don't be stupid.*

"Anyway, what's this Jennifer's deal? She's Satan. And do I turn left here?" I flip on the left turn signal just in case.

"No, turn right."

I take the turn a little faster than I'd intended. Ryan's body swings away from me.

He straightens himself out. "In five miles Reed Road is on your right."

"Thank you."

He nods. "We broke up over a year ago. Those tweets aren't like her. I guess she's changed. Our families were close, but my parents never liked her dad, so when they divorced, their friendship sort of ended. I could call her and tell her to stop harassing you."

"No." I stiffen. Hell, no. Can you imagine? But it's a sweet offer.

"Well, if you change your mind."

We don't speak for the rest of the drive.

I park the van at the warehouse, but before I get out, he clasps my arm. He's so serious. I'm used to him smiling or smirking—sparkling teeth and adorable dimples. Not clenched jaw and sad eyes.

"The pity thing is ridiculous. I hope you know that."

I hadn't realized how tense my muscles were until they all go limp. I look away and smile.

We hop out and meet behind the van.

I throw a rope over one shoulder like a messenger bag, then give him one. I grab two blankets. "Take the crate, please."

He takes it and follows me to the door. It's locked, so he rings the bell. A gray-haired, tan man dressed in a short-sleeve green collared shirt and brown shorts opens the door.

"Hi. Come in. I hope you can get these little guys. My son and I've been trying, and they're too skittish. They've been here a week."

"Inside?" I ask.

"No, outside. I was afraid they'd get hit by a car, and we've got gators in the lake. I coaxed them inside with food, but then they scattered and hid." He walks through the office space and out an interior door. The space beyond is gigantic. Rows and rows of stacked equipment. "I'm a reseller. Got a lot of places to hide in here."

"Yeah." My eyes sweep the vast room.

"Should we spread out?" Ryan twitches. He's full of energy.

I shake my head. Twitchy energy may be good for tennis, but it's not good for earning the trust of a scared pup. "No. We stay together. When we find one, you need to move slowly and calmly. Okay?"

He stops the jittery bouncing. "Yeah." He half smiles and lowers his head.

Was I this excited my first time? It's cute.

The cuteness wears off fast. It's been over an hour, and they've outsmarted us. My agitation maxed out fifty minutes ago, and now I'm biting back insults before I scream them at the top of my lungs.

Deep breaths, Kendall. Deep, deep breaths. He's trying his best.

"I see her," I whisper, and point.

We inch in her direction, closing the gap with each step. He's being brilliantly stealth this time. We look at each other. I sign for him to get the blanket in position, then start to count down. An ear-piercing alarm screeches from his pocket. He drops the blanket and scrambles to pull out the phone. It's mine. He never gave it back to me.

"Give me that." I snatch my phone and open the alarm app.

Ryan peeks over my shoulder. "How many alarms do you set?"

"None of your business." I shove the phone into my pocket.

"Don't be mad at me. That screw-up is all you." His hands fly up like he's under arrest.

I hang my head. "Fine. That one's on me, but the last ten were all you."

We've finally pushed her to the back wall. At least now her options are limited. I enlist the man's help this time. "Please stand there. Just in case. Block that exit." My orders are firm, but respectful. "But don't engage. She could bite."

He nods and stands his ground.

"Ryan. Remember what I told you about the blanket. Throw it over her and fall on top. Forget the rope." His rope-handling skills have proved hopeless.

He gives me the thumbs-up.

I approach her head-on with the food. She's tired and droopy all over except her eyes. They're wide open and ice blue. Her pupils are so small they're almost invisible. She sniffs. Her stomach is hungry. She's wiggling, turning side to side, but she can't back up. This is the closest I've gotten to her. I toss a treat. She eats it lightning fast. Slowly, she ventures a little closer. She sniffs for more food. I'm earning her trust. Finally, she's close enough for me to loop the rope around her. In one fluid motion, I rope her and wrap her in the blanket.

"Got her," I call out, letting the guys know it's safe to walk and talk.

"Aw, little girl. You're a worthy opponent." Ryan feeds her more treats.

"With the feral pups, you want to swaddle them. They're like babies, and the snug blanket makes them feel safe." I tighten the blanket and hug her. "But she still could bite, so you have to be careful. I think she's too exhausted, though."

I put her in the crate and quickly corner her brother. The boy pup runs toward Ryan, who leaps on top of him, smothering him with the blanket like he's wrestling a wild boar.

It's hysterical.

However, Ryan's swaddling skills deserve admiration. He beams at his little bundle like a proud daddy.

I walk over with a handful of treats and a big grin. All my frustration melts away. It was actually a fun adventure.

His eyes glance up and take me in. Something in his stare warms every inch of me. We make a good team.

The dark sky layers with milky clouds that move and disappear with the wind and magically reappear seconds later. It's a cool dance. They mute and shade the moon, transforming it into a sinister gray orb. It's eerie and soothing at the same time.

Go to bed, Tweety, Dad's voice whispers.

I turn toward his photo. "I know, Dad."

Go inside. You'll get a better night's rest for your trip tomorrow.

I grunt. "Why would I sleep anywhere else? And why would changing where I sleep the night before give me a better night's rest? Do you see the error in your logic?" I stare into his brown eyes, my eyes, our soul.

Are you scared?

My face drops and sinks into the mushy beanbag. I bury it and enjoy the softness until I must come up for air. "Yeah."

It's normal. You've never flown before.

I've never flown, never kissed a boy, never had a boyfriend, and the list goes on and on. I push these depressing thoughts out. "I know, but I'm excited too. Having Dragon home is going to be amazing. It's finally happening, Dad. After all these months of begging and pleading and praying. Isn't that what it's all for? Saving an animal's life." A smile spreads across my face, and it might be crazy, but Dad's photo smiles back. It's there in my mind's eye: the part of his lips, the ridges in his teeth, and the sparkles in his eyes as his cheeks round, eclipsing his lower eyelids.

The wind stirs, and I swear someone walked in. I get up and look around, but no one's here in this old beat-up barn—just dirt and dogs.

"Dad?" I turn back to the photo, but it's just an unyielding picture of a remarkable man trapped for a moment in time. My fingers trace the fine lines of his forehead and eyes.

"Come back," I whisper, but he's gone. The cray-cray half has shut off. I'm on my own. I have to fly on my own, go on a trip with Ryan on my own, retrieve the wolf on my own. Tears puddle, then spill. "You should be here. You should be the one taking me to Puerto Rico! It's not fair!"

A solid punch lands in the center of the beanbag, but it doesn't help. Peter still threatens to unleash the pathos.

"Why me? Why take my good dad and not Vicky's shitty one?"

I want to scream and throw, kick and rip everything. I reach to crumple that fucking stupid photo. But I just place it facedown and swallow Peter back into his container. I won't do this again.

Blinking the tears and madness away, I jump to my feet and take in the spooky midnight sky. This is a new chapter. With Ryan, even if we're just friends. I'm going to Puerto Rico. I'm going to get Dragon.

Lucy whines.

"What is it girl?"

She's standing on her back paws, her front paws outstretched, her dewy eyes open wide.

"You're wide awake. This isn't good, Lucy. I really need to go to bed. I'm going to have ugly purple circles under my eyes tomorrow."

She barks.

"Shhh, you'll start a howl-at-the-moon domino." I unlatch the gate and lift her into my arms. Together, we sneak into the house.

Shane lies on the couch, barely awake, watching the news. "Looks like you'll have good flying weather." She slowly rises to a sitting position. She loves to inform me of the weather. "The rain threat goes down to twenty percent tomorrow, and I checked the wind, and it's light."

"That's good." I hadn't thought about how the weather would affect the flight, but now that she's mentioned it, I will. Why do parents always try to help? They just make it worse.

"You know I won't stop worrying until you're safely back here, Dragon and Ryan in tow."

I laugh.

"I put your favorite sweater on top of your suitcase. I just washed it. Thought you might want it, at night, after the sun goes down. You might have a chill." She babbles in her half-awake state.

"Yeah, sure. April in the Caribbean."

She scowls.

"Thank you, Shane."

She smiles. "Ryan's picking you up tomorrow?"

"Yes."

"If I'm not up, but I'm sure I will be, make sure to kiss me goodbye."

"I will. Night," I say.

I lumber up the stairs to my room, place Lucy on my bed while I take a shower, then slip into new pajamas. The muggy air from the barn wasn't helping my inability to sleep. Maybe clean skin and clothes will. Then I slide under the covers and curl into Lucy's warm body, hugging her tightly. She settles into a peaceful sleep, but I think and worry about the weather.

Flying on an airplane. Tomorrow!

Vicky flew all the way to England once. If she was here, she'd answer all my questions, take the angst away.

> Me: U up?
> Jimmy: No—

Then a couple of minutes later—

> Jimmy: What?

I call him and ask a million questions about air travel … and boys.

M echanical difficulties! Our plane has been delayed, and I'm trying not to freak out.

Last night Jimmy never mentioned the possibility of mechanical difficulties. But it makes sense. Of course there could be mechanical difficulties. An airplane is a very mechanical thing that flies in the air, thousands of feet high. How many screws need to come loose before it plummets to Earth? It's terrifying, which is why I refuse to ask any questions.

Thank. God. The sun is shining, and there's no rain, no lightning. Otherwise, I couldn't be calmly sitting in the food court, drinking acai smoothies and pretending it's all okay so Ryan won't think I'm nuts.

"She's a tennis player." I point to a skinny brunette with a huge Wilson bag strapped to her shoulders.

"Gee, that's imaginative. What gave it away?" He grins.

"Okay, fine. The man with the ripped cargo shorts, bloodshot eyes, and dreads is not a drug-smuggling reggae musician like he looks. Instead, he's an undercover CIA—no, DEA—agent about to score his largest bust ever in Colombia." I melodramatically lean in over the table.

"I better hide my Xanax," he whispers while leaning over the table too.

I inhale his candy breath as I've done for the past week, and it hasn't gotten gross yet. He doesn't move. His nose hovers an inch from my nose. Sensational awkwardness arises until a curvy blond slams her heavy tennis bag on my foot.

I glare at this stranger.

"Oh, I'm so sorry." She smiles, places a hand on my shoulder, and appears friendly, but something in her eyes tells me that she isn't sorry at all. The urge to slap her hand off my shoulder consumes me, but she removes it, so I remain politely still.

"Jennifer. Hello." Ryan's voice flattens.

I freeze.

"I thought you were in quallies." His movements become robotic and tight.

"I was. I got bumped to main draw two days ago, then I switched my flight. I won't spend any more time in that place than I have to. Remember last year." She touches his arm and leaves her hand to linger. When he removes it, she rolls her eyes and sits down uninvited.

So far, I'm invisible, which is fine with me.

She opens a protein bar and eats one tiny bite at a time. I want to reach over and smash a normal-sized bite down her throat, but I stay as still as possible and observe Ryan interacting with his own kind.

"Knowing your record, you'll be home soon," he says.

Evidently, this is an insult, because her face turns red, and her eyes narrow. Ha!

"Screw you, Ryan. I heard you lost to Zander." She squirms in the chair as if just pronouncing the name gives her a disease.

Ryan's speechless and losing his charm. His body stiffens. I don't know him that well, even though over the last week we've spent a lot of time together, but apparently he's feeling vulnerable. His lips pout even more than their natural fullness. My stomach does jumping jacks looking at them. Some sort of powerful energy force pulls my lips to him, and I nearly fall out of my chair.

Jennifer looks at me.

Shit!

I pull myself back to sit straight, do a quick check of my surroundings, and exhale, thankful there's no spider's silk drawing me toward him. Heated embarrassment smears over my face.

"Sorry." I lean on my elbow and try to cover my flush cheeks with my hand. "I'm just tired. We've been waiting for too long."

"Do you play?" Jennifer asks. "You look familiar."

"No," Ryan answers for me.

I squint at him. He's protecting me from her, which is sweet but irritating. I can fend for myself. I've been doing it all my teenage life.

"This is Kendall. I work for her mother."

A flash of recognition crosses her face.

I grit my teeth, holding everything inside, the vomit, the words, the anger, and the anxiety demon.

Her cold eyes roll over me, appraising all my unworthiness, then she smirks and turns to sneer at Ryan. "Since when do you work?"

Well, that's confirmed—he's too spoiled to need a job.

"I'm volunteering for community service hours. It's an all-breed dog sanctuary," he says.

"Oh, I already got my hours helping Steve run the wheelchair tournament. That was the longest day of my life. I couldn't wait to be done. He let me skip out on Sunday. If I'd missed Christian's pool party for a bunch of—" she hesitates, looks at me, then says, "Well, you know." She pulls her long, thick hair into a ponytail.

And now I hate her for sure. The legs of my chair shriek against the floor when I push away from the table. "I'm going to go find out about our plane." I grab my carry-on and swing it close to Jennifer's nose. It's my way of saying, *Eff you, from Jimmy.*

She's undoubtedly insulted.

Good! Point delivered.

"Wait. What?" Ryan looks from Jennifer to me, obviously confused.

I hesitate for a second, feeling bad leaving him to deal with her, but I can't stand her shrill voice and sparkling polished nails any longer.

He pushes his chair out and begins to stand.

For a second, time stops. My heart echoes inside my mind, muffled beat after beat. It's like everything has frozen. Ryan smiles, and his ocean eyes gaze directly into mine. I've won. He picked me. Jennifer's glare pulls my eyes away. She clearly doesn't like to lose, and the defeat burns through her. In a flash it's gone—her anger, his smile, frozen time. It all speeds back into place as two guys with tennis bags approach. Soon they're all embracing and fist-bumping and happy to be together again.

Ryan glances back at me, his pointer finger in the air, and mouths, "One minute." His eyes plead for me to wait.

"Just meet me at the gate." I smile and walk away. Let them talk tennis and stuff. It's no big deal. I'm just not in the mood to loiter on the outskirts.

The airport is impressive—a new and fascinating place. People scatter in all directions, wearing all sorts of clothes in many colors, some traveling for business with expensive shoes and cell phones stuck to their ears, others with flip-flops and shorts. Couples snuggle, and exhausted parents chase children; lots of people lie on the floor with their phones plugged into outlets.

Four tennis bags fill the seats in our area as I make it back to gate A-11. The information plaque reads, *Delayed, now boarding at 12:30.* My watch reads 12:10. I itch to get on the plane to get this over with. Now that I'm alone, horrible plane crash images play and replay in my brain.

Mechanical difficulties!

When the woman at the desk begins to call people to board, I gather my stuff and stand close to the line. I search the crowd for Ryan. My hands are full, but I manage to get my phone out of my bag and text him.

> **Me: They r boarding.**

No response.

"Great," I murmur. One. Two. Three. Four. Five. Six. Seven. Eight. Nine. Ten. I inhale deeply and strain to listen to the lady calling out the boarding information. The static of the microphone renders her words unrecognizable.

I can't do this. I bolt into the bathroom and walk in circles, hitting people with my carry-on. "Sorry. Sorry. I'm so sorry." I enter the wheelchair accessible stall in the back, collapse onto the toilet, and think about whom to call.

"Jimmy?"

"Hi, Kens. Aren't you supposed to be on the plane now?"

"Yes. Yes." The breaths come quick, so fast they hurt.

"Kens, relax. Breathe." His voice is a calm and collected reassurance.

I inhale a breath that actually reaches my lungs, and they finally expand. The oxygen flows, easing my pounding heart. A single tear branches down my face. "I can't go." My voice cracks as the failure of my decision sets in.

"Yes, you can."

You can't! Peter's sticky threads spin around my lungs, making it hard to breathe again.

"I believe in you, Kens. You're strong." There's power in his voice.

"I don't think I can," I say.

"You've been after this wolf for months. You've obsessed." At his words Peter's web loosens.

"I know, but I can't get on that plane. I just can't." My hands tremble. The phone clatters against my ear.

"Is Ryan there?"

"No."

"No? Where is he?"

Jimmy's loud question startles me. "I mean, yes. He's not here, here. The lady is announcing the boarding, and he's not here."

"But he's coming, right?"

"Yes."

"Where are you?"

"In the bathroom."

"Kens, he's probably out there looking for you."

I nod. The tears fill my eyes and choke my voice. *You're a failure.*

"It's okay. Ryan can bring Dragon home. It'll all work out." His voice softens, and worry laces the tone.

I nod rapidly. My red, blotchy face reflects in the mirror. I stand and walk toward it, searching my eyes. Dad's eyes gaze back. He's crying, but there's strength way in the back through the pupil, past the lens, to the very, very back. My head goes from nodding to shaking.

"Okay? Ryan will get Dragon. Okay? It'll be all right. Are you there?"

I nod.

"Are you nodding? Because I can't hear nodding, and I'm really getting worried!"

"Yes, I'm here." The words burst through the sludgy saliva coating my mouth. I swallow.

"Do you want me to call Ryan? Tell him change of plans?" He's put me on speaker, probably looking for Ryan's number.

"No, I'm going back. I'm going to try, Jimmy."

"Good, Kens. You got this. I know you do. You're going to be so proud of yourself afterward. Okay?" His voice leaps and skips with encouragement.

"Okay. Thanks, Jimmy."

"Anytime. Call me if you change your mind. I'll be here."

"Okay. Bye."

"Love you, Kens." His words are warm and encouraging. I'm not the only friend he tells that to. He's just that kind of person. He's like human sunshine.

I smile. "Love you too."

I pull tissues out of my bag and pat my face and eyes. Our eyes. They're still red and puffy, but they're tenacious. I'll do this, Dad, for your dream and for Dragon. Desperately, I run cold water over more tissues and press them against my eyes. The redness pales. I straighten my hair with my fingers and put on lip gloss. That helps. I don't look too terrible. I fling open the stall door to a mother with a stroller. By the grim look on her face, she's been waiting for the big stall and is none too pleased I've been hogging it.

"Sorry." I rush out. To my relief people are still lining up, but no Ryan. Maybe he's already on the plane. I jump in line and copy the people entering the tunnel in front of me.

The plane is narrow, and I struggle to pull my carry-on through the aisle without smacking people, scanning each row for Ryan, but he's nowhere. I find my seat number and no Ryan. A woman places her luggage above her seat, so I do the same. I quickly sit down, but I need the headphones out of my bag. The aisle fills with people, and if I get up, I'll be in everyone's way. I remain in my middle seat with nothing to listen to.

The plane is full, and still no Ryan. The empty seat triggers my anxiety. Sweat beads on my forehead and cuts through my underarms.

Think of Dragon. I can do this. Breathe.

The flight attendant speaks. "The cabin doors will be closing soon. Please, step out of the aisle, make sure your belongings are stowed, your seat is in the upright position for takeoff, and your seat belt is fastened."

No Ryan! Peter taunts me.

I fasten, then unfasten my seat belt. I stand, then sit and fasten my belt again. They're going to shut the doors. I'll be trapped. Again I reach to unbuckle, then hesitate. I could leave.

A man sits in the aisle seat next to me. He's blocked my exit. I'm cornered. The suffocating feeling balloons my lungs. I gasp. All my scabs and scars start to itch. My nervous scratching of my arms irritates the man next to me. He slants at me twice, and I force my fingers to still. My arms burn from the unscratched itch. It spreads up to my scalp, making my head tingle and my eyes water.

For Dragon. For Dad. For Mom and Shane.

Peter eyes me with those eight black pearls and threatens to escape from the vivarium I've jammed him into. *What were you thinking, boarding this plane alone? You need to get off. Get off. Right now! Get off!*

I unbuckle and begin to stand, when Ryan appears in the distance at the front of the plane. Huh. I can barrel my way past him and get off this metal flying whale, or stay and do what I set out to do. I'm hovering over the seat stuck between going or staying, between failure or success, between Peter or me.

My butt falls to the cushion. Choosing to stay releases the anxiety. It flows away, starting at the top of my head and rushing out of my toes. Exhaustion follows, filling the void left behind, and I fully collapse into the seat.

Ryan searches me out and smiles eagerly when our eyes meet.

I'm a sweaty, limp mess. Air blows from the little vent above my seat, but it's not enough. I'd need an arctic blast to cool off from the ferocious heat boiling in my belly and stealing the smile from my face.

He acknowledges the change in my expression with a cute grin, dimples and all. His eyes soften. Evidently, he regrets scaring me and making me wait next to some stranger that stinks of beer and onions.

"Hi," he whispers, and squeezes his athletic body past the large man in the aisle seat and then past me to sit next to the window. "Sorry. I haven't seen Jake and Josh in forever, and Jennifer wouldn't shut up. I kept telling them you were waiting for me."

He should apologize. Another second, and you would've lost it. Two years of being incident-free out the door.

"It's okay. I managed." I look away and smile a little, proud that I got on the plane.

The takeoff pushes me into the seat, but instead of feeling trapped, I feel exhilarated. I turn to look out of Ryan's window. He's watching me. I drop my head and stare at my lap.

"You like it?" His voice is kind. He could have easily patronized me, but he didn't.

"Yes." I straighten my back and lift my head to meet his gaze and confront this new, frightening challenge.

Ryan beams like I'm the only person on the plane. He has probably flown all over the world, but he smiles as if we are both experiencing this for the first time.

"Look." He puts his arm around me and slides me closer.

His arm! It's warm and cozy and comfortable, like fresh doughnuts on Sunday morning, as if he's done it a million times.

The weight of his arm absorbs all previous chaos, and I'm free to fly. Together, we lean toward the small oval window. It's like nothing I've ever seen before. The water below is crystal blue with dark spots under the sea.

"Are those dolphins?"

"Maybe?" More grinning.

Seeing the land from high above, there's only beauty. The litter on the beaches and the damaged buildings lining the streets blur and blend into an illusion of perfection. Lush green trees and lawns flow into the creamy, sandy beaches. It could be a painting.

"It's beautiful." I lost myself in the spectacle and didn't realize I had laid my head on his shoulder. I start to pull away, but he presses me to him. His firm, warm chest is so comforting that I don't resist his hold. I'm so exhausted from the battle within that I let him soothe me. My eyes close, and my mind drifts away.

"Good morning." Ryan enters the hotel lobby.

I wave hello, still on the phone with Mom.

He has a bye, which means he doesn't have to play a match today. Yesterday the word "bye" had an entirely different meaning. The merging of our worlds has been cool. He's included me in everything from his practice matches to meals to finding a spot with a good Wi-Fi connection to study. He's introduced me to all the players and coaches. We've managed to avoid talking to Jennifer, but the daggers thrown from her eyes hit their mark.

"Bye, Mom. I'll think about it and let you know." I hang up.

"What's up with your mom?"

"She said the shelter is flexible. They said I don't have to take Dragon on Thursday if you're still in the tournament. I can go home with you, or when you lose, you can come home with Dragon and me."

"What do you want to do?"

"I don't know. I feel bad staying here. There's a lot going on at home."

He takes my hand. "Nothing they can't handle."

I look down at our laced fingers. "I don't know. When Mom and Shane told me about the opportunity to go with you, they kept looking at each other in an awkward way. Don't you think it's strange neither of them came with me?" My eyes rise to meet his.

He shrugs. "I never thought about it. You seem so competent. I guess I assumed you'd done this before."

"I've never even flown before."

"I know, but I mean traveled to retrieve dogs." He hesitates. "It is odd. Isn't it?"

I nod. "Now she's pushing me to stay longer. And three shot pits. They're not telling me something."

"They're tracking down a possible serial killer—"

My head snaps around to interrogate him. "Did she tell you that?"

"Yes, they mentioned it, but of course they're not telling us everything."

Mom and Shane have been busy with other agents searching for the source, trying to link the dogs. But Trax's incident is so much more sensational. The first two were left for dead, one thrown in the reservoir and one hidden under bushes. But the word "serial killer" was never mentioned. It sounds so menacing.

"But they always tell me everything." My insides go quiet. Not even Peter is stirring up trouble.

Ryan lets go of my hand. "It's nothing. It's your spring break. Your moms just want you to have fun. Forget about shot dogs, weirdos, and national news."

"You're right." I long to hold his hand some more. He's right. It's spring break. Let's have fun and not overthink.

The taxi driver weaves in and out of speeding traffic, and it doesn't take long to get to the university. We're dropped off at a beige building.

I tug on Ryan's shirt. "If Daniel says anything about me being sick, just go along with it."

"What?" His eyes pinch.

We wander inside. It's a wide-open room with tons of tanks holding various types of reptiles. The musky, humid air smells of fish and mud. It's tolerable until the underlying bleach smell permeates my lungs.

"Excuse me? Daniel?" I ask the only man in the room.

He stops adjusting a light over one of the tanks and comes to greet us. "Hi, Kendall." He embraces me. "Nice to finally meet you. So glad you're well."

He has an approachable face and endearing eyes. He's just how I envisioned him to be. My guilt over the many lies I've emailed him these past months surfaces. I swallow it down.

"And you are?" Daniel extends his hand to Ryan.

"Hello, I'm Ryan."

"But you're not picking up today, yeah?" Daniel asks.

"No. We're just visiting today. I'm scheduled to bring him home Thursday or when he loses." I apologetically glance at Ryan.

"I'm in a tennis tournament up the road. I could lose tomorrow, and we'd be ready to take Dragon, or I could make it until Sunday. I know it's kind of unreliable."

Now I'm glad he uses the word "we."

"No, no. It's okay. I think Maria talked to Shane about it." He turns away from us and yells, "Maria, *saca a Dragon.*"

"*Bien,*" a voice in the back room shouts.

Maria walks Dragon out on a leash, then unclips it so he can roam freely. He's thin, but his coloring is beautiful and his golden-flecked bronze eyes curious.

"Wow." Ryan's captivated with the lovable wolf. "He's so friendly."

Dragon sniffs us and revels in being petted.

"*Sí,* which is a problem," Maria says. "He's too domesticated. We can't release him into the wild."

"He's a lot smaller than I expected," Ryan says.

"I know. He should be a good thirty pounds more," Maria says.

"I'll plump him up, don't worry," I say.

"*Buena.*" Maria smiles. "Your paperwork is in order. Shane has already signed everything via email, so as long as you approve of his condition, then we are set for you to take him whenever you're ready."

"Okay. Can I take him for a walk?" I ask.

"*Sí,* of course. Spend as much time as you want. We'll be here if you need anything."

I clip the harness onto the grayish-brown wolf. His fur is coarse but still cuddly.

Ryan and I explore the campus. "So what do you think of Dragon?"

"He's cool. When he gains weight, he'll be beasty."

I smile.

"Who's going to adopt a wolf, though?" he asks.

"No one, he's for me. I'm keeping him."

"Oh, very *Game of Thrones*." He laughs.

"Yep, don't eff with me." It's become so easy to tease with him.

"Yeah, he's badass, but we've bonded." He brushes my shoulder with his hand.

His touch scares me way more than Dragon's teeth. Is this what a boyfriend does?

After an hour and a half, we're in another cab heading back to the hotel. We both reek of dirty wolf and reptiles and need to shower.

Bathed and clean, I leave my room to knock on Ryan's door. We're going to dinner early because he has a morning match. I'm starting to understand the intensity of this sport. It's highly competitive and tough. The girls are tough too. I stay as far away from Jennifer as possible but have watched her practice. She's good.

The door swings open. "Hey there." His eyes quickly take me in. A mischievous grin plays on his lips as if he's going to pull me into his room and kiss me passionately.

I shake off these unhinged thoughts, but the tingling sensation filling my blood remains.

"Hi." My arms feel naked, my scratches exposed. Why did I wear a sundress? The feeling gets worse inside the elevator. I'm boxed in with useless arms and no pockets for my empty hands. I put them on my hips, then straighten them, then one on hip and one straight. If he'd just grab one, but he doesn't. I can't stop thinking about limbs. Finally, the elevator door opens but my relief lasts two meager steps when I land face-to-face with Jennifer.

"Showing her the town?" She smirks.

"Uh-huh." Ryan doesn't slow down to talk.

She flings more daggers at me. If looks could kill, I'd be dead three times over. I just grin as Ryan opens the door, and we depart into the dusky evening. A few cars pass on the narrow road, and we have to step into someone's yard.

The rural area has some run-down shacks, but it's also charming.

"You look nice," Ryan says.

"Thanks." The compliment stirs inside me. It's inexplicable, almost painful. A satisfying ache whipping up more steamy fantasies.

"You're going to love this place. It's on the water, and these huge tarpons swim right below your feet."

There are two Ryans: the relaxed-and-sure-of-himself Ryan, who mainly appears when he's alone with me, and tennis-player Ryan, who's reserved and uptight around his colleagues.

"Oh, wow." The old, crappy street morphs into a picturesque fishing town. Wooden storefronts painted in pastel blues, yellows, greens, and pinks. The salty tang of the ocean rides on a cool breeze.

"Are you cold?" Ryan puts his arm around me.

"A little." I let his arm stay in place. The warmth from his body takes the bite out of the wind. It feels like a dream … him … this place. I've never been anywhere that takes more than a fifteen-hour car ride to get to. "It's so cute."

"It is." His voice booms. He smiles wide.

His excitement always takes me off guard. Even though we're almost the same age, he seems much older and more composed. I doubt he falls apart inside every second we're together.

He leads me into an open-air restaurant. License plates, old keys, business cards, and Polaroid pictures cover the walls and ceiling. Oil crackles, and the smell of fried fish fills the air. Large picnic tables are scattered around the room, and we sit at one in the very back, next to the railing. The sea jumps with a school of silver tarpon fish.

Ryan breaks off a piece of bread from the loaf that's on the table and throws it over. The fish attack it, and I start at the viciousness.

Laughter escapes Ryan.

I snarl.

"Here." He hands me a piece.

We toss them in, one after the other, and before the waitress makes it to our table, we've killed the entire loaf. The water stills. The dark sea spans long and wide, merging deceptively into the evening sky.

"Looking out there makes me feel insignificant," I say.

"Yeah, can you imagine how horrifying it was during Hurricane Maria?"

"No. This place is nothing but wood and water."

"*Buenas tardes.*" The waitress places another loaf of bread on the table.

"*Buenas tardes,* can we have the plantain appetizer, please?" Ryan asks.

"*Sí,* and to drink?" she asks.

He looks at me. "Water, please."

"Two bottled waters," Ryan says.

The new bread loaf is warm, and I'm tempted to eat a piece but throw it into the sea instead.

"What do you think?" he asks.

"I like this place. The tarpon are crazy."

"So now you know what I do when I'm not at the rescue. Hit balls and play tournaments."

"You're really good."

"Thanks." He looks down at the table.

"Are you nervous about tomorrow? I'd be terrified."

"Not really. I know the guy I'm playing."

"Here you go." The waitress places the appetizer between us and takes our dinner order.

"Well, I'm learning a lot about you, Ryan Kast."

"Oh, finally learned my last name." He winks.

"Ha. Ha."

"So what have you learned?"

He has a way of making me speechless and putting me on the spot. Last week this irritated me, but right now it makes me feel interesting. "Well, you're very disciplined. You've obviously played tennis a long time, because you're amazing. The other players are not really your friends, although you act as if they are." I pause. *Where are all of these words coming from? Shut up!*

"What do you mean by that?" Curiosity flickers in his eyes, but not anger.

"I don't know. I didn't mean to say that."

"Yes, you did." The flicker of curiosity grows into a roaring flame.

I sigh, desperate to suppress this horrible topic I brought up.

He leans in, waves of expectation, possibly irritation, crossing his face.

"You just seem stiff around them. You seem to only be able to tolerate them for a small amount of time, then leave quickly. Sometimes you make me leave before I've finished eating, which is dangerous." I pop a plantain in my mouth.

"I did that last night. Didn't I?" He half smiles. His dimples are barely noticeable. Thankfully, the agitation is gone.

I nod and smirk.

"I've known most of these people for years. I don't know why, but they do annoy me sometimes. A lot of the guys just want to hook up with the girls. Most of the girls are easy—"

"Hey!" I glare.

"Sorry. Not all of them but a lot of them. I'm not being sexist—I'm being truthful. Some of these players have a lot of money and don't care if they win or lose. I know a girl that smashed all six of her rackets. Twelve hundred dollars."

"That's insane."

"Yep. They just want to be away from their parents, have their own hotel rooms. And I used to be just like them."

"Used to?"

He tilts his head.

"What changed you?"

He pauses. His irritated expression returns. I expect some long explanation, but instead, he leans over the table and kisses me. His lips feel soft. Fiery heat crests around my neck and over my back, sending blazing shivers down my spine. It's not a long kiss, since the table is between us and we're in a restaurant, but it's tender and sincere—my first kiss. His lips are as inviting as I'd dreamed. Even after he's pulled them away, I can't help but stare at them. My cheeks burn. I've probably turned cherry red.

His cheeks don't blush, but his eyes retreat. "I should've asked first."

"No," I huff, because the butterflies make speaking too difficult. "It's fine." I can't stop the smile from taking over my face.

We don't talk much after that. He eats all of his dinner, but I hardly swallow my food and drink loads of water. My insides combust with uncertainty. I felt something between us when we kissed. Did he?

During the walk back to the hotel, he takes my hand. His thumb explores my cold palm. This is doughnuts on Christmas morning, cozy but with the added tingles of an unopened present—and not the kind tossed quickly into a gift bag but the kind wrapped in shimmery ribbons and shiny paper.

Hands are being held!

The walk back seems miles longer. Words catch in my throat. I'm a bundle of nerves, but it's nothing I've ever experienced. It's not anxiety. Peter is steady and quiet.

Ryan's friends gather by the entrance to the hotel, talking and hanging out.

"Hi, Kendall. Ryan." Chloe glances down to see us hand in hand. She glints a genuine expression of happiness.

I knew I liked her when I met her earlier. We had talked about our love for animals, and I had shown her pictures of Dragon.

"Hi, Chloe." I smile, but of course the joyful vibe disappears with one sadistic look from Jennifer.

"Let me guess, you saw the tarpon?" Jennifer's voice chills all the warmth out of me and shreds my perfectly wrapped present.

I'm stunned but pretend it doesn't bother me. It's almost impossible not to tighten my grip on Ryan's hand.

"We had a nice dinner. Thanks for asking." Ryan frowns.

"David just beat Stephen," Jennifer says.

Based on her edgy voice and look of satisfaction, David is Ryan's opponent.

"Barely. He got lucky in a set tiebreak." Jake comes to Ryan's defense.

Ryan flashes his beautiful white teeth at his friend in appreciation.

"He's gotten a lot better." Jennifer won't be deterred.

"Thanks for the update, Jenny."

She cringes.

He's clearly annoyed by her, but it's also clear they were once close. They have a past, a connection. Whatever it is, it hovers between them in the lobby of the hotel. He is back in stiff tennis mode and so involved with her and her mean-girl tactics that he doesn't feel me drop his hand.

I slip away. I've run up two flights of stairs before he calls my name. I continue up two more stories and storm to my room, but before I get the key out of my bag and open the door, Ryan's standing next to me.

"Why'd you leave me there?" His eyes spread wide with sincere questioning.

I want to be angry, to hate him, but I can't. He hasn't done anything, just dated an evil troll. My eyes fall to the floor, too weak to take in his good looks or make sense out of any of this.

"Are you mad at me?" he asks.

"No." I pause. "I just couldn't take another minute of that bitch."

"She's not that bad."

My head snaps up. Is he kidding? He just defended his ex-girlfriend!

"Okay, maybe she is," he adds.

I squint, and pucker, and hate that I'm jealous. "Good night, Ryan." I shut the door.

As soon as it closes, I want to throw it open, take another kiss. My stubborn hands refuse to turn the doorknob, and my insecurities win.

Who are you kidding? This is his world, and you have no business being here. Peters toys with his sticky silk.

I pull Dad's photo out of my bag. Tonight, it's just an image on paper, nothing more. The spiritual connection isn't coming through because of my cluttered mind. I replay the kiss, dissect the possible meanings behind his agitated face, and recall all his words over and over again. It's as if I've taken a test and don't know if I've failed or not.

In bed I leer at my phone, debating a call to Jimmy. I pick it up. Then I put it back down. Up, down, up, down. There'd be zero indecision if I could call Vicky.

I'm not here for Ryan. I'm here for Dragon. *Stop getting sidetracked by great hair and cute dimples.*

16

Ryan warms up for his match. Jake and he perform a sort of tennis ritual. No words are spoken, but they both know exactly when to stop rallying and start volleying, stop volleying and start serving. It's telepathic.

Ryan grabs me from the bleachers afterward. He has shifted into yet another version of himself. His eyes tunnel forward as the sweat rolls over his face from his hairline. He acts serious and offers no conversation, so I stand by his side feeling like a fish out of water, but every other player looks just as solemn. No one is talking. More telepathy.

"Kast. Beckett," the tournament director calls out.

Ryan walks to the desk, then turns back and strides through the crowd of players who haven't been called yet. "Court twelve," he says as he rushes past with his yellow-and-black bag slung over his shoulder and two tennis balls cradled in his hands.

I follow close behind and notice another guy has the same bag and holds one tennis ball. Both guys enter the fenced-in tennis court, and I remain outside, left to scramble for a seat. There's a spot next to an extremely twitchy woman. Her head shifts side to side as the little yellow ball flies over the net, back and forth. The woman cringes every time one of the boys' balls hits the net or drifts out of bounds. She whispers a cheer or a curse to herself, depending on what the boy in the red shorts does. Surely he's her son. She looks foolish, but I soon find myself doing the same thing while I watch Ryan.

Ryan plays with finesse. When he serves, his body extends and curves like a graceful swan, only to crouch and stretch into a position of a much more powerful animal. Once his racket makes contact with the ball, it rockets to the other side, and shivers claim my skin. When he misses, my stomach drops out, like a hole opens up right in the middle of my intestines.

Every point he makes feels like my point, every game he wins excites me, and each point or game lost tugs at my heart.

I torture myself like this for two and a half hours. I'm literally sitting on the edge of my seat. He volleys the last point so close to the line that I hesitate, afraid to cheer his victory, but when the opponent slams his racket to the ground, it's over. Ryan's won. He jumps and fist-pumps the air. At any other point in my life, I would've thought this ritual rude and ridiculous, but today I understand. He worked hard to beat that kid. The thrill of victory courses through my veins, and I'm genuinely happy for him. Kind of like when one of my pups finally accomplishes the agility course after hours and hours of coaxing and training.

Ryan collects the tennis balls and gathers his water bottle then struts off the court. He drips sweat as his eyes meet mine. We both smile.

"Oh my God. That was amazing and horrible. That one point. It lasted ten minutes. Why do you have to win by two points? That's so annoying." I throw up my hands.

He laughs.

"Way to go, Ryan." Jennifer bumps into me, squeezing her short skirt between the two of us.

"Thanks." The genuine smile he gives her smoothers my enthusiasm.

I follow Ryan and Jennifer from the court to the man behind the desk. She says words to him that I don't understand, but he obviously does. "Slice." "Double fault." "Sitter." "Treeing." "Choke." Their arena, not mine, and I fall back. He doesn't even notice I'm not next to him as he slips into the crowd of players. He gets pats on the back, fist bumps, and more mystery words.

Peter unravels more clingy silk.

I leave.

"Hey, I've been looking all over for you," Ryan says.

My long legs form acute angles as I squat on the street curb in front of the tennis facility like some weird grasshopper. He makes me so conscious of my lanky appearance. It's irritating. I shoot to my feet, my knees popping in protest.

I stop myself from saying something snarky. Why give him the satisfaction of knowing how left out I feel? I really don't care. But as the words cross my mind, they're not true. I care too much.

"I knew you had stuff to take care of and people to talk to, so I just thought I'd wait out here till you were done."

His shoulders drop, and his blue eyes pierce my steadfastness. He was actually worried about me.

I'm an idiot.

"Congratulations." It's a weak apology.

"Thanks. It was nice having you in the stands cheering for me."

I should say more, to compliment him on his grace on the court. I should tell him that I enjoy watching him play, that I enjoy being here with him, but the truth scares me, and the fear strangles my vocal cords.

We stand there on the curb, shuffling our feet. When will I stop being awkward and insecure? I wish for that day. I wish for Vicky's attitude and Jimmy's self-assuredness.

"There's the shuttle. Let's catch it," he says, breaking the building tension.

Thank you, public transportation!

We jog to the van. He opens the door and waits. I stand still until he gives me a grin and a tilt of his head.

"Oh," I murmur, and hop into the van. There's a seat in the back next to Chloe, where it's safe, and I can avoid any more gentlemanly awkwardness from Ryan.

Jennifer and two more guys run toward the van, and I pray the driver drives away, but he doesn't. Of course one of the sweaty, smelly boys wedges me between him and Chloe while shining, curvy Jennifer sandwiches herself between Ryan and another boy. She doesn't even sweat; she glows.

My fingers inch up to the top of the back seat where the tip of her perfect ponytail sweeps the vinyl. I snag the teeniest strand of hair and yank it. She slaps the back of her head. Ha, she felt it.

Oh my God, what am I doing? I drop my hands and head praying that

Chloe or Sweaty Boy didn't just see me do that.

"Kendall," Ryan says.

I look up to see that he has scooted away from Jennifer. He leans against the side of the van, one knee propped up so he takes up a majority of the bench seat. Jennifer and the other boy squish together. I can't see her face, but I'm hoping and assuming she's cringing as her pristine, bare arm touches his soaking-wet shirtsleeve.

"I'll shower, then let's go see Dragon." Ryan's hand reaches for my shoulder.

I'm too far away to be touched, but a sensation leaps from his fingertips, connecting us.

"Dragon? What's that?" Jennifer asks.

Connection severed.

"He's a timber wolf."

No, no, no, don't tell her!

"We're bringing him back to the States after the tournament," Ryan says.
Too late.

"Interesting. Can I come see it too?" Jennifer asks.

Ryan's eyes squint, and all his attention shifts to me.

What am I supposed to say? *No, you unworthy bitch!* That's what I should say, but instead, "Sure."

"Great!"

Her shrill bird pitch sickens me. I deflate.

"Can I come too?" Chloe asks.

Chloe? I forgot she was here. "Yes," I say a little too enthusiastically.

"Anyone else want to go?" Ryan asks, but the other guys just shake their heads. A drop of sweat hits my cheek. Disgusting. Then I see that the guy sitting next to Jennifer is about to drip another drop on her, and I'm filled with wicked happiness.

Showered and dressed in a pale-yellow linen sundress, Jennifer waits in the lobby as Ryan, Chloe, and I step off the elevator. My heart lodges in my throat. I'd secretly hoped she'd fallen asleep or forgotten or slipped in the shower or fallen down an elevator shaft. No such luck. She's here, looking beautiful. I smile as if it's no big deal that Cruella de Vil is tagging along.

Once we get to the shelter at the university, I worry Dragon will shy away from the many visitors, and he does at first. But after sniffing all of us and easing into our affections, he soon relishes every scratch behind his ear, rump rub, and head caress. Jennifer lightly pats his back, and by her sour expression, she thinks he smells bad. He doesn't. He smells like an animal, nothing more.

"Oh, his fur is stiff." Jennifer jerks her hand away like the spoiled princess that she is. "Nothing like Dad's German shepherds."

Ryan smiles at her. "I know. I thought he'd be softer too."

"How many dogs does your dad have?" Chloe asks.

"He had three show German shepherds, but now he's down to one."

"Have any of his dogs placed?" Chloe asks.

"Yes, of course."

"He must be good." Chloe sits on the ground, letting Dragon step all over her.

"He just owns them; some guy shows them. I don't know why he bothers. A hobby, after the divorce. He just bought two American pit bulls. They're so awful, constantly mouthing all over each other. It's disgusting."

Chloe stops stroking Dragon to look up at Jennifer, her mouth gaping in disbelief.

"So what are you planning to do with a wild wolf, Kendall? Can people adopt wolves?" Jennifer asks.

"I know a family with a wolf," Chloe says. "It's so cool."

"It's probably a wolf-dog hybrid. You have to have a Class two wildlife permit to own a wolf," I say.

"And you have this special license?" Jennifer asks.

"Yes." I don't, but Mom does, and she doesn't need to know my life.

"So what are you going to do with this guy?" Jennifer asks, her voice accusatory.

She's interrogating me. I level my gaze on her. "I don't know. Keep him as a pet, I guess. The rescue's house dog."

"But it's not a dog." Jennifer narrows her frigid blues at me.

"Cat and Shane are great. Dragon will fit in fine." Ryan turns away. He strolls over to the reptile tanks.

"Oh, well then, I'm sure your dad has everything under control," Jennifer says.

Ryan takes a step back toward us. "It's her moms."

"Oh, mom and stepmom. I get it. My parents are divorced too. It's great that they can work together." Jennifer's lips widen, stretching her model-worthy cheekbones. Her smile isn't genuine. There's a ploy in her eyes.

Peter awakens, but he's manageable. I try to remember the details of her Twitter conversation with Elaine. Doesn't she know the truth?

Ryan begins to explain, when I interrupt, "No, my dad died, and my mom has a wife named Shane. The name can confuse people. Don't worry. You're not the first." *You're nothing special,* I want to add, but I bite my tongue. Peter stretches a long leg, trying to escape the vivarium inside my chest, but I've got this. I inhale deeply, lulling Peter back to sleep.

"My sister's gay." Chloe is still on the floor, playing like a puppy herself. Her voice is sweet and caring.

Ryan and I chuckle at her silliness, but Jennifer just stares at me. She's creepy, and I brace for her next maneuver. It's like she has invisible talons raking my brain. If I'm not careful, they'll grab hold of Peter and wrangle him free, then Ryan will realize what a mess I am.

"Living an alternative lifestyle." Jennifer's nose lifts. "And don't you employ men on parole?"

Ah-ha. She does know the truth. I try her little trick and attempt to assault her mind with my lashing, hateful thoughts, but her smug plastic expression remains intact. I frown and respond, very aware of Ryan's concentration on our girl feud. "Yes, we employ men and women that are getting their lives back in order."

"Be careful. You can't trust people." Jennifer smirks.

"Don't worry about me. I know who I can't trust."

It's 6:55 a.m., and I pace the hall in front of Ryan's door. I've been up for an hour and a half, listening to the obnoxious rattling of the A/C wall unit. He said to be ready by seven. I'm ready. Ready to watch his match and ready to tell him I need to leave tomorrow with Dragon. As much as I like being here, I should be home. Dragon needs to start his new life, and regardless of how much they deny it, my moms need help.

And if you stay here, Jennifer will expose Peter.

The door opens.

"Kendall." Jennifer's unnerving voice bounces off me. Her look of surprise morphs into one of satisfaction. "Ryan's in the shower."

My mouth opens to yell, to interrogate her—as I don't believe what I'm seeing—but then it cements shut. Only a faint whisper escapes. "Huh?"

"Oh, Ryan and I are … well, we kinda … " She snickers and starts to walk away but stops, then turns back around. Liquid venom forms behind her mascaraed eyes, while the rest of her plastic face freezes into a mask of concern.

"I know you like Ryan, and he thinks you're cute. Maybe, if your fling lasts, we'll even see each other at next month's Governor's Ball. I'll lend you a dress. Of course, you'd never fill out the bustline, and everyone would know it was last year's style." The mask disappears for a second, revealing her true loathing of me, then she perks up again and smiles wide. "See you at

100

breakfast." She never looks back.

Peter throws a web, catching all her pretty little insults. They wrap around me, whispering insecure slurs. *You're not pretty enough. You're not rich enough.*

Raw, sour vomit rises up the back of my throat, but I swallow it. A fire in my heart rages. It burns all the insecurities to ash.

I'm a deluded idiot. Me—poor, anxious dog girl—and him—rich, charismatic college-bound guy—will never work. I just want my wolf and to get out of this hotel.

I storm into my room, grab the stack of dirty clothes on the closet floor, and shove them into my suitcase.

"The dress wouldn't fit because I'm not plastic!" I should've said that. But that doesn't really make sense.

I yank some clothes off hangers and stuff them into the suitcase, then I pile the rest of my belongings from the drawers on top.

"No. It'd be big because I didn't get a boob job. Ha. Then I should've glanced casually at her fake chest. Oh, that would've been classic … if it was actually true." Truth is she has a very nice and natural figure.

God, even my comebacks suck.

Broken and miserable, I pick up my suitcase, bring it into the bathroom, and in one sweep, push all my toiletries in. My suitcase looks like Mount Everest. I push stuff into each corner and zip it up.

Packed.

I said nothing. I just stood there and took it. *Why, Kendall?*

In less than ten minutes, I'm at the front desk asking for a taxi. Off I go, all before Ryan's out of his shower. A long shower to scrub her off him, wash away his indiscretion. He told me all these rich tennis kids hook up. He as good as warned me.

Would he do that? Yes, she was in his room. Obviously, they hooked up. Right? I'm not sure, but it's a reality check. We come from different worlds.

In the taxi, my breath fogs up the back-seat window as I lean my head against it. Alone and realizing the finality of my actions, Peter festers. The anxiety, which has been manageable all trip, is now boiling under the surface of my skin, threatening to burn me alive. Questions fly like poison darts: Is the shelter open this early? Can they get me to the airport? How will Dragon react? Can I do this alone?

I don't need Ryan's help. I don't need anything from him.

Maria unlocks the facility door to let me in.

"I'm ready to pick up Dragon."

"What? Now!"

"Um, yeah. Sorry."

She takes me in, and I guess I'm a mess, because her eyes relax with sympathy and she nods.

"I have to get a few things in order before I can escort you to the airport. I'll need about an hour. You're lucky I don't have classes to teach today."

"Thanks." My voice trails off.

"Make yourself comfortable. I've brewed coffee. It's over there, if you want some." She points, then exits the room.

The coffee smells magical, and I can definitely use a cup. The warm liquid assuages the anxiety. I just want to be home, where it's safe and familiar.

I meet Mom in some sort of animal customs at the Fort Lauderdale airport. Her hair knots and tangles more than usual. Her permanent bitch face is more severe than I remember.

"Hi, Mom." I brace for a verbal onslaught of maximum potential, but she says nothing. I have an entire monologue of excuses and answers to give her, but her silence will destroy me.

She walks at warp speed, pushing the crate with Dragon inside. The wheels hit every puddle, splashing nasty water. I'm soaked from the knees down. Heavy sighs and loud grunts escape her mouth. The dark sky and bruised clouds enhance the grimness of her attitude. It's as if I'm in a horror movie. She clasps the metal bar so tightly it might actually bend. We get to the truck, where I try to help her, but her adrenaline must be pumping, because she practically heaves the entire crate onto the truck bed by herself.

Hurricane Mom finally stops and turns to me. The sky above us rumbles, right on cue. Her stare bears down, and I use my most formidable weapon—my best apologetic Dad eyes. It's low, but she looks so pissed off. She looks more than pissed, demonic maybe, or perhaps that's fear in her eyes. Who knows? But I get the feeling all this madness isn't entirely directed at me. Then she turns to take in the beauty of Dragon. Her shoulders give, and she can't help but grin slightly. A tiny ray of sunshine peeks through the thick cover of clouds. This is really starting to freak me the eff out.

"I know you're mad," I say.

"More than mad! I'm furious with you right now! You flew into a lightning storm."

"The weather was fine in Puerto Rico."

She whips back at me again, stopping me mid-step with only a look. "I told you to come home with Ryan. Why do you think I told you that?"

I shrug. Any answer, while she's in this mood, will be wrong, so why bother. All I want to do is get in the truck and avoid any more eye contact.

"Because on the day you flew out, I was a nervous wreck. I couldn't imagine you flying home alone. And then you leave unannounced. You text me from the plane, which I don't get until you're already in flight and I can't reach you because you're thousands of feet in the air!"

She charges to the driver's side of the truck.

I'm shook. "Mom, why are you acting like this?"

"Like what? Like a mom that cares about the safety of her daughter!"

"Uh, yeah! You're always pushing the *Be a strong, independent woman, Kendall, like us queers.*" The words slip off my tongue before I weigh their consequence.

Her head drops. My poisoned dart struck its mark.

We stand on opposite sides of the truck, silent and hurting.

I have to apologize, but how? Finally, I say, "That's not what I meant. It's just that you always push me to be stronger, and I've been stronger, or at least trying to be."

"Let's go." Mom opens the truck door and slides behind the wheel. She drives halfway home before speaking again. "I am proud of your strength, Kendall."

"Thank you." The apology sticks, but I manage to get it out. "I'm sorry."

"Me too."

My phone buzzes in my pocket, but I ignore it. Uneasy silence sneaks back into the vehicle, and I need to break it. "I had to leave."

"Why?"

"Ryan ... he ... well ... "

"Did Ryan hurt you? Did he—"

"No, no, nothing like that. There was this girl ... I mean, he did, but ... never mind about that ... I just had to get home."

Her eyes soften as she reads between the lines, and my admission seems to penetrate her steely exterior. "Boys are difficult."

The mom I recognize is back, so here goes. "There was this girl, his ex-girlfriend. She's horrible, Mom. I had to get away from her. Rich, short-tennis-skirt-wearing bitch."

"Language, Kendall," Mom says, imitating Shane. The teasing tone in her voice gives me a reason to believe we're good now. All is forgiven. "Trax came home yesterday." Mom's eyes gleam.

"Awesome, so she's good?"

My phone buzzes.

"Recovering like the champ that she is. Can't keep a tough bitch down!"

"Mom! Language." The inside joke gets a much-needed laugh.

"Good thing too. We got another pit."

"Shot?"

"No, but badly beaten."

She pales again. This is what's torturing her, and my inconsiderate, unplanned flight home threw her over that razor-sharp edge. I hate that I was the catalyst.

"Hey, but on the bright side. A few more donations rolled in. The debt is shrinking." Mom's tone is not her own. That's Shane's influence.

"Any more news vans taking up residence in our parking lot?" I ask.

Mom's finicky happiness disappears.

Confused by her lack of enthusiasm, I probe on. "I thought you liked the attention, that it brought more money?"

"It does." Mom's voice is unconvincing.

"So we're done with that?"

"Do you want to be done with the media?"

Her question haunts the air. What answer does she want? The truth. "Sort of. I want people to know about the dogs, to see them as victims of inexcusable abuse. If they see it, they'll help us. They'll donate. The Trax video proved that. But I don't like cameras in my face or the mean comments people make."

"I feel the same. It brings the wrong kind of attention." The last sentence trails off as if it wasn't meant to be said aloud.

"Did something happen?"

She hesitates, then covers it with a shifty smile. "Animal Planet is interested in you. I told them I wasn't sure, and we'd get back with them about it."

"*The* Animal Planet?"

"The one and only. They asked about doing a story on you."

"No!"

Mom nods.

"Why me?"

"Well, because they know you work hard to raise awareness. They saw the video and the YouTube thing … "

"And I have a dead dad and criminal friends."

Mom sighs and never takes her eyes off the road.

"Am I right?"

"Well, I'm sure that's part of the intrigue."

This is how the world sees me. How people like Jennifer see me. Now it's my turn to sigh and stare at the road.

"That's why I didn't agree to do the show yet. We need to talk about the pros and cons. I know it's been hard for you. Mr. Young stopped by the rescue the other day."

"He did?"

"Yes. Why didn't you tell me?"

"There's nothing to tell. Mr. Young is blowing this way out of proportion." Like every adult does.

"It doesn't seem like nothing."

"Well, it is." I shudder, dismissing the absurdity of this conversation.

"Alright, but I thought it was nice of him. He seems impressed with you."

I turn away to gaze out the window. I'm not accustomed to people being impressed with me. All my time outside the rescue is spent just trying to keep my shit together. Keep Peter hidden. Be invisible. Get my diploma and be done with high school.

The truck bumps and shifts as we pull down the unpaved road and around the corner to park between the barn and the house. No more is said about Animal Planet, but I get the feeling it will be our next big topic of conversation at the dinner table. Another choice to make. Exploit myself to be on TV as the local freak in order to keep the funds rolling in, or go back to my normal, peaceful, quiet life of poverty. A life I'm beginning to miss more and more. I can't go back to the anxiety-ridden girl I used to be. Look what happened when I stepped out of my zip code for a couple of days. I can't do Animal Planet.

Mom parks the truck. Thankfully, the driveway is empty. Dogs play in the field, and Jimmy's in the yard with Lucy. Home is as it should be, small and ordinary.

Mom turns to me. "Surprise! Look who got Lucy into the yard without your help."

"Awesome!"

My phone buzzes.

"Yes, but I have a bone to pick with you. That poor dog freaked out when you weren't there to sleep with her. She had all the dogs howling. I had to buy a giant stuffed animal to lie down next to her, and then she still cried like a baby. Welcome home; now you can deal with her, and I can sleep."

I roll my eyes at her and smirk.

"Help me with this crate."

We pile out of the truck.

Mom's mutant strength has evaporated with her temper, and we struggle with the heft of the crate as we lift it from the truck bed. We escort Dragon to his fenced run.

Squid is painting the side of the barn.

"Are we finally painting this place?"

"Yes," Mom says—only one word, but it's knife sharp.

She should be excited—the paint has been chipping off for years. But Mom shows no happiness as Squid slaps more and more paint on the wall.

"Squid? Really?" My eyes roll again.

"What's wrong with Squid?"

Shaking my head, I begin, "He's ... Well, he's ... How should I put this? He's dumb. He's glopping it on like he's topping off his hamburger with ketchup."

Mom laughs. Squid loves ketchup more than anything in the world.

"How smart do you have to be to paint a barn?"

I roar at Mom's joke. It's rare for her to be funny at someone else's expense.

"He's not that bad. It looks ... " She stops, sighs, and continues, "Okay, maybe I'll hire a professional."

"He can't even cover up the red things. What is that?"

"Nothing," she says.

It's *not* nothing. Hints of red lines seep through the white primer.

"Help me with this damn wolf of yours." Mom struggles to keep Dragon from pulling the lead. He's sniffing every inch of this place. It's all new and exciting for him.

I grab hold of the lead and tug him into obedience. "Mom? What's going on?"

"I said it's nothing. Let's go!" Her voice turns.

That's the there's-no-arguing tone, and I don't dare unleash the storm of emotions I just experienced, so I keep my mouth shut. I'll talk to Squid later.

My phone buzzes.

"Jesus Christ, Kendall, answer the damn phone. Is it Ryan? Did you tell him you left?"

"I texted him that I'm safe. That's all he deserves to know."

She closes the gate with Dragon and me inside. She looks through the run's fencing. Her tough exterior lessens a little. "Got it. But he needs his community service hours for school, and I have to honor my commitment to him. Are you going to be okay with that?"

That's my mom—practicality trumping hurt feelings. Gotta keep going, gotta push through. Don't let 'em bring you down. Her mantra.

As expected, I add a sarcastic jab. "Yes, but he got all of his hours days ago. Now it's just pathetic."

"He's a good worker, and he's free." She levels her gaze. "He won't be the only boy to screw up. You have to kiss a lot of frogs before you find your prince."

I snort. What am I, twelve? But she's trying to understand, and I appreciate that. I stay with Dragon for a little while until he seems comfortable in the run, then head over to Jimmy.

"Hey, world traveler." Jimmy winks.

"I wish."

"So, how was it? I hear the Kardashians vacay there."

"Not where I went." I laugh, trying to picture Kim K. in the dump hotel I stayed at. "Legit, there are horses tied up to fences like in the Wild West. The countryside was pretty, and the people were friendly, but the hotel sucked."

"How'd Ryan do?"

"He won." Not going there! Subject change. "Heard anything about V?"

"No. I'm glad you're back. Spring break's been rough without you guys."

"I bet."

"Was the water blue? Did you at least get to go to the beach?"

"No."

"But you're glad you went, right?" His hazel eyes bulge and coax.

"Yeah." My voice isn't as strong and convincing as it should be.

"Where's Ryan? I thought you weren't coming home until he lost. I looked up his record, and he's a baller. Ranked three in Florida and, like, twenty in the nation."

I huff out a noise, not really a word, sort of a loud sigh. Ryan never brags, so I'm a little stunned, but after watching him play, I'm not surprised he's ranked that well.

"Yeah, he's really good." I nod.

"What happened?"

I guess my downcast eyes give me away. Come clean or ignore him? I wish Vicky were here. Maybe BTR has visiting hours.

"So you got Lucy in the yard. She looks so happy." I change the subject.

"She's doing great. It's you I'm worried about."

"I'm fine. Drop it."

"Alright." He shakes his head, and I notice something's different.

"You shaved your hair." My mouth gapes.

"You finally noticed."

"I'm sorry. It's been a rough day."

"You can touch it. I know you want to." His freckles spread.

I laugh. "I do." I slide my hand over his sleek cut.

"Do you like it? Should I grow it out again?" He turns his head side to side.

"Hmmm. Not sure. You're cute either way."

"Don't I know it." He bobs his head and smirks.

The levity dissipates. We awkwardly watch Lucy sniff the grass.

"Party at Jeff's tonight. It's gonna be lit. Wanna go?" His hazels flash enticingly.

"You know I don't do parties."

"You also don't do Puerto Rico with a boy either. It's the spring of new things." His hand sweeps across the air in a grand gesture.

"Yeah, and look what that got me. Bad example."

"Kens, it's spring break. Come on," he pleads.

"Not tonight. I'm tired, and I have a lot of work to do with Dragon. I need to get him over to the vet for a checkup. The Mayaguez shelter claimed he was clean, but Mom won't let him near the others until Dr. Ferrera gives the final all clear."

"I'll let you off the hook today, but then we're partying."

"Okay." I can try for Jimmy's sake. How bad can a party be, right?

I unpack Dad's photo and pin it to the wall. "Maybe I overreacted." My head shakes dismissively. "No, I'm right. It's true I don't fit into his world, and Jennifer blatantly pointed it out."

Dad's voice echoes, *You can fit in wherever you choose.*

"Yeah, right!"

His eyes beam like only those of a dad who's blinded by the love for his daughter can. He doesn't see the reality.

Kendall, he doesn't see anything. He's a piece of fucking paper!

I unpin the photograph and turn it facedown on the shelf. "He's just a piece of paper," the whisper trails off.

Here come the what-ifs—What if Dad were still alive? A life without therapy flashes through my mind. It's a peaceful life, and the image of it brings so much pain.

I refuse to go down that path again, a fool's dream that morphs into a torturous nightmare. Dad's gone; he's not coming back, not even for one second. I can't play the what-if game, the poor me pity party because it'll give Peter life and break me down.

Peter rattles his container harder than he has in months.

The edge is too close tonight. Why? Because of a stupid boy and an overprivileged princess. Her evil words still stick to me, thanks to Peter. They try to seep through my skin—*you're not good enough*—but my skin is thicker now. It's a battle to stay shielded, but I've been on this war field before. It'd just be so much easier if Vicky were here.

Why did she have to leave now? What would she think? She'd say I'm better off without him. She'd tell me not to listen to a word of Jennifer's hate speech. But it's not *what* Vicky'd say; it's *how* she'd say it. Somehow, she'd make me believe it. Somehow, she'd push Peter away.

I glance at my phone and contemplate texting Jimmy. Maybe a guy's perspective would help, but the red dot on my text icon reminds me of Ryan. Not gonna read those texts.

Red dots tag my Twitter and Snapchat apps too, like blistering chicken pox. Just looking at my phone makes me want to scratch. The itch creeps up my neck, like a thousand spiders. I'm close to a relapse, to an episode, to a blackout. It's just under my skin, so close to the surface. Too close, like that train. My sanity depends on my escape from that train, from these red dots. I have to stay far away from all of it. There's no way I can consider Animal Planet. No way!

No boyfriend and no TV. A long exhalation sears my throat but eases the anxiety. *Breathe.*

I remain silent. The decision soaks in and calms the itch. My eyelids quiver as I force them to shut. No voices in my head, not from Dad or Vicky. But words zoom across my mind: "Dog Girl," "less than," "out of place," "alone." I rush to my feet and out of the barn.

With the ground between my toes, I knead the earth. Exhaustion weighs me down, yet at the same time, I'm twitchy with restlessness. At least the panic is gone.

Lumbering around outside, I find myself standing in front of the painted wall. There are the lines. Something had been written on the wall, but I can't make it out. My hands follow the peaks and valleys of the meaningless lines.

I step back and concentrate on its entirety. Nothing. Maybe, in the morning, sunlight will reveal whatever's hidden under that sloppy white paint.

I n the bright morning sun, every cruel word bleeds through the white paint. *Dyke perverts! DIE! ur gutter trash thugs 2! Get out a MY hood or else!*

It's the last four words that scare me the most. This horrible person lives around here. Where? Which house? The slashes and strikes of the paintbrush cut into the very soul of the barn. I can't stop staring at it. The tears turn hot and inflame my skin. I own them and stomp into the house, purposely waking everyone.

Shane appears first in her delicate flowered pajama set. This is not the image of a dyke pervert.

She takes in my appearance and jolts backward. "What happened to you?"

"You really thought Squid could hide that shit from me!"

Shane deflates in a sigh. "No." Ragged breathy sounds leave her mouth. "We didn't have time. Pretty much when you texted from the airport, we discovered the graffiti. Your mom was beside herself. She and Rock got into a fight over it because he wanted to call the police. He stormed off." She pushes the coffee brew button, then collapses into a chair at the kitchen table. "There's been phone calls too, and hateful postings on the Facebook page Ryan set up. But we wanted the two of you to have a nice spring break. I'm sure Ryan can delete them when he gets back."

"I know how Facebook works. Vicky has one. I can report it and delete it. I agree with Rock. The police need to know."

"I know." She slumps further. The circles under her eyes darken. "Cat just freaked out. With all you've been through. Everything was looking up. We paid off some of our debts. You hadn't missed a day of school in a long time. We saved Trax and Dragon. She wanted to make it disappear. She won't discuss it with me."

"Discuss what?" says a rough voice in desperate need of coffee. The words float in from the hallway, followed by Mom's disheveled body in black sweatpants.

"I saw the graffiti."

"Oh, that stupidity. Just some dumb kids." Her hand swats at the air, and she pours her coffee.

"Mom, this is serious. You have to tell the cops."

"And then what? All that will do is bring more news reporters. It's painted over, so there's no news."

"It's not painted good enough. Kendall was able to read it," Shane says.

Mom shakes her head, and her stare drills me. "You just couldn't listen to me, could you? One more coat and it'll be fine. Over and done with. Isn't that what you want?" She slices the air with a rigid hand, then ninja chops the counter.

Mom's right: I don't want any more publicity, any more hashtags or hate mail. I want our old life back. But something stirs inside, and it's not Peter. It's a strange rage. Anger is familiar—after all, I'm a fatherless child—but this rage is different. "Mom, people like this need to be called out. I'm telling Fred."

Again, Mom levels her hard, hazel eyes on me. This time the madness is gone; she's totally lucid, and I feel the burn. "Kendall Marie, so help me God, if you drag Shane's brother into this mess. You know about these kinds of people. Ain't nothing Fred can do about it except say I told you so. This is the life we chose, and we just have to ignore the devil."

"*I* didn't choose this." The words sour on my tongue as soon as I say them.

Mom coils like a snake ready to strike. Shane wilts, and my heart heavies with regret, then plunges to my stomach.

"This is over. Do you hear me? Over!" Mom ends the conversation, venom spewing from her glare.

I try to replicate the poison of her glare, locking my brown eyes on hers.

Look into Dad's eyes. Look at the choice you made, not me. I'm surprised she holds my stare. For the first time, she wins the staring contest.

I leave. The front door swings so far open that it snaps back, but I hop out of the way and let it slam shut.

"Kendall Marie!" Mom hollers.

I grab my bike and ride. I need to get far away from that repulsive red spray paint, but I barely make it out of the driveway. Dr. Ferrera's car is at the clinic. Dragon has an appointment this morning. Shit! I can't go back inside, not after what I said.

I begrudgingly walk my bike back to the barn and search it for something to eat. Rock usually leaves a protein bar lying around. Nothing. No food.

The growl and ache of my stomach force me back to the house. Shame from the argument nests in my conscience, and I'm thankful the kitchen is empty. I couldn't face Shane right now. I bite into a bagel. The doughy bread is difficult to swallow with Peter lodged in my throat. Eventually, I eat the entire bagel, swallowing it along with Peter's taunts.

Stay strong! Don't break!

Dragon checks out fine at the vet. He's acclimating well to his new environment. The somber morning turns into a pleasant day filled with peace, until Mom informs me that I have two hours to decide on Animal Planet. Apparently, whoever's in charge requires an answer before five o'clock.

Pros—money and money. Cons—my alternative upbringing on display to the nation, hate mail, more graffiti, and, oh yeah, let's not forget, Peter threatening to retake control. I can't risk it, not even for two hundred dollars an hour with the possibility of much more if the show takes off.

My final announcement to decline hangs in the air.

"It's your decision, honey." Shane plasters an enormous smile across her face to suppress words of persuasion.

"I don't blame you. I'm not sure I'd even want you to do it, considering the circumstances. A lot of money, though." Mom attempts to look cool but fails miserably. Her arms pull so tightly across her midsection that if she lets go, she'll lurch forward and knock me over.

"You could put it toward college." Shane looks from me to Mom, nodding.

"Of course, you'd have to keep those grades up." Mom's fake chuckle bounces around the room.

I smile. I appreciate their effort to try to accept my decision. They can't force me to risk my sanity for money. How could they, after everything they've been through? After the cruel threats were written on our barn. Even so, it's obvious they were hoping I'd accept the show deal.

"Are you sure?" Mom asks for what feels like the thousandth time.

I want to scream, *Hell yes!* But instead, I say in a respectable, steady tone, "I'm definitely sure."

Mom holds Shane's hand, and they both nod and claim to understand, but they don't. No one does. I exit the house, decision made, moms disappointed, and head to where I belong—with the dogs.

After two days the decision has rooted, and everyone's accepted it. Nothing more's been said or argued. Shane's been busy hiring professional painters, and Mom's been investigating the increasing dog abuse, traveling from Miami to Vero Beach. Life is back to normal again, and surprisingly, it's content. Broke, but content.

I stroll outside to the barn. It isn't until I've placed Lucy in her stall next to her stuffed bear that the quiet sets in. I've never been fearful in the barn, surrounded by lots of sharp teeth, but tonight's different. Someone trespassed on this property to spray paint words of hate. That takes a lot of balls. Someone must really have it in for us.

A rustling sound comes from over there. "Who's there?"

A giant silhouette exits the barn office, and I gasp. It's Rock, and I exhale, nearly falling over.

"What are you doing here?" I ask.

"Sorry I scared you, Peanut." Rock puts an arm around me. He's sweaty from a long day of hard work but smells of cocoa butter. Louisa, his wife, packs scented towelettes in his bag. He's constantly wiping his bald head with them.

"Yeah, thanks a lot, Shrek."

He laughs, and we both sit down, I in my corner and he in a lawn chair.

He glances at the photo of Dad. "He was a good man. Only person that'd hire me."

"He said you were solid, that you'd be my *rock* forever." It's a saying I've repeated a million times, but it's true.

"I know, Peanut. I know."

Rock's worked here twelve years, at least. He was here when we got the news that Dad had been killed in a car accident. He held me as I cried. He made me feel safe then, and now I feel safe knowing he's here, just in case that creep decides to come back.

"What is it?" I ask, as his deep, black eyes cloud with strangeness.

"I don't want you sleepin' out here tonight." His voice is stern.

"But I always sleep in the barn." I swivel to look at Dad's photo.

"Listen, your mom's worried even if she don't say so. She called Fred."

"She did?" I snap back around, focusing all attention on him.

"Yeah, these threats are serious. You hear me?"

"What did Fred say?"

"Not much he can say, 'cept he's keeping an eye out. This ain't his jurisdiction. I don't like it." Rock's lips thin, hiding gritted teeth.

"Mom said it was just kids being stupid. She said she wasn't going to bother Fred," I say.

He shakes his head. Clearly, he knows more than he wants to tell.

"She lied to me."

"Come on. I'll walk you back up to the house. Then I have to get home. Louisa's already gonna yell at me, put me in the dog house." His eyes stretch at the mention of his wife's name, then he chuckles.

"No. If I'm in danger out here, then the dogs are too. I'm not leaving them."

"Kendall, don't you do this to me. Don't make me get mad at you."

I laugh, but he's dead serious, and my smile flattens. "You know I don't sleep. I'm fine. That way, if I hear something, I can alert Mom or the police." I shove my phone in his direction. "Look, phone's fully charged. I'll call 911."

"No, not tonight. The cameras and alarm will be in soon, but not tonight!"

"Cameras? Alarm?"

"Yes, Fred suggested it, and your mom got on it right away. You know your mom when she sets her mind to somethin'."

"Yeah." I nod as panic webs up my spine. "Mom thinks the graffiti and Trax are related, doesn't she?"

"Not exactly." His arms cross as he ponders how much to tell me. "All these hateful things are coming from the buzz Trax started. If the same person did both, don't know. Seems kinda far-fetched that one person is doing all this."

"A serial killer."

A deep gurgling grunt is conjured up from the depths of his belly.

"I know Mom's looking into it. I know that's why she's been visiting the other rescue agents."

His nostrils flare, and his eyes bore into me. They're two bottomless lagoons, rippling with suspicion. "You know I've seen and done some bad stuff. So I know." He nods. "And what I know is it takes a cold person to shoot a dog without reason, but the person that did what they did to Trax, now that's evil, or some kinda sign. And whoever did this writing on the barn is just plain cowardice. There's a whole lot of stuff goin' on. Don't seem to me like it's all one person, but could be related."

Rock lifts me up and places his massive arm around my shoulders. I may be tall, but he's a giant, and there's no escaping his bearlike grasp.

"I guess I'm staying in the house tonight."

"That's right, Peanut."

Sundays at the rescue are usually casual and slow, and today was no exception. I'm not complaining. After all the craziness of Puerto Rico and the vandalism, I'm thrilled to lie around on a beanbag reading. Tomorrow's my last day to chill before it's back to the grind and the drama of Atlantic High.

"Peanut," Rock calls from the other end of the barn.

"Yeah."

"Since you got time on your hands, go check on Cruz," he says.

This blissful laziness was too good to be true.

There's a lot of meds to be sorted out at dinnertime, and Cruz is still messing things up even though he's been here awhile.

Cruz is a talker, which is why he's constantly distracted and screwing up. I've had my share of babysitting duty with him and learned to keep my answers short. The police haven't caught the vandal yet, and that's all he wants to talk about.

"Any more been done about that guy?" he asks.

"No."

"That's too bad. But they got leads, right?"

"Yes."

"What kind of leads?"

I shrug. If I explain the little that I know to Cruz, he'll never shut up.

"Ain't nothing." His phone lights up. After a brief glance at it, he shoves it into his pocket, then fidgets. "Ain't nothing," he mumbles again, then starts snatching bowls and sloppily scooping out food. Whatever was on his phone bothered him. He places Trax's pills in Duke's bowl.

"No, wrong. Why is Trax's meds out here anyway? She's still in the recovery area." I grab the bottle and storm off.

"Sorry," Cruz calls out.

Guilt insists I reply, "It's okay." I give him a little smile, and he starts in with a story, but I cut him off. "Hold on. I'll be back in a minute."

He nods, and I get out of there as fast as I can. With the medication in hand, I rush over to the recovery shelter and come to a complete halt, dropping the bottle and spilling pills everywhere. My heart wedges in my throat.

Ryan kneels next to Trax's kennel.

Why does he have to be so cute?

"What are you doing here?" My tone is unfriendly, with an added eye squint and lip snarl to make sure he gets the point. Without waiting for a reply, I feign an air of indifference and bend to gather the pills.

He helps collect the medication. He stares directly at me with his adorable half smile that makes tiny dents in his cheeks.

The pills keep slipping out of my fingers. The loudest sigh I've ever made escapes me.

"What did I do?" He drops his pills into the bottle.

"What are you talking about?" I stand.

He stands. "You left without saying goodbye. You took Dragon and got off the island. I think I'm entitled to an answer as to why."

He's so diplomatic and stiff. But I'm stiff too. I can't move, and I just stand like a soldier with a blank face.

"Are you mad at me?"

I snap out of it and head toward the food pantry to put down the medication and scoop kibbles into Trax's bowl. "No." I grab a pill pocket and fold the giant white pills into the doughy treat.

"Okay." Confusion slashes his face. "It was a pretty shitty thing to do to me."

His harsh tone slices me apart. Me? It's him. Jennifer was in *his* room. I want to scream out how we come from two different worlds. Mine is full of red spray paint, and his is full of pretty tennis girls. But the words lodge in my mouth. I just stare at him, mouth agape. The itch and tremors slowly materialize. I turn away. It would devastate me if he experienced a true episode, not just a fainting spell after a *Good Morning America* interview. So I breathe deeply, ignore his rude comment, and return to the chore of feeding Trax.

Still not looking in his direction, I feel the heated frustration radiate from his body. I sneak a glace, but his eyes laser beam to Trax. In strangling silence, we watch her eat, until I can't take it anymore. "How did the rest of the tournament go?"

A modest smile stretches his lips. He's trying to downplay his excitement. "You won?"

"Yes. I won."

Guess he wasn't too broken up about you leaving. He still won matches. Must've had Jennifer cheering him on. Her special winning kisses.

I shake off Peter's pessimism. "Great." My heart flutters, remembering the match I had watched him win, and I'm genuinely happy for him.

"Thanks." He strolls out of the recovery shelter.

"Where're you going?" My feelings tug and pull. Do I want him to stay?

"To see Cat. She wanted me to come over right away." His stare awakens annoying, tingly butterflies.

Apparently, they were gathering in my gut, awaiting his return. I've missed him, but I don't let on and struggle to keep my air of indifference. "Did Mom say why?"

"She's upset about some bullying on Facebook. I told her I could probably change the settings, but when your site is public, all you can do is delete it and report it."

"Seriously! I told her I'd do that." I march past him.

He follows.

I throw open the door, and the setting sun hits me square in the face, blinding me for a second. Once my vision clears, I stumble over something or someone.

"Jimmy! What are you doing here?"

"I'm fine. Thanks for asking after steppin' all over me. I'm okay, really." His eyes widen.

I laugh, and so does my shadow.

"Hey, man. Like the new cut." Ryan clasps Jimmy's hand firmly in a bro shake.

"Thanks, Ryan!" Jimmy runs a hand along the side of his head. "You win, man?"

"Yeah."

"Way to go. Congrats!"

"Thanks."

Their eyes light up at the word "win." Competition is their drug. Jimmy is sincerely excited for Ryan.

Interesting.

Makes me wonder if Ryan won simply for the joy of winning, and it had nothing to do with Jennifer or me.

"Why are you here?" I ask.

"And it's nice to see you too," Jimmy says.

I sigh, not in the mood for his sarcasm.

"Just bored. Thought I'd come see if anyone else has vandalized the barn. It's always exciting over here."

My eyes nearly pop out of my skull. I don't want Ryan to know about that.

"Is that why you left Puerto Rico? What happened?" Ryan asks.

"It's nothing."

"It's not nothing, Kens. Somebody used red spray paint to write nasty threats across the barn."

"Who?"

"They haven't caught the guy yet." Jimmy shakes his head.

"I'm sorry, Kendall. I didn't know." Ryan reaches out to me, but I step away.

"It's fine. Really." Even though his hand never touches me, its warmth does. I want to accept his concern and hold his hand. We are friends, right? Friends console each other. But I freeze in place and lower my head.

"I'll go see what Cat needs," he says. "Talk to you later."

"Sure thing," Jimmy says.

I say nothing. Just watch him walk away.

"What happened?" Jimmy asks.

"What are you talking about?"

"I know I'm not Vicky, but it doesn't take a pint-sized queen bee to know you and Ryan got into a fight."

"We didn't fight." I squirm inside and out.

"Then what."

"His ex was there, and she's a real bitch, and I just didn't want to deal with it."

"What'd she do?"

I explain everything as we head back into the recovery shelter.

Of course he follows the bro code and sticks up for Ryan.

"Why are you taking his side?" I set Trax's pill bottle in the appropriate cabinet. Hopefully Cruz won't misplace it again.

"I'm not taking anyone's side. I'm just saying, don't jump to conclusions. Talk to him about it. I think this Jennifer girl wanted to drive you away, and you let her."

Every part of my body seems too heavy to hold up, and I slump against the wall. "Do you really think so?"

"Yes." He nods.

"Wanna help me pick up dog bowls." I peel myself off the wall and grab Trax's stainless steel bowl.

"Sure." Jimmy wheels behind me as we leave the shelter to go over to the barn to gather the rest of the dinner bowls. "It's our last night to party, which is why you're coming out with me tonight."

"Jimmy!" I protest.

"You have to."

"Why?" I whine, then chuckle, knowing I sound like I'm two, or maybe ninety-two.

"Because it's on the beach, and I need help wheeling out there."

I look at his strong, muscular arms, chiseled chest, and rugged tires and shake my head.

"What?" he asks sheepishly.

He brags about those tires on the regular. His chair is custom-built for rough terrain because he lives in a beach community and helps with the dogs in the dirt. But he gives me his best puppy dog eyes.

I cave. "Okay."

"Yes! Jay-Z has his Beyoncé!"

"It's more like Luke has his Princess Leia."

"Okay, that's good too."

"A party might be fun." *I guess.* Dragon's safe. I got past seeing Ryan without Peter weaving any webs. I can handle going to a party.

T he blazing bonfire marks our destination. The rumble of people and the sound of music are heard way before we actually get there.

Of course Jimmy's welcomed with bro shakes and hooting hellos while I stand in his shadow. Most of the parties Jimmy attends are a mix of students from various schools. He knows everyone south of Palm Beach. He played a lot of sports growing up and became a football legend freshman year of high school until a bad tackle sent him to the hospital.

I get the occasional nod of recognition, and some people even make small talk, but most pay no attention. I'm not wearing designer flip-flops or the latest short shorts that every girl has in an array of colors.

"I didn't realize my shorts were supposed to go up my ass."

Jimmy frowns.

"What? Insensitive sarcasm isn't charming? Vicky would've laughed."

"I'm sure."

A girl wearing short cutoffs and a huge smile approaches.

"Chloe! Hi."

"Hey, it's great to see you." She envelops me in a big hug.

The embrace is unexpected, and I reluctantly, but happily, participate in the intimate welcome. Then a shocking chill of fear slaps the happiness right out of me. "Is Jennifer here too?"

"No Jennifer sighting yet." And her smile gets even bigger.

Chloe is adorable with her round, tanned face, big blue eyes, and wavy brown-blond hair. It's as if she's bouncing with electricity, and joy spills out of her and onto me.

"Let's hope she doesn't show up," I say.

"She lives with her mom in Miami, so it's a hike up here, but there's a rumor she's moved in with her dad right down the street."

Jimmy clears his throat.

"Chloe, this is Jimmy." I turn to Jimmy. "We met in Puerto Rico."

"Hi, nice to meet you. Cute shorts." Jimmy grins like the devil incarnate.

"Thanks."

I kick his tire.

"What's been up with you?" Chloe steers the conversation back to normal.

The weird events of my life form a list in my mind, but I shove it away, not wanting any of her electric joy to abandon me. "Not much, just enjoying my spring break. How'd you do in the tournament?"

"I lost in singles but got to the finals in doubles. We would've won too, but the other team was local, and the refs were *so* biased. It was ridiculous some of the calls they got away with. Huge cheaters."

"Sorry. That sucks," I say.

"Did you get that wolf?" she asks. "I'd love to come see him."

I nod and smile. "Yeah, that'd be great. Just come to Delray Dog Rescue. Anytime."

A painfully good-looking guy, tall, with his shirt open—revealing a six-pack that weakens my knees—loops his arm around Chloe's elbow and begins to drag her off. "Sebastian, hold up." She digs her bare feet into the sand.

"Chloe." He kisses her.

I almost drool from his hotness.

He looks over at Jimmy and me. "You don't mind if I snag my girlfriend, do you?"

Suddenly my mouth has rocks in it. I shake my head and smile.

"Sorry, Kendall. I'll find you later. Nice to meet you, Jimmy," she says with a cute wave as he pulls her away.

"Jackson has that awesome grapefruit beer you like so much," the boyfriend tells Chloe.

I'm dazed and gawk at them stumbling away in pure teenage bliss. She probably has two (not dead) parents, lives in a big house, and plays tennis in cute skirts with no crazy haters gunning for her alternative family. My eyelids drift shut for an instant as the depression slides down my spine. Well, at least for a brief moment, I felt comfortable at a party. That's progress. I hope she does visit Dragon. That would be fun. I laugh. Vicky's reaction to my new bubbly friend would be classic, but she'd like her.

"I approve of the fabric-to-ass cheek ratio of her shorts." Jimmy laughs.

"Yeah." I sigh.

"You okay?" Jimmy responds to my lack of cynicism.

"Oh, sure, I was just envisioning Vicky here," I say.

"Ha! That would never happen." Jimmy's bright smile bumps his freckle patch. "It's a miracle you're here."

"You're a master of persuasion." Or I just needed a distraction.

"And you're having fun. Admit it."

"Never." I glower.

"Uh-huh! I'm gonna get a beer, do you want one?"

"I'll go too."

"Um, no. I'm okay." He glances behind me.

I turn around. Ryan waltzes up. His powerful shoulders and tanned legs glow against the indigo sky. Chloe's boyfriend may look like a fallen angel, but Ryan awakens my butterflies. He's nodding and acknowledging a lot of people in the crowd, but his path cuts straight to me.

"Hey there," he says.

"Hi," I say.

"I didn't expect you to be here."

My eyes squint at this remark. How do I take that? What does he mean? And it's not true. Jimmy must have set this up.

"What's that look for?" he asks.

"Nothing."

"Always so secretive. Do you ever let anyone else in?" he asks.

"Sure." I breathe and remind myself that he has no ulterior motive, and that I'm here to have fun—be a typical teenage girl. "Okay, maybe I'm a little guarded."

"You want a drink?" Thankfully, he shifts the conversation.

"Okay." I prepare to wait alone and count, but he takes my hand and gently tugs me toward the big plastic coolers. My head spins, and my skin tingles as we part the sea of high schoolers. A guy high-fives Ryan, and I recognize him from Puerto Rico. Most have beers, but some are drinking soda or water. I whisper to Ryan, "I guess rich kids don't get caught underage drinking?"

"At this house? Not likely." He huffs.

I hadn't looked beyond the bonfire. We stand in front of an enormous pool in front of an epic waterfront house. "Who lives here?"

"I think Jackson's dad helped invent some sort of plastic surgery procedure. Mich Ultra, Corona, or some sort of grapefruit German beer?" He looks at me with those almond-shaped blues, rendering me speechless for a couple of seconds. "Would you rather have water?"

He's been holding the cooler lid open for far too long. "Uh-uh. Ultra's fine."

Like a gentleman, he opens the bottle before he hands it over. I've drunk alcohol twice, and both times I vomited. Granted, the first time I was way too young and stupid. The second hurl came after Elaine's nose-picking post. Vicky and I snuck into her mom's liquor cabinet while watching *The Hunger Games* for the gazillionth time. Needless to say, I sip cautiously as we stroll to the fringes of the crowd. Vomiting in front of Ryan would seal my fate—girl that can't hang in his world.

He keeps walking, and soon we're at the edge of the water. He takes off his shoes.

I copy.

The air is warm, but the water holds a chill from winter. As it cascades over my toes, shivers run through me, and I'm not sure of the cause—the sea or Ryan?

We drift down the beach, away from the party and my shoes. I need those shoes. They're my only good pair of sandals. Ryan probably has twenty pairs of the same adorable Sperrys.

We haven't spoken in minutes, and he seems entirely at ease as I squirm and die. And once this beer is empty, what will my hands do?

Ryan stops and turns. His deep-blue eyes settle on mine. I freeze. He smiles. I smile. Then he pivots and begins to stroll back toward the party.

That's it? But what did I want to happen? I'm still angry with him. I just want friendship, right? Why would I want to kiss him anyway, after he hooked up with that horrible girl?

"Are you okay?" His question is far away on a ship in the Atlantic.

My face tenses and wrinkles. Is that why he's asking if I'm okay? Do I look that miserable? I consciously relax my face muscles. "Yeah, I'm fine."

"I wouldn't be fine if I was you."

"Well, you're not me." God, that sounded so bitter. "I'm sorry. I don't know what I'm doing." I stop walking and turn to face him. "What do you want with me?"

"Want with you?" He questions with both his words and his eyes.

"I mean, do you like me or not … Are we friends … Why was Jennifer in your room?"

"What?"

Peter wrings his hairy legs and extends his fangs, desperate for a juicy reason to sink them into me, so I don't reply at first. But I need answers. Washing away Peter and gaining courage with a big gulp of beer, I say, "I saw her leaving your hotel room first thing in the morning. She implied that she spent the night." Each word is like my last breath. It's incredibly difficult to carry on a conversation while the anxiety threatens to take over, but I force the strength to the surface. This is my body, my mind.

He rakes his hair with both hands while cleverly preventing any beer from spilling. "That's why you left me!"

I nod.

"She was in my room for one second. Her coach called me to ask if I had any KT tape. She came in to borrow KT tape. I put it on her shoulder." He throws his hands up, spilling beer this time, and paces. "That was it! Fucking KT tape!"

This is the answer I wanted. The reasonable explanation. But he's pissed, whether at me or Jennifer, I don't know.

"I'm sorry. I should've talked to you before I left. I just got angry … and scared." My heart pounds.

He kicks the sand. "I can't believe her." He takes my hand. "She's out of my life. I don't want you to ever think there's anything between us."

"Okay." Relief wafts over me like a blast of arctic air, but something nags. "So you're fine with the fact that we come from opposite worlds."

"Yes. I mean. No. There's only one world."

"No, there isn't. There's the world of fancy tennis tournaments and the world of nasty hashtags and dirty dogs."

He pulls me to him. "Don't insult yourself or your moms by giving credence to those comments or the trolls that post them."

My head falls to rest on his shoulder. For a few seconds, maybe minutes, we embrace while our feet sink in the sand and the ocean licks our toes.

I break away first and renew our stroll.

He follows. "I'm worried about your safety."

"Don't be. Mom has a gun, and we're getting cameras and an alarm, and anyone stupid enough to mess with Rock won't be able to walk after he gets done with them."

"Okay," he says.

I'm an idiot. He's trying to be chivalrous, and I'm shooting him down. "Thank you, though."

He jerks his head in my direction.

I huff an awkward laugh. "For worrying and for helping out at the rescue."

"Just please tell me next time … when something happens."

"Hopefully there won't be a next time."

He squeezes my hand, and we trudge back to our shoes.

My phone rings. "Hi, Jimmy."

"I'm catching a ride with Gina and Susan to another party. Do you want to come?" he asks.

"I don't know. Let me ask Ryan." I face the phone away and ask, "Jimmy's going to another party; do you want to go? Or should I go with him?" Why am I asking his permission? I begin to ignore Ryan and tell Jimmy I'll be right there, but I hesitate.

"Up to you, but I can take you home later," Ryan says.

I hesitate some more. Jimmy calls out from the phone.

"Kens … Kendall … Make up your mind. Gina's leaving," he says.

"No, I'm good. Ryan will take me home. Are you okay with that?" I ask.

"Of course. Have fun. See you tomorrow," Jimmy says.

"Bye."

We don't walk back to the crowded bonfire. Instead, we skirt around it to the sidewalk and continue strolling down the street. We cross the road and go down the finger of land to a large three-story house. Ryan punches numbers into the keypad next to the garage door, and it opens.

"I assume this is your house?" I ask.

"No, we're breaking and entering." He smirks and escorts me through the immaculate garage, through a laundry room that Shane would kill for.

I pause to admire the fancy navy-blue washing machine. How many dog towels could fit in that huge cylinder?

Ryan stares at me, probably wondering why I care so much about his appliances.

That's embarrassing.

We move on.

"Holy wow," escapes my lips before I can stop it. The kitchen is as big as my living room—no, my entire house. It's gorgeous even with a pile of dishes in the sink and several paper towel wads littering the counter. I'd probably be a lot messier if my parents left me alone for days.

Ryan takes my beer bottle and tosses it into a garbage can marked Recycle, then he pulls two water bottles out of the fridge. "Hungry?" He holds the fridge door open.

The fridge is nearly empty. What does he think we're going to eat—pickles?

"My parents have been out of town awhile, but I have ham and pickles."

"I'm okay." My stomach growls.

He grins. "Let's order pizza."

"That sounds really good." I nod.

He gives me an abbreviated tour of the place while we wait for the pizza. Photos of Ryan line the stairwell wall leading to the second floor—cute chubby baby Ryan, elementary Ryan in plaid prep school clothes, young Ryan in tennis clothes, current Ryan in his senior class picture. All attractively framed.

As the wall continues to the third floor, more photos map the chronology of a boy with similar features. I want to follow this boy's developmental changes and see if he morphs into another handsome Ryan. Can there be two such marvelous creatures? But instead, we settle on the second-floor loft, where a television screen spans the entire wall, facing cushy lounge chairs that invite casual viewing or gaming.

"Here's my classroom," he says.

"Way cooler than Atlantic High."

"Yeah, but it can be lonely and distracting."

"You poor thing, distracted by this incredible view of the Intercoastal."

"No, distracted by *GTA*." He smirks but doesn't acknowledge my sarcasm.

"Boys and that violent game."

"I know. We're awful." His eyes pin me in place. It's an intense look that arouses the butterflies and scares me to death.

I wander away, through the archway that leads to an enormous bedroom.

"Do you have the entire floor to yourself?"

"Yes."

"I hate you." My eyes bug out of my head as I twirl around to take it all in.

"Sorry." He shrugs.

The view is spectacular because the windows span floor to ceiling and the entire back of the house. The windowless wall is covered with shelves holding trophies, books, or vinyl. An old-fashioned record player sits open with a record on it ready to be played. Scattered album jackets from classic rock to indie to rap fan across the room like an edgy, eclectic rainbow. The light bounces off the gold, silver, and glass trophies. They range in shape from balls to triangles to three-foot-tall tiers with miniature men poised mid-serve on top.

I spin around some more, my mouth gaping in awe, then my eyes land on Ryan. He's leaning against the archway, observing. "Do you like it?"

"Yeah."

He comes closer.

Hot flashes and ice tingles shudder through me with each step he takes.

"That's Jim Morrison." He points to a man's face on one of the vinyl covers. "He's the guy Jimmy and I—"

"I know." My abrupt interruption brings silence, and silence seems more intimate.

He looks at me to say more.

I don't speak.

He takes another step.

I have nothing more to add to the conversation, and he's inching closer and closer. Am I ready to kiss him again? I don't know. "So your brother must have the top floor to himself, right?" The question blurts out.

He stops and stills. His face shifts from seductive male hotness to confusion to … I'm not sure. The mood has successfully changed, which was my intention, but now I want to go back. I do want to kiss him.

Rewind.

Rewind.

Rewind.

I really want to kiss him. Where'd those intense eyes disappear to?

Can you handle a boyfriend?

"That was his room." He takes a step back.

The doorbell rings.

"Pizza's here," I say, finally breathing again.

Ryan brings the box outside on the patio by the pool. The breeze ripples the water, and the palm trees sway, swooshing, hypnotic music.

"Your view is pretty." I slide a slice of pizza onto my plate, thrilled to have something to concentrate on other than his remarkable eyes.

"I like it. It's going to be weird not seeing the water every day when I go to Northwestern. I'm definitely a beach boy."

"Beach Boy and Dog Girl. We could be superheroes," I say in a movie trailer–announcer voice, and immediately regret my corniness. But Ryan laughs.

"What would our powers be?" he asks.

My mouth is full of cheesy dough, but I have no idea how to answer that question.

He continues to entertain my silly idea. "I guess I can build impenetrable sandcastles and you can run really fast."

He's amazing. He's actually rolling with this. I laugh and add, "Or you can breathe underwater."

"That's way cooler. And you can talk to animals." His husky laugh makes this conversation seem much more sophisticated than it really is.

"Yeah."

We finish the pizza and end up back in the enormous kitchen.

"What time do you have to be home?"

"Midnight. I guess. I don't go out much." My moms are so happy I went to a party with human friends that they won't care if I waltz in at two in the morning. I start for a second. Did I say that out loud?

"Alright, do you want to watch a movie?"

"Sure," I say.

I unfold onto his stain-free sectional and sink into the cushions. A lush throw drapes over the back. I grab it and curl up. Everything about his home is comfortable, yet elegant. What does he think of my house with its beat-up old furniture?

Ryan turns on the television and searches for movies. He settles on *Mission Impossible,* and I nod. It doesn't matter what we watch, just as long as I don't have to continue to make conversation. Not that Ryan isn't easy to talk to. He is. But I've already started a superhero debate, so my stupid topic allowance has been met.

Soon, he's snuggled next to me, sharing the blanket. His bare legs rest next to mine. More butterflies. Thousands of them. The movie ends, and neither of us moves. I have to go home, but all I want to do is fall asleep on this couch in his arms.

He stirs, and I begin to separate myself from his embrace, but somehow he's maneuvered in such a way that our noses are practically touching. He stares at me. I can't blink. His eyes fascinate me, and while I'm taken in with their beauty, I feel a gentle tug on my lips as he kisses them. My eyes involuntarily close. His mouth discovers mine. Hours and seconds pass at the same time. Then it's over.

As he pulls away, he takes a part of me—a piece of my heart or gut or soul. I'm not sure. But he cradles it tenderly, and I'm glad to have given it to him. He has given that same wonderful part of himself to me. It clicks into place like the snap hook on a lead, forever connecting us. This is so far beyond doughnuts, even fresh-out-of-the-oven-on-Christmas-morning doughnuts. This is completion. This is my real first kiss.

He drags me to my feet, his arm around me to keep the chill away. The air-conditioned room is brutal after being snug under the cozy throw.

"Come on," he says. "I don't want to get on Cat's bad side."

I smirk. "No, you definitely don't."

It's twelve thirty.

"Is that you, sweetie?" Shane calls from upstairs.

I yell up, "Yes!"

She saunters down and gives me a quick kiss. "Cat's asleep, and I'm going lights out now. Did you have fun?"

"Yeah, it was fun hanging out."

Her eyes light up. "That's great, hon. Did you lock up?"

"Yes."

She gives me one more peck on my head, then a smile. "Love you." She travels back upstairs to the bedroom.

I'm not tired and want to go to the barn, but the security system is still not installed, and orders are to stay in the house. A tub of chocolate ice cream cures the frustration. I mutilate its smooth swirls with the prongs of my fork, nearly devouring half a gallon. Vicky thinks it's so weird that Mom and I eat ice cream with a fork. I wonder which utensil Ryan uses?

Before going up to my room, I survey the barn from the window and notice Ryan's car parked outside. That's strange.

I sneak out.

"Why are you here?"

"I don't know." He shrugs, then blinks the sadness from his eyes.

I walk up and stand next to him in front of the empty stall.

"Where's Rascal?" he asks.

"Cruz knew someone that wanted a bull terrier. Trax will stay here starting tomorrow. She's not a hundred percent, but she's ready to get out of the recovery."

"How do you do it?" he asks.

"Do what?"

"Not miss them."

"I do." Ghosts of dogs past cross my mind. "Some I miss more than others. Some remind me of good times, while others, not so much. Some leave scars, like Trixy. She was Dad's favorite. After he died, Mom adopted her out as soon as she could." The memory stings.

"Rascal was cool." His voice fades. He seems a million miles away. Maybe he's reminiscing about Rascal's goofy smile or disturbing farts.

I had wished for Rascal to be adopted. Every time I had looked at him, he had reminded me of Ryan and the day we first met. At the time I didn't want to think of Ryan—it hurt too much—but now I miss the dog that connected us. Does Mom miss Trixy?

"He was," I say.

He turns toward my corner and studies the photo of Dad. "So what do you do here?" He gestures to my spot in general, not just the photograph.

My body shrinks as my mind automatically compares my pathetic corner to his posh room. "Hang out."

He picks up my journal but doesn't open it. "Do you write?"

"No. I jot down things or draw but nothing good. It started out as an idea from my therapist to help ease my dad's death, but now it's just habit." I search his reaction. Will he think seeing a therapist is bad?

"Oh." He puts it back down, and his fingers brush the pinned photo. "That was taken the day before he died," I say.

He nods. "I see the resemblance. You look so much like him."

"Yeah, and nothing like Mom."

"No." He shakes his head. "Cat said it was his idea to hire parolees."

"It was. He'd gotten a second chance after screwing up and going to jail, so he wanted to pay it forward."

"Cool." His eyes reflect that sadness again. Something's different. I want to ask, but there's something raw and delicate about them. Prying questions could break him.

"It's weird that I'm here. Should I go?" he asks.

The thought of him leaving crushes me. "No."

His feet shuffle. He's obviously undecided about being here.

I force a question to make him stay. "Why did you come here tonight?"

He hesitates. "After you left, my house seemed oddly vacant."

"Do you miss your parents?"

"Yes and no. They're gone a lot, but I've never felt lonely. I mean, I've always been kind of a loner anyway. I guess I liked having you at my house. I didn't want you to leave." A breath escapes him, and his eyes dart around until he lowers his head and nervously laughs. "You must think I'm ridiculous."

"No, of course not." Words of consolation swim around my brain but either won't form complete sentences or seem stupid to say out loud. All I know is he's here, and Peter isn't. This feels right. I have no other intimate relationships to compare this one to, but I like whatever it is we're doing together.

His head lifts, and his eyes lock onto mine. I've looked into them for days now and never really seen them or the soul behind them until now. His good looks have been blinding me all this time. There's a caring, complex person standing here, leaning in, kissing me. Our bodies fuse, and the strain of our tethered lead slackens. It's heavy and fluid. Waves of warmth ripple through my body, making me weak, too weak to stand, and I pull him down.

We fall as one onto the beanbags.

I can't stop kissing him. I don't want to stop kissing him. Why in the world would I ever stop kissing him?

Not sure how long we make out, but he stays over, and I sleep like never before. No Peter inside my chest. When I wake, I'm wrapped in his arms, and Rock stands over us, scowling.

I shoot to my feet.

Rock's clenched face loosens. Apparently, he thought we were naked under the blanket.

I laugh.

"What's so funny?" Ryan asks, still half-asleep.

His shirt is off, and for a split second, his bare chest captures my undivided attention before reality comes crashing back. Rock is about to kill us.

"Nothin'! Get up, boy," Rock growls.

His menacing baritone wakes Ryan up instantly. He stumbles to get his bearings. He's blinking and trying to focus, not used to being tossed out of bed.

"I told you not to sleep out here." Rock frowns.

"I know ... I didn't plan on ... I mean, I was with ... "

"I know who you're with. What's he doin' sleepin' over? Does Cat know?"

Rock tenses again, so much that the veins in his bald scalp bulge to the surface and pulsate.

Ryan's safety may be in jeopardy.

"No ... I don't know ... Let's not tell her." I use my best puppy dog eyes.

He looks down his nose, nostrils flaring, and it's evident that he's not going to keep my secret, but he says nothing for a long time.

"Humph!" he sighs. "Well, as long as you're here, you can get to work."

Rock turns his back on us and stalks toward the other side of the barn.

My armpits burst with sweat. Thank God, he isn't going to kill Ryan.

Ryan's disorientated gaze falls on me, and I say, "I'll go get us coffee."

"Don't leave me alone with him," he whispers, wide-eyed.

I laugh and whisper, "He's a big teddy bear under that raging bull. You'll be okay after coffee."

"I guess." He frowns. "Coach doesn't like me to drink coffee."

A shovel comes whirling through the air like a missile aimed straight at Ryan's head. I catch it and glare at Rock.

"Stall five." Rock's voice barrels through the barn, sounding like the boom from a cannon.

Ryan's eyes expand, and he looks as if he's about to vomit, but he takes the shovel. "Cream and sugar, please." His voice rumbles with sleep, and maybe fear. "And water, if you don't mind."

My sympathetic smile is met with a panicked stare, and I leave, giving Rock a death glower. He better not ruin my perfect night.

My constant companion, Peter, returns. *Ryan is never going to want to go out with you again. Why would he if it means the wrath of a man the size of Hulk?*

I hurry to the kitchen. The coffee is already brewing. A half-eaten doughnut sits on a plate on the counter. It's Mom's, because Shane doesn't eat doughnuts. A gentle touch swipes my shoulder, and I jump. Mom is on her phone, listening intently. Her face pales. Something's wrong.

The last thing she says is, "I'll be right over."

"What is it?"

"Someone brought in another badly beaten pit mix last night to the hospital, so Dr. Ferrera needs me to get Bubba right now."

"Okay, well, his kennel's ready. Do you need a hand?" I ask.

"No, I'm good." She hasn't been sleeping. The dark circles under her eyes are proof of that.

"Any leads?" I don't know much, but I do know she's sick over these dogs. She's been spending a lot of time with other animal control agents trying to piece this puzzle together. The desire to catch this monster consumes her every waking hour.

"Not really." Concern shades her face as she sips the last of her coffee and rushes out the door.

I skillfully take three cups of coffee into the barn. The guys seem to be getting along. Rock no longer scowls, and Ryan's eyes have normalized.

"Stall ten is ready, right?" I ask Rock.

"Yes, why?"

"Mom just got a call from Dr. Ferrera. She went to pick up Bubba," I say.

"Humph. Vet said three in the afternoon," Rock says.

"Apparently, another pit mix has been beaten up badly enough to need Bubba's bed." I sip my coffee and sit with Ryan.

"I'll do the feedin'." Rock leaves us.

The dogs rustle restlessly, but I think Rock's being polite. He must approve of Ryan.

"Thanks, Rock," I say.

"Don't mention it, Peanut," he responds with gentle eyes and a tensionless scalp.

"Cleaning stalls is a great way to wake up." Ryan's lips curl on one side, so only a single delicious dimple appears.

"Sorry." I crinkle my nose.

"It was worth it. What are you doing today?"

"I don't know. I guess I'll check on this new dog and take Dragon for a walk." Then school pops into my mind. "I have some homework that I've blown off all break."

"Oh yeah, you start back tomorrow."

"Yep, must be nice to be homeschooled."

"I've got work too. If I don't finish on time, NCAA could revoke my eligibility. But I'm ahead." He cocks a brow.

He's ahead in school. You've never been ahead in school, not once. And he's going to Northwestern this fall.

Stop staring dreamily at him.

"Do you think you'll get more reporters here because of the new dogs?" he asks.

"I don't know. I mean, we get neglected dogs all the time. The whole Trax explosion was unusual."

"Shane mentioned Animal Planet?" he asks.

"Yeah." I can't hold his questioning gaze. *Tell him you wimped out. Tell him you couldn't handle it. Go on, Kendall, remind him of how much of a loser you are.* Peter's taunts cut deep.

Ryan coaxes me from my silence. "Are they coming here?"

"No, that fell through."

"Oh, too bad. You and this place would make for a great story."

He doesn't mean to unhinge me, but his words slice like a jagged knife through my gut. Am I just an interesting story? Again, what does he see in #dirtydoggirl?

Stop! Last night was real. One world. Remember!

He tenderly kisses me. It's not a big kiss, just a sweet, kind gesture, lifting me out of pity party central. Impeccable timing.

"I have a lot of back-to-back tournaments coming up. Be safe, and tell me if anything else happens."

I huff a laugh. "Don't worry about me. I'll be fine."

"You did it again," he says.

"Did what?" I ask. "I haven't done anything."

"Looked at your dad's picture."

"I did?"

"Yeah. You glance at it a lot."

I lower my eyes. He's going to find out that I actually talk to the photo—and that it talks back, which is even more nuts. His phantom kiss vanishes from my lips as my mouth dries, with only the bitter taste of coffee left behind.

"I'm sorry," he says.

"No, it's fine." I shake my head. "I didn't realize I looked at his picture so much."

"It's cute." He smiles but only at the edges.

I force my nerves to stop quivering, wanting desperately to look away, to run away. He leans in, and I'm motionless, until his lips touch mine. It's a longer kiss than before. A sweep of nausea tingles through me, and my heart pounds wildly. I'm going to fall over. What is wrong with me? Luckily, I don't faint. He draws me up by the leash that bonds us.

Our phone alarms go off. We lock eyes.

"I have to go. I have practice," he says.

"I have morning chores," I say.

We stand still for awkward seconds.

"I gotta go. Coach makes me run three extra laps if I'm late. I don't think I could handle that today."

"Okay." I freeze with nothing else to say. Why is this so hard today when it seemed effortless last night?

"I need to do school too, and laundry. My parents won't be back for two more days. Can I see you tomorrow after school?" he asks.

You have to ask? Of course! Yes! "Sure."

"Thanks for the coffee." He sets his cup down and bewitchingly stares at me.

"Bye." I barely say the word.

"Bye."

I watch his black Range Rover drive away.

An hour later I walk out of the barn with Dragon on a lead but halt abruptly.

Shane approaches with Jennifer and an older man.

Jennifer's dad is tall, with a well-groomed blond beard. He's dressed in dark jeans and a loudly patterned button-down. He struts and doesn't smile. Jennifer plows toward me in a white shorts outfit.

Who wears all white to a dog rescue? Could I possibly hate her any more? Yes, I can.

"Hey, Kendall, this young lady says she knows you and Dragon." Shane wears an inquisitive look on her face, relaying that their visit is unexpected.

"Hi, Kendall." Jennifer oozes fake delight at seeing me.

"Hi, Jennifer." My tone doesn't match hers.

Shane's eyes land hard on me.

"See, Daddy, isn't he beautiful?" Jennifer claps her hands together.

Vomit hurling could happen.

They share an undeniable resemblance. He's a more exaggerated version of his daughter. Where she's angular, he's pointy. Her nose is sleek; his is too long. Her hair is naturally blond; his is dyed.

"It isn't about the looks. I've told you that." His impatient tone cuts sharply.

Jennifer's proud shoulders wilt. She struggles to keep smiling.

"He's fascinating." The man stares at Dragon.

"Thank you, Mr.—?" I force politeness.

"Mr. Turnberry." He nods. He's a serious man. Not an ounce of warmth in his demeanor. "But he's underweight."

Dragon sits alert but quiet, just as I have trained him to do over the past few days.

"May I?" He holds his hand out for Dragon's leash.

Shane gives me a nod of approval.

Mr. Turnberry leads Dragon with confidence. It's clear he has handled big canines before. He pets under his chin, admiring Dragon's regal charm. Dragon actually seems at ease with him, but Dragon is used to being handled by many strangers, and he has a good disposition, so the credit isn't Mr. Turnberry's.

"What do you think, Daddy? Can we buy him?" Jennifer asks.

My eyes shoot out of my head. I forcefully grab the leash out of Mr. Turnberry's hand and lead Dragon away. Dragon senses my angst. His ears shift, and he half growls, half barks, unsure if there's a threat.

"He's not for sale." My voice is unyielding.

Mr. Turnberry looks at his daughter with cold eyes. Now I know where Jennifer gets her charm.

I look to Shane for help. "Tell them he's not up for adoption. Dragon's mine."

Shane's astonished expression says it all, and I wonder what lies Jennifer has fed her.

"Oh no, I apologize, Mr. Turnberry, if I gave you that impression. Dragon isn't for sale or adoption. It's illegal to own a wolf without a license."

"No need for an apology. My daughter should be the one apologizing for wasting everyone's time." He smiles at Shane and me, then overtly gazes along the landscape of our worn-out rescue and continues, "I have a license. I could pay ten thousand for the wolf and make a considerable donation to the Delray Dog Rescue. And I assure you, the wolf would be in good care."

Trembling but standing firm, I state, "Not for sale." Without saying goodbye, I storm away with Dragon.

"Bye, Kendall. Hope to see you at the Delray ITF."

Her saccharine voice is like a thousand tiny needles puncturing my skin. A few needles make it dangerously close to Peter's container. I shake it off and continue walking away, sensing her stare on my back.

Why is she doing this? She couldn't even bring her snooty self to pet Dragon in Puerto Rico, and what the hell is a Delray ITF?

I'm on the dirt road, the one that I travel every day to school. A couple of lost thoughts later, I've walked for an hour. It's hot. Sweat drips down the side of my face, and Dragon pants laboriously. I end up along Atlantic Avenue, where bowls of water dot the sidewalk in front of cafés and stores. I don't have any money, so I'll have to remain thirsty, but at least Dragon can get a drink.

A few stares pass over us, some admiring and some fearful of the giant canine. But seriously, what's weirder, a dachshund in a Gucci tutu or a wolf on a leash? Half of this town dresses up their designer dogs and parades them down the sidewalk in baby strollers. If you ask me, that's crazier.

We amble back home before attracting too much attention. The Florida heat exhausts both of us. My face and arms shine bright red, which sucks because my burnt skin will be peeling off during class, giving everyone another reason to think I'm strange and gross.

After I feed Dragon and secure him in his kennel, I enter the house. The smell of meatloaf wafts through the front door.

"Hey, hon, where ya been?" Mom asks as she's setting the table for dinner.

"Just around," I say.

"I know meatloaf isn't your favorite, but we made a Caesar salad too." Shane rips the lettuce over a large bowl.

"Great, I'm starved." I grab a glass, fill it with water, guzzle the entire thing, then refill it.

"You're sunburned." Shane hands me the bowl and the carafe of dressing. I mix the salad. "I know. I didn't mean to be out so long. I was just so mad."

"Yeah, I got that impression earlier," Shane says.

Mom slices the meatloaf, then brings the platter to the table. "What happened?"

"We had an offer to buy Dragon," Shane says.

Mom freezes before setting the platter down. "How much?"

"Mom!" I slam the salad tongs on the counter.

"What? We need the money!" Mom shrugs and sits down.

"What about all the Trax donations?" I bring out the salad and join her.

"I paid my debts, and now we're getting an expensive security system. It goes, Kendall. Too fast." She dishes a slice of meatloaf to me and one to Shane, who is still on the other side of the counter in the kitchen.

"No, I won't let you sell him." My piece of loaf looks like something I should be feeding to the dogs.

Mom swallows, then says, "It's not up to you. I never promised you a pet. I promised a rescue."

I stare at her, my stomach knotting and the smell of dinner no longer appetizing.

Shane sits next to Mom and softly says, "He's offering ten thousand."

Mom nods.

"And he has a license. He owns farms all across Florida. He has a lot of animal licenses on file," Shane says.

"Are you kidding me?" My heart drops to the ground by my feet, an ideal position for them to stomp all over it.

"No." Shane shakes her head and pushes the ketchup bottle toward me. "Eat, Kendall. And he shows German shepherds. I thought Jennifer was your friend?"

I squeeze the bottle with unnecessary force, and loads of ketchup dump out. "No. We are *not* friends. I met her in Puerto Rico, and she's a manipulative bitch."

"Kendall!" Mom scolds.

"Humph!" Hypocrite. She curses ten times as much as I do when she's working. She's like two people—a cursing redneck on the job and a perfect lady in the house. It's Shane's presence.

"She's the reason I left Puerto Rico. Mom, she hates animals!"

"How do you know that?" Mom's brow furrows. She always assumes I'm exaggerating.

"Because she barely touched Dragon before and kept her distance from him today."

"Yes, it's the father that wants Dragon. He seems to be the animal enthusiast. Jennifer had a lot of nice things to say about you. I had no idea you disliked her so much until I saw how you acted," Shane says.

"Well, I do. And she wasn't nice to me. She's lying. She just wants to hurt me." I chew with difficulty.

"Honey, I think you're overreacting," Shane says.

"As always." I clear my throat as the food sticks.

Shane cuts her loaf delicately. She's a slow eater. "She just seemed so sweet."

"Well, she's not. You wanted Dragon too, Shane. Why would you sell him?"

"Believe me, if I had all the money in the world, I'd be happy to keep him, but we are a sanctuary, and the more funds we have, the more dogs we can save. We're not their forever homes. We would never have rescued Dragon in the first place if it wasn't for all the money that people donated for Trax." Shane sets her fork down and sighs. The piece of meatloaf never makes it into her mouth.

Mom's finished her meal. "Oh, that reminds me. Ms. Shapovalov came by again to check on Trax. You were right; she's going to adopt her. I told her Friday."

I wish I'd been here to see her. My fork swirls the ketchup, but I don't eat the loaf. Two bites of the salad and I can't even taste it. My taste buds are stunned like the rest of my body. I've never had a pet. Never. I give all my love to the dogs, knowing they'll get adopted. Over and over and over! I'm surprised I still have any love leftover.

It was stupid to think you'd be able to keep Dragon.

They're right—our job is to save as many canines as we can. For ten grand we could save a lot of dogs. The tears sting as they bite my eyelids, but I refuse to give in to them.

"I'll think about it, sweetie," Mom says.

I nod, trying to understand, and leave the table silently. The tears are winning the battle, and crying in front of them would make everything worse. Mom and Shane struggle with keeping this place running and keeping me fed and dressed, but I'm afraid. *I'll think about it* is code for *So sorry, honey, but we need the money.* The Turnberrys of the world can buy whatever and whomever they want ... and the Kasts too.

On my bed, the tears fall. As they roll down the side of my face, I remember my social studies journal. I haven't made one entry in nine days. Without moving my head from the pillow, I raise my phone and open my Twitter. There are too many notifications for me to count. The assignment is on trending topics, and—thankfully—a teenage rock star's nude sexts are all over the feed.

I rush through all nine entries, then search my hashtag. This isn't a good idea, but apparently I'm a sadist. It's the same old, same old. Some people have crossed over to my corner and root for Team Kendall. That's comforting.

It takes a minute to find the original tweet that everyone has attached the replies to. It's a boomerang of me while I walk Dragon. There's nothing terrible about it. In fact, it's kind of funny. But it's frickin' creepy that a random stranger took a photo of me on Atlantic Avenue without my consent.

> @charlee_FAU—Dog Girl on point with that tan! #doggirl #2moms #nomoreemo

I fumble to the mirror and take a long look at myself. My skin has calmed and cooled to a deep tan. The sun has lightened my hair. Huh! Turning my head, I inspect my jawline and cheekbones. Not model-worthy but decent. However, I'm highlighted in other ways too. The fine scratch lines no longer blend into paleness; now they stand out like white dashes and hyphens on bronze paper.

I roll into bed and take one last peek at my phone. Big mistake!

> @Jenlovestennis—Outrageous! That wolf looks exhausted and underfed. It needs a proper home. #dirtydoggirl #rescuethewolf

I stare out the window in disbelief for a few seconds, then scream, "Fire! Fire!" I run to Mom and Shane's bedroom and fling open the door. "The barn's on fire!"

"Oh my God," Shane shouts. She grabs her phone and dials 911.

We all hustle downstairs and burst out the front door, rush across the yard. It's the middle of the night, but the fire blazes as bright as the rising sun.

Mom and I disappear into the smoke to unlatch all the stalls. The terrified dogs cry and howl, but their instincts force them to hurry away from the flames. Stampeding paws follow us outside, where we corral them into the run.

"Mom!" I scream and cough as she runs back into the fire. My lungs ache from the smoke. I wrap my hands, burnt from the hot metal latches, around my throat, but there's no relief from the sting. I need water.

Mom reappears with Trax and Bubba in her arms. I turn, count all the dogs, and realize Lucy's missing. My feet step back toward the flames, but Mom's sweat-slick hand stops me.

Tears stream out, forming black trails down my face. "I have to find Lucy!"

Mom coughs, and her hands blister worse than mine, but they determinedly cling to me. "Absolutely not! I won't lose you. Lucy'll be fine."

"You can't know that." I remember Dad's photo, cut loose from her grip, and sprint into the barn, ignoring the harsh, thickening air.

Mom curses and screams but follows.

The smoke is blinding, but we run on instinct to the photo's location.

We're too late. The hungry fire has already consumed my corner, and nothing's left of Lucy's stall. My books and beanbags. Dad's photo. It's an uncrossable wall of red and orange. The smoke debilitates my lungs as it sucks the last drop of oxygen out of me. Mom snatches my arm and drags me back outside.

Mom doubles over, coughing and gagging. She staggers but catches herself before falling over.

I gasp for the fresh night air. It cools until Peter's venom burns through. I spit slimy pink mucus onto the ground. It tastes bitter and dry.

Lights flash and sirens howl as big red engines barrel into our parking lot. Soon, water gushes from the tremendous hoses, drenching the ravenous flames. It's under control quickly. Thankfully, there are no dead dogs, but there's no Lucy either. In her panic she must've scurried away, probably to hide in the bushes. Relief, worry, and guilt-ridden tears prick the corners of my eyes.

I wasn't there for her. I was tucked safely away in the house. She probably feels abandoned. The need to find her hollows me out and brings the bitter taste back to my mouth.

I leave everyone behind and scour the woods. "Lucy! Sweetie!" My voice rasps, still dry and damaged from the smoke. She's nowhere in sight. Anger gives rise to a fierce determination inside my heart. "Come here, Lucy, come here, girl," I push through the searing pain in my throat and repeat over and over until the bushes rustle, but it's too loud to be Little Lucy. "Who's there?" Rage has made me foolishly brave.

A hooded person runs away.

"Stop!" My scream cracks. I swallow and attempt to yell to the first responders, "Over here! Over here!" No one comes. My impaired voice won't carry over the many loud noises.

I sprint to the police. They question Mom while the paramedics tend to her wounded hands. One of the officers catches my frantic stare. "I saw someone. Over there." I point.

She immediately leaves us, seizes her partner, and they jog over to where I had just been.

Hours pass. The sky has lightened. Ryan has come and gone but promises to return after his tennis practice.

The hooded person got away.

Atlantic High's first day back after spring break is halfway over, but I'm not there. It's just another absent strike in the teacher's roll call book for weird Dog Girl. There's no way I could have handled the gawking eyes of students or the pitiful stares of teachers or the principal's obligatory pat on the back. A ton of homework was most definitely given out today. I can only imagine how far behind I'm going to be, especially since I'm not sure I'll have the courage to return tomorrow either.

I loose a long sigh to expel some despair. No sense wasting time worrying about school.

Six sleeping dogs cover the floor next to the couch by the open window. Nothing but the smell of smoke and the whisper of wind slip through. Lucy still hasn't returned. Dragon takes up the closest spot next to me. His warm head rests on my legs, and his watchful eyes never shut.

Johanna Wells, from YouTube's *Get Out and Off Your Ass*, shows up at the front door. For some odd reason, it's a comfort to talk to her. I'm sure I look like death, but she holds my hand and assures me everything will be fine. "With the help of my viewers, we'll catch the assholes that did this. And we'll pressure the police. That's the beauty of the internet. Unfiltered truth. For the people, bitches!"

Her enthusiasm ignites me, and I believe her. This tiny titan is fighting for my family and for me. It's inspirational. But all my hope disappears when a fancy car rolls down the drive.

"What's he doing here?" I mumble.

"Who is that?" Johanna asks.

"Mom!" I yell, and as I do, she runs down the stairs. "Why is Mr. Turnberry here?"

Her woeful expression says it all.

Peter tangles my heart in the web and squeezes.

"I'm sorry, Kendall. But we need the money."

"No! You can't do this!"

She has no answer.

"What about the insurance money?" My voice cracks, but Mom shows no sympathy, only steadfast determination.

"Honey, this is a piece of dirt in a crappy part of town. The insurance—" She hesitates. Exhaustion may have finally caught up to the she-warrior inside of her, or maybe her lungs are still recovering from the distress of smoke inhalation. "It's shitty, and we need the money today, not months from now. Today."

"Wait and see what Johanna can do." I look to Johanna, but her brightness fades.

"Everything's destroyed—food, blankets, collars, the office. I have to go buy a computer and a printer, right now!" Mom's red, swollen eyes reveal more than her obstinate words.

I stand in a haze, gazing at her, the person who's supposed to have my back. The indescribable pain of betrayal claws through my insides, ripping and shredding and damaging worse than Peter ever has. So what if she's cried. It's about time. I only wish she'd cried with me instead of behind my back.

"I had to. He tripled his offer when he heard about the fire."

The rage within bursts through the binding web of angst, and I explode. "Great! That's just fucking awesome, Mom! You're giving *my* wolf to an opportunistic asshole. That's my blood, sweat, and tears. Mine!" I pound my chest. "This is fucked up." Yes, I'm cursing out loud in her face, and I don't care. What can she do? Nothing could possibly be worse than this.

I dare her. I dare her!

Madness swells, and more curse words dart across my tongue, then die because I can't even breathe. I teeter in different directions. I should say goodbye to Dragon, but the tears will upset him. And I won't give Mr. Turnberry or his awful daughter the satisfaction of seeing my breakdown.

Johanna stands in the background—a shadow, an echo. She's witnessed everything. She turns and glances out the window as Mr. Turnberry inches closer to the front door. Fear, dislike, and recognition shoot from her eyes as they volley from him to me. Her fierceness lessens. This is a man you don't argue with. He finds a way to get what he wants and has enough money to offer the right price and use the best opportunity to close the deal.

I look at Johanna one last time.

"I'll try," she says, but her eyes close, and her shoulders shrug. As much as she wants to help, she can't cross a man like that.

I nod, then run up to my room, slam the door, and bawl. I don't want to see any of them. Not Mom. Shane. Jimmy. Especially not Ryan. He brought that horrible family into my life.

My phone lights up with text message after text message. I turn it off, then hurl it across the room.

Aren't you happy with all his attention? What do you want from Ryan, and what could he possibly want with you? This is what people with money do. They take and take and take. Don't be a fool, Kendall. One world. What a joke!

Peter pushes for control.

Every article of clothing inside the chest of drawers lands on the floor. I rip shirt after shirt, pair after pair of pants off their hangers and add to the pile. Blankets and pillows fly through the air. My fingernails dig into the Black Widow poster, then the two of Thor. I shred them. Last, I shove the mattress off its metal rectangle and bury myself under Peter's makeshift web trap.

The sobs rise from the pit of my stomach, forceful and endless. They're a repetition of tiny tingles of torment that grow into a tidal wave of agony. It hurts so badly. I pull more clothes over my face, trying to feel something soft and cool. I curl into a ball and stop. Stop crying. Stop feeling.

"Stop, Peter! Stop!" The pleading scream has no breath to build on. It's a hoarse, scratchy sound.

Someone knocks on my door.

"Go away!" I wait and consciously breathe.

Silence.

Time passes. It could be two hours or two minutes. I don't know.

Peter's hold loosens one millimeter at a time, but my brain activity increases to near warp speed, replaying all the day's events. It won't stop until it does.

More silence.

I'm buried … beneath underwear. This is dumb. Why am I doing this again? It's okay to be angry. Right? I'm allowed to be angry. Anger feels good. It's better than anxiety or sorrow.

Someone knocks again.

"I said, go away!"

I peel a piece of clothing off my face. It's probably Shane. She's the peacekeeper. She's come too soon this time. I'm not ready to forgive and forget. Peter's barely restrained.

"Kendall?"

Ryan's beautiful, stupid, blue eyes stare down.

God! No! He can't see me like this.

I explode from the pile like a mutant monster. My hands shove his chest. "Get out!"

"I'm sorry ... I thought ... "

"Get out!" I shove him into the hall, slam my door, and make sure it's locked this time.

The pile in the middle of my room looks like a broken rainbow. It's mostly gray, with a blue bra hanging from the bedpost, a red shirt crumpled in the corner. Yellows, greens, and oranges scatter the mound. It's untamed and manic, and he saw it. I drop to my knees and crawl back under the mattress. Just when sanity is within my grasp, the convulsing sobs start again. "Stupid ... perfect ... idiot!"

When the house seems peacefully empty, and I'm adequately numb, I stand. All of the clothing and bedding fall away. I leave my broken room just as it is. I *want* the mess. Neatness is for neat little lives. I *need* the mess. Besides, Ryan's already seen it. He's seen the crazy. Whatever we had? It's over.

I venture down the stairs and out the front door. News vans idle, but I sneak around the opposite side of the house and into the woods in pursuit of Lucy.

The sun sets as I call Lucy's name. The darkness richens, so I must have searched for hours by now. The exact time remains a mystery, since I left my phone at home on purpose. Ryan's not going to call. That's for sure. And I want to hurt Mom, and the phone would just be a temptation. She'd persuade me into compromising. Screw compromise. Screw her. I'm never talking to her again. In fact, why do I even need a phone anymore?

She put money above me! And weak Shane couldn't talk her out of it. That's how you want to play it, Mom, well: game on. I can be tough too.

Jennifer wouldn't even know I exist if it wasn't for Ryan. The day he set foot on this property was the day Peter snuck back into my life. No Jennifer. No Mr. Turnberry. No Ryan. No Peter. A simple math equation—zero plus zero equals zero.

Peter doesn't want to be zero. *You could've saved him. You could've accepted the Animal Planet proposal. You could've made enough money to keep Dragon. It's just as much your fault as anyone else's. You had an opportunity, and you blew it. You chose to hide when you should've chosen to be brave.*

I'm not brave.

My racing heart devours the oxygen. The air won't reach my lungs. The ground spins beneath my feet. Life is a tilting blur of random colors. Then my face smacks against the cool dirt. Blackness.

A droplet of rain wakes me. I look to the sky, heartbroken. "I needed you hours ago." More raindrops fall. Something tickles my side. "Lucy!" I pull her into my arms and nestle my nose in her dirty, leaf-covered fur. She smells like she rolled on a dead fish, but oh well. She's all I have right now, and I'm holding on to her forever. We need each other.

I embrace her tighter than I've ever hugged her before. She's so resilient. I'm going to be as tough as she is. If she can survive a fire, then I can be strong and fight against my anxiety. Build a wall of strength and never let someone like Jennifer or her dad break me ever again.

Having her nestle in my arms lightens my mind. I peer into her glossy brown eyes and ask, "Why do they want my wolf?"

In answer she licks the salt off my skin.

"I'm getting him back. This fire was no coincidence. They set it. But why?"

My phone buzzes on the walk home from school.

"How long are you going to make that guy wait? It's not his fault, Kens," Jimmy says.

I sigh but don't answer. How can I face Ryan? I'm a freak. Who buries themselves under a mattress? What kind of crazy does that? I can't. I just can't.

My phone buzzes.

"Answer it."

"Shut up!"

We keep walking and rolling in silence. The ground squishes below my feet and his wheels. The dirt road has turned to mud from the constant rain.

More buzzing from my phone.

"Kens!" Jimmy barks as he reaches for it.

I jerk my arm away and turn it off.

He gives me the evil eye, then rolls on. His muscles bulge as his wheels trudge through the thick mud. He shoos my help away, and he won't turn on the motor. God, he's more stubborn than I am.

Then he stops. "What's with you?"

"Nothing … everything."

He won't let me pass. He's very talented with that chair.

"Bullshit. Why is any of this Ryan's fault?"

I shake my head. I want to explain. I really do, but I can't. All words are crammed in my throat, trapped.

"Talk, Kens. I'll listen. I'm your best friend."

I throw up my arms, and the words spill out. "He saw me."

"Saw you where?"

"No, he saw the crazy in me."

"He wouldn't be blowin' up your phone if he cared about whatever it is you think he saw."

"I had an episode. I hid under a pile of clothes. I pulled my mattress off my bed and hid under that too. Can you imagine what he thought when he saw that?"

"You had a reason to be upset."

I huff. "What's gonna happen when the news coverage ends and Trax is adopted? When Mom finds the sicko, and there's no more story? When the fire and vandalism are gone, and Ryan doesn't have to worry about me anymore? When he goes to college. Then what?"

Jimmy shrugs.

"Exactly!" I mirror his shrug. "I'm just a thot."

"You're not a thot."

"Just someone to pass the time. I'm not a Kast or a Turnberry. I'm a Shepherd. No matter what he says, there are two worlds, and they don't blend."

"Huh." Jimmy's brow furrows, puzzled.

"This is my miserable life. Train and support the dogs until someone else gets to love and live with them." The word vomit stops as the tears form. They sting and burn, but I fight them and force them to stay behind my eyelids.

"Forgive me for not feeling sorry for you." The freckles flatten as his eyes sharpen.

Shame burns through me.

"Ryan isn't like that," Jimmy says.

"How do you know?" The tears trickle, and I quickly wipe my face dry.

"I just know."

"No, you don't."

"Okay, fine. How do you know he *is* like that?"

I say nothing.

"That's right. You don't."

"People like Ryan and Jennifer just decide, *Hey, I want that. I think I'll take it. Everyone has a price.* Well, no one is taking me, and I'm not wasting my time on someone just for them to turn around and love somebody else."

"That's not fair."

"God, Jimmy. You of all people should know life isn't fricking fair!" My voice cracks.

The disappointment flashes across his face. He shakes his head, then rolls away from me.

I want to apologize. This is why I didn't want to talk about it. All talking did was dim the sunshine kid. My goal is to be strong, build a wall of impenetrable steel, not to argue and complain.

We finally reach the barn and go straight to work. Our newest rescue, Rocky, is a whippet with an identity crisis. We're not sure what he thinks he is, but he has no idea he's a dog. We've worked all week just to get him to accept the collar around his neck. Jimmy has discovered that Rocky likes the theme from *Rocky*. It's ironic, but whatever works.

Jimmy starts the song, and the annoying lead-in plays—Dant-dant dant dant—dant dant daaaaa! I want to puke, but out strolls Rocky with his head held high, tolerating the collar. Now for the leash. It's tricky, and I end up slipping in the mud.

"Shit!" I scoff, when someone offers me a hand. Instinctively, I grab it, and as soon as my skin touches his, I know it's Ryan. Those treacherous butterflies! "Thanks."

He doesn't let go.

"Let go." I tug, but he holds firm.

"No, not this time, not until you tell me what I did wrong."

"Nothing. You did nothing wrong."

His face. His chiseled face. My heart caves in. What did he see when he looked at me under that pile of stuff? What did he see?

His blues storm. He's not smiling. No dimples.

I try to hold his gaze, to find a strength and confidence within. My lungs tighten. The tears puddle. I yank out of his grip and sprint into the house before my protective wall collapses.

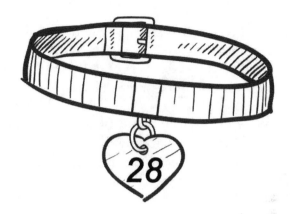

Jimmy has a doctor's appointment, so it's a lonely lunch. Amanda from social studies comes over and invites me to hang at her table with some people I know well enough. We've all shared the same school since kindergarten. Apparently, she feels sorry for me after Johanna's segment on the fire and heart-wrenching plea for more donations. Plus, today's round of *Let's Make Kendall's Twitter Less Humiliating* in Mr. Young's class.

"Thank you, but I have a book."

Amanda nods and retreats.

What kind of answer is *I have a book*? God, Kendall!

I open said book. A half an hour will fly by. Thirty minutes isn't a long time.

Ten minutes stretch out painfully. Sweat droplets dot my forehead, and the horrible itch strikes again. I scratch viciously, drawing blood, but get no relief.

"It's all in your mind, Kendall," I mumble. Terror hits as a boy from the table in front of me turns around because I'm obviously nutso. A nervous smile creeps across my face, and I bow my head. The humiliation tops off my anxiety, and that's it, Peter's been released. I can't break down at school as I did at home. I bolt out of the cafeteria and into the parking lot. I'm not going to leave. I'm just going to get some fresh air and wait for the bell.

A familiar Range Rover waits around the corner. The windows are dark, and I can't see Ryan, but I recognize his car.

He pulls up and lowers the window. "Hey."

With just that one word, I'm crushed. He completes the offense with a lopsided lip curl and dimple.

I feel the lead that connects us snap back into place, but does he feel it too? "What do you want?"

"To talk."

"How'd you know I'd be outside of the cafeteria?"

"I didn't."

My brows draw at this strange twist of fate. Pushing him away is too exhausting right now. The fact is, I'm happy to see him. Maybe it's because I want to ditch school so I don't have to face people like Amanda and her pity or … just because … just because he's Ryan.

"I was going to sit here until two and make you talk to me."

"My school ends at three."

"Then I would've waited."

"How long have you been here?"

"I don't know, forty minutes. Will you get in, please?"

I hesitate and cross my arms. Anger, fear, confusion, desire all blend into a paralyzing smoothie.

"Please."

He's right. I can't repeat what I did in Puerto Rico. We should talk. I stroll around to the passenger seat and slip in. My red, itchy neck evolves into a red, itchy chest on fire, and I can't get away from Atlantic High fast enough.

As I pull the door shut, my eyes land on a cardboard box in the back seat. "Wow! That's a lot of tennis balls."

"Oh yeah. I got some old practice balls for the dogs."

"Cool," I murmur. I've been stupid, lumping the Kasts in with the Turnberrys. Ryan is different. Maybe he didn't think the mountain in my bedroom was weird. All I know, he's exactly what I need right now. "Drive!"

"Yes, ma'am!" He winks. His car bumps as he misses the turn and runs over the curb.

The grab bar is my salvation. "Are your parents home?"

"They're at work. Why?"

"Can we go to your house?"

"Sure." He looks at me and not the road.

"The road." I release the grab bar for a second to push his chin forward. I snatch a piece of the hard-cherry candy in his cup holder, then prepare to be terrified.

We get to his home and walk into his lavish kitchen.

"Ryan," a woman's voice calls from another room in the house.

"Yeah, Mom," he answers.

I soundlessly mouth, "You said your parents were at work!"

He shrugs. "I thought they were."

Footsteps click down the hall until a woman in black pumps and a knee-length black skirt suit steps into the kitchen. She holds her cell phone and coffee in one hand as she wrestles with her briefcase-sized designer bag in the other. She doesn't miss a beat once she sees me.

"Hello, I'm Patricia Kast." She extends a long arm with nude-colored nails tastefully clipped short.

I shake her hand. "Hi, I'm Kendall."

"It's nice to meet you." She dashes around the kitchen, seizing a pencil, a business card, and a protein bar. She pours coffee, then says, "Hope to see your mom again soon. Goodness, it's been years." Her phone buzzes. She glances at it and stiffens. "Got to go. You two have fun. I'll be late, honey. Order whatever you want." She pivots and waltzes out of the room. Before we hear the door open and shut, she hollers, "Love you."

"Love you, Mom," he yells back, then turns to me. "That's Patricia."

I nod, still sucked into the whirlwind she's left behind. I struggle to remember what she looked like, but like her son, she's left her scent behind—vanilla and lavender—and a feeling of importance, like I was in the presence of a judge. She's the kind of woman that makes you feel sloppy, as if you're not putting enough effort into your appearance or your life.

"She's always in a hurry," he mumbles.

We exit to the back patio. The sun shines. It's warm; luckily, I'm in shorts. I remove my long-sleeve shirt, and the tank top underneath feels adequate for the heat.

"I'm not going to let you push me away," he says.

"I can see that." I grin and try to be cool, as if hot guys always try to win me over. On the inside Peter zips around trapping butterflies.

"I'm not like your dogs; I'm not going anywhere."

"You talked to Jimmy." I scowl.

"Yes." There's no apology in his tone or expression.

"Are you sure you really mean that?"

"I do mean it." No smile. No dimples. Sincere eyes.

The tingle of tears sparks relief. "You're not freaked out about my ... " I search him to make sure his sincerity is real.

"Just because you had a meltdown in your room doesn't change how I feel about you." The half smile develops.

I bite my lips and blink.

"I'd be surprised if you didn't freak out. I know how much Dragon means to you." He puts a hand on my thigh. My skin warms. Then as if a bottle of itching powder dumps all over, the itch spreads. It's all I can do not to scratch.

Itch.

Trap butterflies.

Itch.

Trap butterflies.

Peter, stop! Please!

I stand up and walk it off. The designer patio furniture, the waterfront mansion. I'm sipping fruity soda, not a generic grocery brand, with a guy that's everything a guy should be. And he wants me, the #weirddoggirl, the girl that buries herself under bras and blankets.

I can't concentrate. This is not my life. This is not my element. I kick off beat-up sneakers and back right into the pool. The water smacks the back of my legs so hard it leaves a mark and makes a cringe-worthy *thwack!*

Ryan cannonballs in, then swims over. "Are you okay?"

"I'm fine."

"You're crazy," he says.

My heart drops. He thinks I'm a fool.

"I'm sorry." My clothes float and bubble.

"No. Don't be sorry. You're crazy in a good way." His hair slicks back from wetness, and it's even sexier than when it's dry.

Peter traps and traps. Sticky folds everywhere. My God, how many butterflies can fit inside a stomach?

"My anxiety isn't just teenage girl cray-cray. I have a therapist. I've been diagnosed with a mental illness." Peter and all the butterflies go still. I've opened the gates and let out the truth.

"It's okay." He wraps me in his arms and kisses me. It's a tenacious kiss, full of teeth and longing.

As the water swirls around us, I drift in both my mind and my body. His electrifying tongue sends a chill down my body.

He pulls his lips away from mine, but we continue to embrace. He takes me in with his blues and smiles that perfect-teeth smirk. "Don't ever push me out of your life again."

Tiny explosions of glee crackle and pop through my veins as the blood races up my arms from my fingertips, down my spine, and through my legs. Even my toenails tingle, and my untamed heart nearly beats out of my chest. Suddenly I want to touch every inch of him. Right now. I need to touch him. Now!

"Deal?" he asks.

"Yes." My mouth locks on his as my legs wrap around his waist and my hands run through his wet hair, then down his back. Our connection cable reels in tightly, until there is no give in the lead that bonds us.

He carries me out of the water, never releasing my lips and never stumbling, and lays me on a giant chaise in the sun. "You're shivering."

Goose bumps cover my legs, but I'm not cold. His body is my blanket.

For the next half hour, we lounge in the warmth of the sun, letting it dry our clothes. I'm relaxed, but the fact that I'm skipping school again snakes into my thoughts. I breathe calmly, trying to think only of holding the hand of the guy I'm falling in love with.

What's Vicky going to think?

"The renovation sketches look great." He breaks the silence.

His mind is probably running wild like mine. I've never been much of a sunbather. Just sitting around, doing nothing. It's a pathway to dark thoughts.

I turn on my side to face him. "Yeah. It's going to be a lot better for the dogs."

"What about you?" His finger drags along the length of my arm over the many bumps and dents.

"Me too. If it ever gets completed."

"I'm sorry you lost your dad's photo."

"Thanks." I roll back and close my eyes, not feeling particularly upset about the photo but happy he cares enough to mention it. Sadness is relative after losing a father. Sure, I hate that the picture and my stuff burned to ashes, but that loss is nothing in comparison. "What time is it?"

"One thirty."

"Okay, Ms. Shapovalov is taking Trax home today, and I want to make sure I'm there to say goodbye."

"She's ready?"

"Pretty much; she has to take it easy, of course. Very light exercise for another month."

We fall back into silence again.

My mind yearns to know more about him. "Can I see your poetry?"

His head whips around as if he's going to say *no way*, but then he pauses in reconsideration.

"It's okay. I don't have to read them. I just thought—"

"I want you to read them." He slides closer.

The lounge chair we share is narrow, and I can feel every inch of him.

"You do?" My words barely pass my lips. The butterflies block my air passageway. I'm surprised I can even find words when my mind focuses keenly on the touch of our bodies.

His head falls to the cushion, positioning his lips a mere millimeter from my ear. "Sure, but I'm not a great poet."

His breathy words tickle, delivering shivers of heaven. "I doubt that."

"No. Really. They're not good."

We leave the sunny patio for the brisk air conditioning of his second-floor bedroom. My damp clothes chill my skin and goose bumps race up my legs. This time it is because I'm cold.

He grabs a notebook and plops onto his bed, waiting for me, but I remain standing. "Sit," he says.

"My clothes are still a little wet."

"So?" He leans over and picks up a blanket that's crumpled on the floor and hands it to me.

"Thanks." I wrap up in the fleece fabric and settle down next to him.

It's strange being in his bedroom. It's the only boy's room I've ever been in before. Jimmy shares his bedroom with his younger brother, so we always hang out in the living room.

Ryan shuffles past several pages, each with one or two paragraphs of handwriting, stopping and skimming through a couple until he lands on one. He places the open notebook on my lap. "I like this one. I wrote it while traveling across the middle of Florida. There was a coach at Saddlebrook I really liked, and I went over to hit with him about twice a month, so I got used to the drive." He lowers his gaze, shaking his head. "I don't know; it just seemed cool being in the middle of nowhere. I liked the drive."

His compact and angular writing squeezes a lot of words into a small amount of space. Disciplined and clean like he is. I read the poem, and apparently he gets nervous, because he stands up and paces the floor.

The road is my church, miraculous and deadly.
I gaze across the land,
Green, Yellow, Gold.
Vultures perch on mile markers.
The corpse of an alligator rots on the pavement.
Skid marks appear from nowhere, then die abruptly.
Evergreen trees clump together like families,
Cows take shelter under the branches,
One bull sits in the yard,
Monstrous in size but serene in posture,
Horns outstretched—his regal crown.
One awkward-shaped tree stands tall on a hill,
Watching, Judging, Being!
I drive on.
The scene shifts.
Freedom continues behind fences.

"It's beautiful," I say.
"Thanks."
"Can I read more?"
"Sure."

I lean back against furry pillows and read a few more pages. Some of the poems are jagged with hard ink slashes and abrupt exclamation points. They're all without titles. Frustration and anger leap from the paper, and I like it. They're messy and full of energy. It's a glimpse into his dark side.

Brother, where are you?
Protector from the storm—
Player, WINNER, Loser!
Frayed! Fractured! Asshole!
Die?

I look up and want to ask him the meaning behind these darker poems, but he's pacing and fidgeting. Am I invading too much of his personal space? Should I close the book and do something else? But he'll think I don't like them, so I pause, keeping the notebook open, and stare at him.

He stops pacing, lets out a deep breath. "Do you want to spy on Dragon?"

"What?" I rocket to a sitting position and wobble from the softness of the bed and pillows. The notebook folds shut.

I didn't want to think about Dragon. It's too soon, too fresh. Tears prick my eyes, and a dull ache forms. Ryan's supposed to be the dream that pulls me out of the nightmare, not the demon that shoves me back into it.

"I know where Jennifer's dad lives."

It doesn't take us long to drive to Jennifer's house.

"And we're here. Already. Humph!" I cross my arms, annoyed.

"Yeah. That's it." He points to a long driveway lined with trimmed dwarf hedges, ending at an impressive house. An immaculately tailored lawn surrounds the sprawling estate. I can't see the entire backyard, but it appears extensive. A German shepherd spots our car and raises its ears on high alert.

Just before Ryan reaches the entrance to the drive, the garage door lifts.

"Ryan," I gasp.

"I see." He slowly drives down the road undetected. He pulls over to park.

The car leaves Mr. Turnberry's driveway and turns onto the road. It continues past us. A large animal is in the back of the Escalade. The windows are tinted, so I can't tell if it's Dragon, but it's large enough to be.

"Follow him." I hysterically pat Ryan's arm.

Ryan glances sideways and nods, then stomps on the gas pedal.

I drum the dashboard as if that will make the car go faster. We pass the railroad tracks where Trax was left for dead, and a chill runs the length of my spine.

After miles the Escalade turns off the main road, through a secluded neighborhood where each house sits on an acre or two. They turn down a long driveway and park.

Ryan stops the car and hands me the fancy binoculars he'd brought to spy on Dragon at Jennifer's house.

The driver of the Escalade opens the back hatch. Dragon leaps out. He looks me dead in the eyes, and I freeze, but the man yanks the leash, forcing the wolf to enter the house. When the man comes out, he's holding a folder.

"Where's Dragon?"

"Still in the house." Ryan squints and takes pictures with his phone.

With the binoculars' zoom, the symbol on the folder is clear. It's a circular design with bulky muscular arms folded above a dog's head.

"Duck." Ryan pulls my head toward him, hiding us from the Escalade as it whizzes past.

I lift my head. "This must be some sort of dog training facility."

"Maybe."

I shiver in disgust.

"What?" Ryan asks.

"Why didn't he bring Dragon to me? I would've trained him. I *had* trained him. He doesn't even need training. Take me home … Please." This was a bad idea. I can't bear the heavy sadness any longer. Not even Ryan's gentle touch on my shoulder can haul me out of this funk.

Another news van sits in my driveway. I exhale roughly. They're here to follow up on Trax and Ms. Shapovalov.

Ryan looks at me. "I'll handle it."

My knight in shining armor. But I'm not running away anymore. No more hiding. I already made the mistake of passing on Animal Planet and all that money. It's time to woman up. "It's okay. I need to do this."

With a comforting wink, he takes my hand. "Let's go."

But it's not the news media.

Shane and Mom walk out of the recovery shelter with two students wearing University of Central Florida T-shirts. They're both tall and lanky. The boy's red hair shoots up from his scalp like fire, and the girl's slicks back to a point, then escapes in a ponytail.

"Great, honey. You're home just in time." Shane rushes over to us. "I want you to meet Adam and Marie."

"Hi." Ryan and I shake their hands.

"They're film students and want to do their senior project on us," Shane says.

"It's a documentary. They will be around here a lot with their cameras." Mom fiddles with the rope slung over her shoulder. She talks slowly while her eyes feel me out.

I smile to reassure her I won't break. We haven't spoken since she sold my wolf.

Ryan places a hand on my back. "Sounds interesting."

The gesture draws Mom's attention.

"Yeah." I nod.

"The focus will be on rebuilding the sanctuary. Showing how these hate crimes devastate real people and affect the community as a whole. You guys do a much-needed service." Adam sweeps his hand, rounding us up in an imaginary circle. "You get strays off the street, and now you're limited. Also, the possible serial killer is a tantalizing angle. We'll definitely include it. Heck, we might even find a clue." He talks fast. He's obviously passionate about this project, but he looks to Marie to continue.

"Most people aren't aware of how dangerous your job can be. Trax is a perfect example of that."

"And the arson." Adam tosses a conspiratorial glance at Mom.

Marie smiles. "But we're not solving crimes. We'll leave that to the police. It's basically an account of your daily lives. We'll work around you. No need to do anything differently. We'll take tons of footage and edit it into a twenty-minute film. We'll premiere it at UCF, and you all can come see it."

"Can we see it before, too, while you're doing it?" Ryan asks.

"Sure," Marie says.

I shuffle away from Ryan and pace out my leeriness. "Do we get paid?"

"I wish." Adam smiles.

"Unfortunately not, but you will get recognition. A lot of UCF's films go on to win awards or get used for marketing. You and the dogs will definitely capitalize in many ways." Marie nods.

Adam points to Marie. "She has five dogs. All rescues. And I have two goldendoodles. My mom's allergic." He shrugs.

"Do you want to do it?" Shane asks.

All eyes fall on me.

"Yes." I inhale and exhale loudly and look at Ryan.

He smirks. "I like it."

"Terrific." Adam claps. His face beams with excitement, then calms as he leans in and says, "You never know what our state-of-the-art equipment will capture on film."

Life without Dragon gets a little less sucky each day. Ryan and I drive by Mr. Turnberry's on the daily and catch a glimpse of him. Plus, I keep busy with work and the new UCF project.

After school Ryan is at the rescue, but he's not in the barn or the field. I go straight into the house, leaving Jimmy to tend to Rocky on his own. Ryan sits at our old kitchen table. He fits. He's become part of the family already, like Jimmy or Vicky.

"What's up? Where's Mom and Shane?" I ask.

"Oh, hi." He glances up from the computer.

He didn't even hear me come in.

"Come here. Look at this." He pats the chair next to him. "Cat and Shane just left."

"Where'd they go?"

"The feedstore. I think."

"Okay." I scoot in next to him and examine the video footage on the screen. "Is this the documentary?"

"Yes. From the randoms they shot yesterday. Adam sent me this link, but look. Look at Cruz's wallet."

It's footage of the parolees getting their paychecks, and I don't understand what he's trying to show me. His face is enthusiastic, but I can't return his excitement, because I'm completely clueless.

"See it?"

"No."

"Okay." He slows the action down until he pauses on Cruz opening his wallet to put his check inside, then he zooms in. "There."

"Oh my God! Ryan. Is that what I think it is?" I ask.

"Yes." He places his finger directly on the card nearly falling out of Cruz's wallet.

The symbol jumps out as plain as day now.

"Isn't that what you described? A round symbol with a dog head and crossed arms?"

"Yes. That's it."

"Why does Cruz have their business card?" he asks.

"I don't know."

"What was Cruz in jail for?" he asks.

"Theft and carrying a gun without a license." I pause. "He definitely has another job. It might be mowing lawns."

"That could be why he has the card—he mows their lawn. But I don't believe in coincidences."

"Me either."

"And isn't he the one that knew someone to adopt Rascal?"

"Yes." My voice shoots up a decibel.

Ryan shakes his head. "Cat and Shane didn't use any sort of data storage server, did they?"

I laugh. "Are you kidding?"

He sighs. "Where are the records on the animals?"

"In the barn. Probably burned up." I sigh too.

"Let's take a look." He stands, and we bolt out of the house.

"Hey, Ryan," Jimmy hollers above the music from the yard.

"Hi, Jimmy," Ryan yells back, then turns to me. "Music Appreciation on Wednesday? That's not on the schedule." He mocks my obsessive-compulsive dog routine.

"Ha ha. The schedule went AWOL the day I met you and Trax."

"I bet your phone alarm is set to go off in about thirty minutes." He snickers.

I scowl, then yell to Jimmy, "How's it goin'?"

Rocky doesn't have on his collar, and he's being difficult.

"Not very well. I could use some help," Jimmy shouts.

I look to Jimmy, then back at Ryan. "Be there soon," I call to Jimmy. But I have a feeling Ryan and I will be in the office for a while.

I step past charred wood and glance over my shoulder at what used to be my corner. The spot where Dad died again when his photograph burned to ashes. My chest tightens, but I refuse to let it strangle me. I can do this. *Be strong.* I force my gaze forward and plow on.

The office is dark. We're not supposed to cross over the caution tape, but we do. Using the flashlights from our cell phones, we shuffle through the files. Some of the metal cabinets escaped the funeral pyre, but the heat still damaged the folders.

"Here's Rascal's file." Ryan hands over a manila folder that smells acrid like burnt microwave popcorn and has turned a weird brownish-orange color but remains intact.

"Look for Sampson, Oliver, Scotty, and Rival. Cruz helped with their adoptions too," I say.

"I have Rival and Oliver, but that's it. The others might be in this mess that's totally destroyed."

"That's okay. These are good enough."

We bring the files outside into the sunlight, and Jimmy rolls up next to us, frustrated.

"That's the most difficult dog I've ever dealt with." Jimmy scoffs. He's covered in sweat, and his eyes droop from exhaustion.

I laugh, then try to express my sympathies.

"What are you two doing?" Jimmy asks.

"Double-checking the dogs Cruz found homes for," I say.

"Why?" Jimmy wipes his hands on his shorts, leaving dirt skid marks.

"On the UCF footage, I spotted this symbol. It's the same one Kendall saw a few days ago when we followed Dragon to that house." Ryan hands Jimmy a file. "Here, man."

Jimmy takes it. "And Cruz is involved how?"

"He has a business card in his wallet with that same symbol. My eye caught it as I watched the clips." Ryan shakes his head, apparently astounded by his discovery.

Rummaging through the folders, our fingers tinge with black ash. Every flip of paper conjures a cloud of smoky dust.

"Nothing unusual here except the person moved here from Nevada, and isn't Rascal's guy from Nevada too?" Ryan asks me, since I'm holding Rascal's file.

"Yes." I find the page with the person's former address on it.

"My guy's a local, been living here for ten years," Jimmy says.

"But they're all single guys around thirty." Ryan's eyes narrow, and his forehead wrinkles as his mind turns.

We follow Ryan back into the house. He starts searching the internet. His fingers fly over the keyboard while his eyes focus, and he bites his bottom lip.

I ask, "What are you looking for?"

"I'm trying to find a match to that symbol, but it's hard when there's no name. I've tried the words dog, train, kennel, breeder, and nothing comes up." Ryan bites his lip harder. He leans back in the chair and runs his hands through his hair, obviously discouraged.

"Try dogfighting," Jimmy says icily.

My head snaps around. A stone-cold face, a face I'm not used to seeing on Jimmy, looks back at me. Air as thick as canned dog food weighs on us as we sense the truth. My heart jumps into my throat, and Peter's sticky silk clogs my lungs. It takes a minute for me to recognize Peter's presence. I haven't drifted into the dark side for days. I almost forgot what it was like to doubt, to feel the slime of anxiety smother my happiness.

Ryan jolts back and resumes typing madly. His face pales as he angles the screen toward us.

The round symbol with the dog head and crossed muscular arms screams out in bright red and blue, along with an article about a ring of dogfighting houses that had been raided and shut down in Nevada five years ago.

I collapse onto the kitchen chair, smash my head into my hands. All emotions hit me at once, and my brain can't handle it.

"We can't jump to conclusions. It could be a coincidence. Five years is a long time ago," Ryan says, forever the diplomat. But the deep impression his teeth left on his lower lip tells a different tale.

"You just told me an hour ago in this very room that you don't believe in coincidences," I argue.

"You're right," he sighs, attempting to mollify his frayed appearance and bring his dimples to the surface but failing miserably.

Obviously, he's trying to put me at ease, but he's doing just the opposite. I'm not in the mood for his white-knighting, and it takes all of my inner strength to keep Peter in lockdown.

"Cruz is from Nevada," Jimmy adds.

"How do you know?" I ask.

"We talked about it one day. Not sure how the subject came up, but he said he was saving money to get back home to Nevada. That he missed the desert."

I get up from the table and walk over to the counter to browse the work schedule. "Cruz comes on duty in an hour. Let's ask him."

"Dogfighting is no joke. These kinds of people are murderers," Ryan says.

"I know, but I also know Cruz. He's unreliable and annoying, but he's not a dog killer. He loves the dogs." I shake my head. "There's just no way." There's no way I would've missed that.

"He's a convict," Ryan says, his upper-class prejudice slapping me in the face.

I sigh and close my eyes. One world or opposite worlds? "Yeah, he is, so what?" The words come out a little more defensively than I mean them to.

"So, he's broken the law." Another swipe of his luscious hair, only this time it's not sexy. It's arrogant.

I throw my arms into the air and pace. "Of course you wouldn't understand. You live in a mansion. You've never had a problem like these guys."

"I have problems," he spits.

"Oh, really? Like where your next meal will come from, or if the bank is coming to take your house away? Those are real problems, not which tennis tournament to play." I can't stop the bitterness from branding each word, and they singe. His vacant stare absorbs me, and I shut up.

"Why are you getting so upset, Kendall? I'm on your side."

"You'll never understand."

Jimmy's head volleys between us, caught in the middle.

Ryan sneers, then snaps, "I'll be back tomorrow after you've calmed down." He stalks out of the house.

"Jeez, psycho," Jimmy says.

"What do you mean? Come on, he's wrong. To come down that hard on Cruz just because he went to jail for stealing so he could survive."

"You're overreacting, and you know all these guys had a choice, and they made the wrong ones. They're guilty, Kens. I agree with Ryan. This looks bad. If Cruz is linked to this symbol, then he's dangerous."

"Or he's just mowing their lawn and has no idea."

"That still doesn't explain the homes he's found for these dogs."

I jab my fists at my hips. "He's a go-getter."

Jimmy tilts his head in disbelief. "How many homes have Rock or Digit miraculously found for these dogs?"

I bow my head. "Point taken."

He's right, and I don't know why I'm stubbornly fighting it. I rely on certain definitions of life and people, and before Ryan those definitions were clear and precise. Now it's all blurred and confusing. Doors are opening, lines are being crossed, and it's scary. It's the red words of hate—and Mr. Turnberry purchasing Dragon—manifesting in a comment made by Ryan. A lifetime of prejudicial assumptions thrown in my face because of the parolees I call friends.

"You know Ryan has had real problems. You know about his older brother, right?" Jimmy asks.

I'm shocked. I always forget he has a brother. The family photos in his house are the only evidence of his existence.

"He's at college or something." The mystery sours my tone. "Sorry, I didn't mean to ... What happened to his brother?"

"Drug addict. Bad. The parents forced him into rehab, where he stayed for several months, acted rehabilitated, went home, and left the country the next day. Cleared out his bank account and disappeared. Ryan hasn't seen his brother in two years. He said they used to be best friends. He gets post cards. Ryan worries he'll never see him alive again."

I stare, dumbfounded, tears building. *Now who's making assumptions, Kendall?*

"He knows real problems, Kens. People with money are still human."

"I'm such an idiot, Jimmy." I look at my friend in awe. Everyone talks to him, and he listens. He's such a great person, and I'm so lucky to call him my best friend.

"You didn't know?"

"No," I murmur, and recall the vague poem about his brother. Poor Ryan. I feel like the lowest of the low, like the garbage truck has just dumped its entire load of trash on my head. Like the lead that binds us is wrapped around my neck. We rarely discuss his life. He's always consoling me, helping me. I'm the worst girlfriend ever.

My phone's ear-piercing buzz goes off. It's feeding time. I turn off the noise and call Ryan to apologize. He doesn't answer.

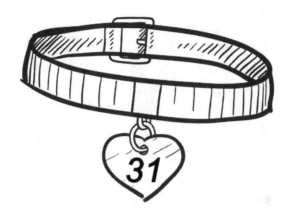

No sleep. I'm exhausted, but my brain wants to dissect the random fight I picked with Ryan. I amble to the barn for answers, push past the yellow dividing tape, and step into my spot. I'm not supposed to be here. No more beanbags or books, just ashy soot and the smell of woodsmoke everywhere. My hands blacken when I pin another photo of Dad to what's left of the wall.

"Dad?"

Silence.

Beyond the field and the light from the moon, the woods darken and shadow. The vandal hid there. Possibly planned and plotted the fire right in that spot. Fire that destroyed. Destroying us was his or her mission. It doesn't seem real.

"Dad, it's been crazy around here. I need to hear your voice." I sigh.

Silence. The soot and dirt rest calmly. Everything remains eerily still. Even the dogs on the other half of the barn, the side damaged less, sleep soundlessly.

I continue searching for any remaining piece of the original photo, my favorite photo. Warmth blossoms on my cheek. A kiss. I kneel and close my eyes. Slowly, his face appears. "Why am I like this? He saw the crazy and accepted me anyway. And I push him away all the time. Telling him he doesn't understand when he does. I've screwed everything up. *Again.*"

Silence.

"Dad?" I wait for a response that doesn't come. "Do you think it's true?

Cruz … and the dogfighting. Can it really be true? I would've known, right?" My eyes smash shut.

Dad's ghost remains speechless, but his worried eyes glow behind my eyelids.

"I'm afraid it's true too." I slump. "What do I do?"

Silence.

I'd hoped coming out here would bring clarity. What's clear is I'm scared. Everything's wrong.

I stand and pace with my eyes still closed. "Since when do cute, rich guys like me, and why? Since when did a dogfighting ring set up in Delray, of all places? I was just getting strong, accepting Ryan's affection and Dragon's absence, making sense out of it all." I grab my hair and pull, allowing the pain to pierce through my thick skull. "Nothing makes sense. What am I supposed to do, Dad?"

Silence.

The tears blur Dad's image. My heart pounds. I inhale deeply, reaching for the strength. I have it somewhere. I shove past Peter's influence and feel the seed. *Grow!* It sprouts one tiny little shoot, and I open my eyes. Dad's image vanishes completely now, but I don't feel alone anymore.

Two shiny dots glow in the distance, race along the fence line. The branches rustle and leaves crunch under galloping paws. That gait's familiar. I jump to my feet and bolt toward the fence.

Dragon runs to the gate, and I open it. I hug him so tightly, not wanting to let go, ever. My head swivels. No one else is in sight. It's just Dragon and me in the field under the stars. Panic rushes through.

"What am I going to do with you? If Mom finds you, she'll send you back to Mr. Turnberry. I've got to get you out of here."

He has no collar. I rummage through what's left of the tack room and put one on and hook him up to a leash. My ratty slippers will suffice for the jog to Ryan's house. His parents are out of town again, and now I wonder if they are traveling for work as Ryan tells me, or if they're out searching for his brother.

The garage door opens. Ryan got my text.

"Get in here," he whispers.

I enter the darkness with Dragon, and the door shuts behind us.

"Thanks. I didn't know where else to go. And I'm so sorry. I was a massive idiot. I had no right to act like that. I'm sorry." The words spew, but he only smiles, his eyes still heavy with sleep.

"Get in here," he repeats, as I stand frozen in the garage until he takes the leash and tugs us inside.

Dragon nuzzles up to Ryan, and Ryan pets the top of his head. I keep my distance for several reasons. Ryan's probably mad at me for my horrendous behavior, and I smell—bad—like humid earth, from the long run here.

"Please, tell me you didn't steal Dragon from Jennifer's dad's house?"

"No, Dragon came to me. He ran away. Can he stay here? Your parents are out of town, right?"

"Yes and yes, but Mr. Turnberry is going to want his money back, money your moms have already spent, and I think my neighbors will wonder why I have a wild animal here. They'll call the cops." Ryan scratches his head and pours beans into the coffee maker.

The loud noise of the beans grinding to fine dust, followed by the inviting aroma of percolating coffee, monopolizes my attention. We are soon sipping coffee at the kitchen bar counter while Dragon curls up at my feet.

"I'm not giving him back. I'm not! Not when he's involved with that place. … That … that dogfighting place."

"We don't have proof. Jennifer and her dad are many things, but I don't think skeezy dogfighter is one of them."

"I do."

"Then we need to make a plan."

"Yes!"

"Fine." He sighs and puts his cup down. He looks at me as if I've just asked for mission impossible. "I'll keep him here today, but I'm driving you home before the sun comes up, and you better go to school just as if it's a normal day."

"Thank you." Relief and desperation lace my voice. Captured inside the moment, I forget my sweaty smelliness and throw my arms around him, burying my head in his neck.

He hugs me back and kisses my hair. "I'll think of something." Then he laughs.

"What is it?" I pull away from him and see black streaks on his face and clothes. Then I glance around. I've left a trail of ashy skid marks all over his kitchen. "Oh my God, I'm so sorry. I'll clean this up."

"Don't worry about it. I'll clean it later." He surveys me and laughs some more. "Let's get you home fast before Cat sees you like this."

It's fifth period before I'm called to the principal's office. Mom, Shane, Mr. Turnberry, and a police officer await my arrival. I play dumb and express complete shock at seeing them.

"Honey," Shane says in her sweet, concerned voice. "We're here because Mr. Turnberry seems to have lost his wolf." Her tone shifts to a keenness that stabs his coiffed appearance. Her doe eyes morph to stone. They dart to him in warning.

It makes me smile.

He lashes out. "I didn't lose my wolf. She stole him." His arm flies up from his side, and a long finger jets out, pointing menacingly at me.

Mom steps between us. "Don't accuse my daughter of stealing."

"Dragon ran away from you. He's a good judge of character." A half second later, I'm scared at what I've just said and the way I've said it.

"Kendall!" Shane turns her warning eyes on me.

I fold my arms. "I don't know where your wolf is." Then I turn to the principal. "Sir, may I go back to class now? I was in the middle of a quiz. I don't want to fall behind again."

Our principal retired from the Marines and still dresses and acts accordingly. He respects hard work and expects politeness. And he has an inexplicable fondness for me. Perhaps he feels the slow improvement in my grades and school attendance are a direct result of his pep talks. Whatever. I just want to stay on his good side.

His eyes question me, then turn on the adults. "I need to send Miss Shepherd back to class. It's apparent she doesn't have a wolf here at school."

Mr. Turnberry huffs and gives me a beady-eyed squint. I glare back at him until something in me empties, and I look away, unsure.

Mom and Shane quickly step toward me before I'm entirely out of the room, and Shane says, "Love you, sweetie. Sorry we interrupted your class." Her kiss on my forehead soothes my trembling nerves.

Mom leans in to whisper. "You're lucky you're in school right now."

She knows. She's not smiling, but there's a twinkle in her eyes telling me she's relieved I was smart enough to go to school. There's also a hidden warning that I've got some explaining to do. So glad I listened to Ryan.

After school Jimmy, Ryan, and I raise the volume on the speaker. We're in the yard with Rocky discussing our next move.

Ryan frowns. "I can't keep Dragon any longer."

"Why not?" I ask.

"Land mine in your parents' bedroom?" Jimmy grins.

Ryan laughs. "No. Dragon's been a good boy, but Jennifer called, and I played it off, but her dad's going to start snooping around my house soon."

"No." I shake my head.

"Kens, you have to give Dragon back. Ryan could get arrested," Jimmy says.

"No, he couldn't," I argue, but Ryan gives me a look that says otherwise. "Fine," I whine.

"I'll sneak him back to her house tonight after dark," Ryan says.

"I'll help," I say.

"I don't want you walking to my house in the middle of the night. It's too dangerous!" Ryan says.

"Thanks, *Dad.*"

"He's right. It's one thing to walk at night with a giant wolf; it's flat-out stupid to walk alone," Jimmy says.

"Fine!" Again with the pouty voice. *Stop it, Kendall.* "I'll walk to the end of my street, then you pick me up."

Ryan hesitates. "Okay, what time?"

"Two."

"Okay." Ryan nods.

"But this doesn't mean I'm leaving him there!" I point hard at both of them.

"What do you mean?" Jimmy rolls closer.

"What do you think I mean? He's not staying there forever." The thought of Mr. Turnberry petting Dragon or giving him commands makes my skin crawl.

"And how are you … What are you … Gotta plan?" Ryan asks.

"Not yet. But if he ran to me, then he's not happy there."

The boys glance at each other.

"Good luck convincing Cat," Ryan says.

"That requires actually talking." Jimmy crosses his arms and tries to act like my older brother.

"You're still not talking to your mom?" Ryan's eyebrows arch.

I sigh and roll my eyes.

"She's not." Big bro smirks.

"I'm getting my wolf back. One way or another." I cut the air some more with my finger.

Ryan grabs my hand mid-slice. "What about the others? I think we should follow up on all the dogs Cruz found homes for. We have the addresses. We could snoop around, make sure they're safe."

"Great idea." My heart leaps.

Rock marches over, stirring up clouds of dirt and ending further conspiring.

"It don't take three people to train that silly dog," Rock scolds. "Ryan, get in the house. Shane needs you. Somethin' about another hate letter."

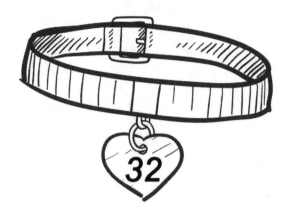

It's two in the morning, and I'm standing alone in the dark. Images of mutilated girls post inside my head, one after the other, like a gruesome photo gallery. The guys were right. It's scary out here without sharp teeth by my side for protection.

Swoosh!

I twist around violently, eyes wide, but there's no one. I'm flipping out. The bushes have swooshed a million times in the last five minutes. Raccoons, I guess. I hope.

Blinding-white headlights turn onto my road, then cut to black.

Finally!

I hop into the passenger side. I can practically smell the safety and security.

"I already returned Dragon," Ryan says before I even click the seat belt.

"What? Why?"

"For one, if I got caught, I didn't want you to get into trouble. I don't really trust Jennifer. She might jump at the chance to throw you in jail."

"I thought you said I was overreacting!" The syllables stick to my teeth.

He nods and smirks at the jab. One dimple pops, and maybe I shouldn't have teased him. Nah.

"What's the other reason?"

"I got restless. I wanted to get it over with. It was tough, really tough. It would've been too hard for you."

I sigh and turn away to peer out the window. There are only shadows and gloom, but I keep looking. Tears prickle, forcing rapid blinking.

"Do you want to go back home?"

"No." I'm still blinking and gazing into nothingness. "I'm too awake. Let's drive by that kennel place. The house we saw Dragon get dropped off at."

"Okay."

He cruises by the house-kennel. One light fixture shines outside by the front door. The inside is completely dark.

"Doesn't look like anyone's here," I say.

"Yeah, it looks quiet."

I spin to face him. "I'm up for a mission!" The excitement in my voice sounds almost sinister.

He rasps a laugh. "Alright."

He parks on the opposite side of the neighbor's home, several yards away. "We'll walk from here." He reaches into his back seat and hands me a black hoodie.

I put it on and slip the hood over my head, taking in the spicy smell of boy that clings to the fabric.

He pulls on a navy-blue hoodie. "When we get close to the house, we need to look for cameras. Keep your hood up to hide your face."

"Got it. You thought of everything. Have you done this before?" I smirk.

"I've done my share of stalking." He rolls on his hood and mocks wickedness.

"Hmmm." I lean back.

"Joking!"

I lean in.

His hands reach inside my hood, cradling my face as his hooded lips close in, and he kisses me. My body screams, *Let's nix this spy mission and make out*, but instead I pull away, determined to find a way to get Dragon back. I breathe, then slowly open the passenger door and step out onto the vacant road. My footsteps pat lightly on the asphalt, then crunch on the grass.

Ryan tiptoes in front, and a breeze carries his citrus spice. I almost swoon, which is irritating as hell. When did I get so ridiculous? But dang, he smells so deliciously sexy. Then he stops walking, and I stop next to him. He's casing the floodlights.

"I think if we stay this far from the roofline, we'll avoid the sensors. We'll have to reassess once we get to the fence. I'm not sure we should go into the backyard."

"I want to look in the windows."

"Not a good idea," he says. "Maybe we can look in the garage window without tripping the light."

I follow his lead, and we sneak to the window, remaining in darkness. Inside there are several lawn mowers and stacks of tires.

"No cars and no dogs," Ryan says.

"Good, no one's home."

"You said Cruz mows lawns." Ryan walks away as if our mission is over.

It's not over. I step toward the backyard. My heart flutters. My sweat stings like minuscule razor blades slicing my skin.

"I don't know." He reaches for me and shakes his head.

"I'm going," I say, decisively. This place is bad news. My bones ache just being here. I need to find out why.

He hesitates, then swallows his apprehension. "Okay."

Ryan isn't a big guy—he has a tall, lean build—but he would and could protect me. I've witnessed his strength on the tennis court, and he's fast. I'm fast too, but he'd probably be dragging me behind if we get caught.

Not only is the gate locked, but the floodlight sensor is angled directly at it, so we move farther away to climb the fence and stay in the shadows.

I take each and every step with caution, expecting a huge rottie to come charging at us. The backyard is darker as the house eclipses the streetlamp. Tons of cages tower against the back wall of the house. All but five are empty. All five dogs are muzzled but highly alert to our presence. Three are bounding off the metal bars, trying to bark through the restraint and simultaneously wagging their tails. They're scared, excited, and instinctively territorial. The other two barely raise their heads. They appear weak, beaten.

"Rascal!" I rush to his cage. "Oh my God, Ryan. What is this place?"

"I don't know, and I don't want to know."

Rascal only lifts his head an inch and flops his tail pitifully. That's all the energy he has. The tears spill, and the rage pools in my gut. Something explodes inside me, but it's not Peter. The wrath that's stronger, harder, ignites my resolve to pummel these people into slivers of flesh.

I open the cage and gather Rascal into my arms. "Get them all."

Ryan doesn't answer. He's creeping around, peering into the house, when an American pit bull crashes into the sliding glass doors, rattling them nearly off their tracks. "Whoa!" Ryan jumps back. "This big boy looks healthy and pissed."

"And loud." Impatience fills my tone. I do a double take. "That's Oliver."

"I don't think he recognizes you."

"No." My heart sinks.

"There's nothing here."

"What do you mean? Look at Rascal; look at this dog." I point to the other lethargic, straggly canine.

"Yes, but look at these. They're fine and healthy." He points to the three in cages, then turns to Oliver, who pounds the glass again.

"So!"

"And there is no evidence of dogfighting or anything else. Just despicable animal care."

"They have muzzles on! They're in cages way too small!" My voice gradually rises to an almost yell.

Ryan's pointer finger shoots to his lips. "Let's get out of here before Oliver breaks the glass." Ryan's eyes dart between the pit and me.

The rumble of an approaching car freezes us. Without another word, he grabs the other weak dog, and we carefully maneuver around the yard. Then we haul ass. We get to the fence. He puts his dog on the ground, then snatches Rascal out of my arms and lays him down too. Next, he practically throws me over the fence. He chucks Rascal over, and I barely catch him. I'm sure Rascal would've howled in pain if he wasn't muzzled. I hardly place Rascal on the ground, when the other dog comes flying over. Ryan scales the fence like an Olympian, and we take off in a sprint, the limp dogs bouncing in our arms.

Soon, the house is lit up like Friday-night football, and we hear shouts and curses, but we get to the Range Rover before the man gets back to his car. Ryan pulls out onto the main road, tires skidding. It's empty, since it's three in the morning. Panic flashes across Ryan's face as he scours the open road ahead, looking for a place to hide. Before I can make any suggestions, he swings the Rover into a McDonald's parking lot, turns off the engine and lights.

His chest heaves, and I squeeze Rascal. He whimpers to be free, but I hang on. The hateful muzzle does its job. Fortunately, it's a twenty-four-hour

McDonald's, and there are cars parked and one going through the drive-thru. We sit as still as blocks of ice for what feels like an eternity.

Ryan now breathes normally. His hand covers my knee. "We did it."

"Do you think he saw the car?" I ask.

"I don't think he got close enough to make out exactly what kind of car I have, but he obviously knows we were there."

My head drops, and the terror slides down my throat, tasting rancid. I'm shaking from the roar of anger and fear in my blood. I'm nauseated with confusion. But no Peter. My focus is clear, even though my heart hurts worse than it did after losing Dragon. The bone ache returns, because whatever's going on in this town is an evil that's beyond the depths of imagination.

"It's okay, Kendall. We got Rascal." Ryan tracks the tornado of emotions whirling through me.

Trembling hands clutch Rascal. "I know, but we left dogs in that hellhole." My voice cracks as I fail to keep the tears from falling.

Ryan reaches over and removes the muzzle from Rascal's nose. The other pup is cowering in the back seat. She doesn't trust us, and after what she's been through, I don't blame her. Ryan starts the Range Rover and drives home.

After Mom freaks out for several long minutes, she makes us recount the entire evening. Before we're done, Rock hurtles through the door. He charges straight to Ryan, and I propel my body between them.

"It's my fault. It was my idea. I made Ryan help me!"

Rock halts, but his eyes widen, the vein in his scalp pulsates, and his hands clench to soccer ball–sized fists. "Boy, if you had gotten my little girl hurt in any way, so help me, Louisa!" He swears using his wife's name.

"I'm sorry," Ryan says. "I—"

I interrupt him. "Look at Rascal. Look! He would've died if we hadn't gone there tonight. And there's another one like this. And Oliver was there too."

"Yes, but you should've let the police handle it." Shane's full cheeks sink from the force of her swallow.

I've never seen her face this contorted with worry before.

"We didn't know if there was anything illegal happening. We wanted to check it out first. In hindsight, it was a bad idea," Ryan says in full diplomatic mode.

How he always remains so poised, I'll never understand. We're different breeds. I'm a fiery mutt, and he's a sophisticated purebred.

"It wasn't a bad idea. We're fine, and we saved two dogs! And now we know Cruz is involved," I argue.

"You could've gotten yourselves shot. I would've shot you." Mom tugs on her crunchy blond ends, spreading the dark roots and magnifying her crazed appearance.

"I'm fine, Mom. That's not the point."

"Like hell, it isn't!"

"Dragon running away and coming to get me was some sort of sign. Dragon's trying to tell me something." I lose my voice and swallow. They need to understand the gravity of this place. All they care about is my safety, and that's been established. "Mr. Turnberry is a bad man, and he has my wolf. My baby!"

"Honey, you need to keep that information to yourself," Shane says.

"Why? Don't you get it? Rascal, Cruz, the house-kennel, Dragon, Mr. Turnberry. It's all connected. There are no coincidences." I share a glance and a knowing smile with Ryan. He gets it. He understands.

"I'll call Fred," Shane says.

At the mention of Fred's name, Mom throws up her hands and falls into a chair, completely lost for words.

"What?" Shane asks. "You want to call 911 *again!*"

"Of course not. You know I've already consulted him." Mom shakes her head. "No. I want Fred's opinion on this." She doesn't sound very convincing.

Fred is a cop, a church-going Baptist, and Shane's brother. To say the least, he wasn't keen on his sister shacking up with a woman, but last year they reconciled. His Chihuahua got lost, and I found her. I didn't know who he was until after I gave him his dog back. He was so grateful that, even though our rescue was out of his jurisdiction, he'd periodically cruise by and check on us. He'd come in for coffee, and our conversations soon broke through his bigotry about Mom and Shane's relationship. Mom still holds a small grudge.

Thirty minutes later Shane has brewed a fresh pot of coffee. There will be no more sleep for any of us. Fred shows up and pours a cup. In a strange way, it feels like a typical visit from Fred.

I begin the story with my accusations about Mr. Turnberry and eventually get to the weird kennel-house. Ryan finishes the tale, as my voice is now so loud and irate that Mom has shushed me six times and Shane has threatened punishment for my multiple curse words.

Fred nods when Ryan stops talking, processing our story, then he says, "First of all, Lucas Turnberry is an influential man in this area, and I find it difficult to believe he knows what he's gotten himself into. That's assuming this is a dogfighting establishment. From what you've told me, this could simply be a case of animal cruelty."

"There's nothing simple about animal abuse," Mom says, her expression hard and defiant.

Fred sighs. "I'm making a comparison, Cat."

"Well, will you check it out?" I ask.

"Of course, but without probable cause, there's not much I can do." Wrinkles ripple Fred's forehead all the way to his receding hairline.

I point to the two sickly dogs. "There's your probable cause. Two weeks ago Rascal was full of life, and now his face is cut up and his spirit defeated."

"And if I use the dogs, you and Ryan could be arrested for theft and trespassing on private property."

That shuts me up fast. I don't want to join Vicky in BTR. And if Ryan got in trouble because of me, I'd never forgive myself.

Fred stands.

Shane walks over to him. "Let us know what you find, will you?"

"As soon as I know anything, you'll hear about it."

They smile at each other. It's the tender smile of two people who've known each other all their lives and shared both good times and bad. If anyone can help us, Fred can. But his concern manifests in pursed lips and drawn brows. Probably worried about the backlash from interrogating a billionaire like Mr. Turnberry.

I rush out the door and catch Fred just before he gets in his car. "Uncle Fred, thank you. I know they're dogs, and you have worse crimes to deal with."

"Some dogs are worth a lot more than some humans in my opinion.

I'll see what I come up with. But you stay away from that place and Lucas Turnberry."

I say nothing.

"I'm serious, Kendall. Promise me."

"Fine. I promise."

"I don't want anything happening to you, or Cat and Shane. And keep Rascal close to you, and don't let anyone know he's here."

The past weeks have been rough. Mom, Shane, Rock, and Fred hover over me like hawks. The annoying alarm system beeps every time I open or shut the door, alerting the parentals of my coming and going. I've assured them a million times that I'm following the rules, not that I want to, not that I have a choice. When Mom leaves the property, she checks the cameras remotely to make sure I'm home doing my job, even though I've agreed that Fred and the police should handle the takedown of these lowlifes and I've promised to stay out of it. So far my only disobedient activity is my daily spy mission with Ryan.

The Range Rover hums outside the front door. *Awww—the sound of freedom.* I hop in. We get breakfast at Starbucks, then drive by Mr. Turnberry's house. Lately, that's been our only time together. He has a critical tennis tournament coming up and hasn't been able to work at the rescue, which also puts a damper on any devious detective work I might scheme up. It's hard to spy on a bicycle. Plus, he fears the wrath of Rock. If I even mention the house-kennel or the dogfighting ring, he and Jimmy gang up, telling me not to worry, that justice will prevail.

Blah, blah, blah. It hasn't prevailed. Justice might be blind, but it's also slow.

Luckily, Vicky comes back this weekend. She has a car and a weakness for vengeance and spy missions.

This morning Dragon is nowhere in sight. I usually catch glimpses of him either standing behind the front gate or sitting by the window. I hate to admit it, but he looks well cared for, which contradicts all conclusions that Mr. Turnberry's involved with these scumbags.

"Sorry." Ryan echoes my disappointment.

"It's okay. At least I saw him yesterday."

He smiles. "We're early. I'll park for a minute. Maybe we'll see him."

I've missed those dimples at the rescue. He's been training insanely long and hard. It's paying off. His shirt clings nicely to his muscles.

"The tournament starts tomorrow," he says.

"This must be a big deal." A strong urge to drag my finger down the outline of his deltoid overtakes me.

His shoulder shivers from my touch, and he takes my hand in his. "It is, I guess. I mean, higher-level tournaments are coming up this summer, but the ITF in Delray is … "

I interrupt with a groan.

"What?"

"Nothing." I drop his hand and pick up my Mocha Frappuccino from the car cup holder.

He tilts his head.

I smile because I've come to recognize that tilt. He knows I'm not being honest.

"Jennifer mentioned that tournament the day she brought her dad to the rescue."

"Oh, sorry."

"Whatever." I sneak another peek at the house. No wolf.

"Will you still come and watch me?"

"Sure." I must make a weird noise or expression, because Ryan looks at me sideways. Embarrassed, awkward girl alert.

"You probably won't even see her. If she's on a court close to me, I'll try to hit her with the ball." His eyebrows rise sinisterly.

"Ha! Thank you. It's not that; it's just V's home this weekend, and I sort of wanted to spend time with her," I say.

"Oh. I'm looking forward to meeting her."

I cringe. Those two meeting will be like two worlds colliding. She's the complete opposite of him.

Ryan laughs. "Don't worry, she's going to like me."

I laugh. "Cocky, much?"

"Bring her to the tournament."

"Maybe that'd be fun." I've run every scenario in my mind of these two meeting. Most go well, some don't.

"Maybe?" He leans in and kisses my neck, then whispers with ice-cold breath, "Am I that boring?"

"No, not at all," I stutter, and shiver.

He pulls away, a coy grin playing on his face. "Okay, then, bring her."

I smirk. "You better not welcome her like that."

"Like this." He repeats the offense.

I slap him teasingly. "Stop. I'm serious. What if you lose? And you're in a dicky mood."

"I'm not going to lose." He sips his Frappuccino.

"Wow! Cocky."

"No." His brows rise in offense. "I signed up late, so I have to play the qualifying. It's stupid. I'm the first seed, and I'm going to beat everyone, easily, because I should be in main draw, but with everything that happened with Dragon and the rescue, I completely forgot to sign up."

"Oh." The small word draws out, highlighting his cockiness.

He nods and holds my hand. "Okay, yeah, that sounds cocky. Just come to the match. I promise, if I lose, I'll be nice."

We leave the Turnberrys' neighborhood and drive to Atlantic High in silence until Ryan says, "That sucks about the inspection."

I sigh. "Yeah. They hid everything. I know it."

"There wasn't much there." Ryan shrugs. "The legal system sure took its sweet time, though."

"What sucks is if we'd left the dogs, not touched anything, then maybe Fred would've had evidence."

"Or maybe Rascal would be dead."

My heart skips a beat. "I know. It's a lose-lose. Maybe we even made it worse. Now these scumbags will be more discreet, knowing the police are watching. Something really bad is going to have to happen before they realize we're right." I shake my head.

"I know how you feel."

I lean in. "It's weird too."

"What?" He perks up.

"You're going to think I'm crazy." My head and back fall against the seat. "I already know you're crazy."

"Ha, ha!" I chuckle at the sunroof.

"Seriously, what is it?" he asks.

"Sometimes I feel like Mr. Turnberry puts Dragon on display so I'll see him. Like he knows we're checking him out, and he wants me to know Dragon is totally fine." My gaze slips from the ceiling to him. "Stupid, right?"

He pulls the car into the school parking lot, throws it into park before it's completely stopped. We jerk forward. He turns to me, entirely unaware of his horrendous driving skills. "No, it's not stupid. You might be right."

My face hurts from the smile spreading across it. Having him in my corner is more than I could ever imagine. He finally sees the injustice, the lack of progress, the red tape. After the tournament maybe I can convince him to delve deeper into the surveillance of Mr. Turnberry, Cruz, and the house-kennel.

He leans in and kisses me on the lips this time. All thoughts of dogfighting disappear, replaced with the desire to skip school and spend the day curled up under a blanket, wrapped in his arms. The daydream shatters when a hammering thud slams down onto the roof of the Range Rover. We jump, and our lips rip apart.

A gang of jocks peers in.

"Woo-hoo! Hit that, Brah!" They yell.

"Humph! I hate everyone at this school." My jaw clenches.

"Except Jimmy," Ryan says.

"Except Jimmy. Who isn't in school today!"

"Can you manage?"

"Yeah." My forehead falls on his.

"Bye, Dog Girl." He hooks his arm around my waist.

"Ha! Get on with your superpowers, Beach Boy!" My hand searches for the door handle, while my forehead twists but remains stuck on his.

His mouth is so close to my ear. "Off to leap sandcastles in a single bound."

"Bye." But I don't leave. Instead, we kiss some more. "I gotta go." It's torture, but I finally peel myself away.

Ryan always waits to make sure I get inside. It's kind of nice to have a boyfriend that cares enough to make sure I'm safe, but I don't venture into the halls. Instead, I mill around for a couple of minutes and exit the building once Ryan's gone. While other students walk toward Atlantic High, I jog away from it.

The last few days when I've kissed Ryan goodbye and headed to first period, I've thought only of school and his kiss, but today is different. My mind clings to Dragon and Rascal and Trax and all the other dogs. All the truths everyone else wants to ignore or wait for time to tell us we were right.

Sorry, your dogs are dead.

Forget that. I'm not waiting for more crushed spirits like Rascal or shot bodies like Trax. Enough is enough.

The long trek through the neighborhoods relaxes me. The warm spring air slips into the depths of my lungs. Sweet jasmine infuses the breeze. Birds chirp and hop from tree to tree. I'm keenly aware of the vibrant echo of their voices and the colors of their feathers. It's like the universe agrees with me, whereas, usually, it's against me. Not just against me—hurricane-force winds against me.

The lawns become more and more manicured closer to the Turnberrys' estate. It's incredible the difference a couple of streets can make. One mansion after the other boasts beautiful front doors of solid oak and intricately carved glass. I can only imagine the imported stone and expensive decorations within. But the angles and cuts of that sharp glass are like the teeth of a guard dog—pretty from a distance, lethal up close.

These homes are untouchable, with alarms, cameras, fences, and gates. And according to Ryan, this is Mr. Turnberry's *small* house. Apparently, his *big* house is on an island somewhere.

I stand at the entrance of the lengthy drive, wondering what the next move should be. Ryan and I never go past this point. We always remain inside the safety of his car. How can I penetrate this fortress and find my Dragon?

God! What am I doing? This is beyond stupid. But for some odd reason, I can't walk away.

The next-door neighbor is less proud. I'd probably like them better. No fence to climb or wall to scale, and no sign of an attack dog, so I cross over. A large hedge separates the two properties along Mr. Turnberry's wrought iron fence.

I plod on, hidden inside the shrubbery, until I can look into Mr. Turnberry's backyard.

The two pits Jennifer complained about eye me and freak out. Luckily, they're trapped in a long fenced run, but they're loud and will give me away.

I crouch, making myself as small as possible, and keep silent and still.

The dogs don't give up. They continue to violently bark and glare in my direction. Thick muscles, pointed fangs, and determined stares intimidate exactly the way they're supposed to.

They're gorgeous warriors. Those jaws could shred me to a pulp.

The pits' commotion draws the attention of someone inside. The back door opens. Someone yells. Cruz emerges and struts the bricked pathway from the house to the run.

My blood chills.

Looks like that lowlife found a new job. Oh, what I'd have given to see Jennifer's face when she learned her father had hired an ex-con. I hope I do see her at the tournament so I can ask her about her new friend.

Poetic justice!

"What is it, boys?" Cruz asks the dogs. They've calmed but still glance over and bark. He looks toward the bushes, where I scrunch into the smallest ball my height will allow, hidden by the shadow of the tall shrubs.

As soon as Cruz opens the gate to release them, they race. Fangs stop inches short of my face. The fence doesn't give. They bark and sniff and pace the fence line, but they can't get me. I don't move. They're not happy, but I've convinced them I'm not a threat, so when Cruz calls them back, they obey. I'm a stranger, but they've been trained impeccably and listen to their commands.

Cruz brings the dogs into a miniature house in the backyard. It looks just as posh as the main house, nothing like our barn even with the improvements. Before Cruz shuts the door, he glares back at the fence line.

I don't breathe or blink. My body aches from the crouched position. When he finally turns his back and shuts the door behind him, I exhale and fall to the ground. All the muscles in my legs cramp for minutes before finally letting go.

I flatten onto the ground. I don't trust that Cruz didn't see me. I wait and wait and wait. After what feels like an hour with no sounds from dogs or humans, I stand and decide it's safe to leave.

All this work and I won't even get to see Dragon.

I brush the dirt and leaves from my clothes and rid the negativity from my thoughts.

The backhouse door opens, and dogs barrel out, but it's not the pit bulls from before. It's Dragon and a German shepherd large enough to be a wolf. I hate to admit how healthy Dragon looks. He has put on the appropriate pounds. If I didn't know him, I'd be petrified. He's beautiful and fierce and regal, and I miss him. He should be mine. He's gonna be mine.

I linger in the hedges on the other side of the fence, watching. His exemplary grace and powerful stride mesmerize me. He plays with the German shepherd. They have a bond. I'm happy for him. He has a friend. My broken heart leaps with joy.

Could I be wrong about Mr. Turnberry? Maybe he is an animal lover and has no idea about the dogfighting.

"Maybe," I mumble, still inwardly doubting. But Cruz is definitely dealing dogs to those sleazeballs. He's weaseled his way into the Turnberrys' good graces for a reason. I get restless for more information. Remaining stone still becomes impossible.

The dogs tire from running and playing. They prance around and sniff. They catch my movement, and the two of them charge just like the pits had. I freeze. Teeth and nails attack the fence, but it holds. I'm safe. Dragon's fierce bronze eyes bore into me like I'm a stranger, like I'm his enemy, then recognition flashes through those big golden-flecked orbs, and his face morphs from vicious demon to beautiful friend. His ears perk, and his lips curl into a smile. His bark fades away, but the German shepherd doesn't know me and continues his pursuit to kill.

Dragon rounds on the German shepherd. They scuffle. Dragon is the alpha, and he warns the other dog not to harm me. Reluctantly, the German shepherd takes two steps back. His barking settles to an occasional low growl, and his eyes dart back and forth from me to Dragon. He will submit to his alpha but hasn't completely accepted it. His hind legs set in a position to charge if necessary.

I shove three fingers through the fence, and Dragon nuzzles his nose in them. "Hi, boy. I've missed you so much. How ya doin'? You're a good boy." Sudden, forceful tears rush my eyes. The pain of loss scorches and stings and strangles. It's almost worse to pet him, but I can't stop. I place my cheek against the fence, and he licks it. The void in my heart deepens, threatening to swallow me whole. I wish it would.

The German shepherd's face softens, and his tail wags. He finally sees that

I'm no enemy, I'm a friend—but wait. Something's wrong.

Mr. Turnberry grabs my shirt and yanks me from the bushes. Dragon growls, but he's conflicted. He sees us as two masters. This is a testament to Turnberry's training and treatment of Dragon. I'm impressed.

"Do I need to get a restraining order, Miss Shepherd? You're trespassing on private property." His cold gray eyes evaluate me.

I open my mouth to spit venomous words of anger and hate but think better of it. That will only land me in trouble, possibly in jail—or worse, he could hurt Mom and Shane. I swallow my pride along with my bitter words and mumble, "No, sir."

"What are you doing here?" he barks, but his composure remains flawless.

"You took my wolf." I loathe the tremble in my voice and the tears in my eyes.

"No, dear, I purchased your wolf. He's mine now, and you need to learn to deal with that."

His tanned face tenses behind a trimmed blond beard like an evil Florida Santa Claus. I can't bring myself to say anything.

"Look, I'm not this nefarious man you think I am. I have a daughter your age. I don't want to have to hurt you. Don't force me to call the police."

I tuck his threat into my memory to dissect later. Right now I just want to get away. I still say nothing as I squirm out of his grip.

He lets go and orders, "You need to leave, right now. If you don't, I'll have no choice but to hold you accountable for your actions."

I turn away and sprint down the path. Cruz stands near the street like Mr. Turnberry's bodyguard, his duty to catch me, hold me down for the police if needed. But I've struck a silent deal with the bearded devil and retreat without a fight.

I sneak one last stubborn glance back at Cruz. We share a sneer. He's changed. He no longer looks kind. They're hiding something, but my wolf— my big, beautiful wolf—is healthy, so I turn around, stare ahead, and race home.

Covered in sweat and dust, I reach the barn. It isn't finished yet, but all the burnt wood has been replaced. Soon, the exterior will have fresh red paint with white trim. Each kennel sports shiny new metal fencing with brand-new latches. Concrete fills in the cracks and holes. Shelving to rival any celebrity's closet leans up against the wall, awaiting hanging in the new walk-in feed-and-gear room. Bags of dry dog food pile high in the corner until the room is ready, alongside new leashes and collars without rips and teeth marks, in sizes from extra small to extra large.

I love it and hate it. The new and improved version of our rescue has been bought with Mr. Turnberry's money. The security of my future I owe to him. Mom could probably afford to send me to college now, where I could learn how to run a business and make sure we're never indebted to a man like Mr. Turnberry ever again. The fresh concrete seals more than just the cracks in the barn. It's a forever bond to his blood money. I've hardened with it, and so has my resolve to protect these innocent dogs, to find the truth.

Mr. Turnberry made a mistake. He should've turned me in to the police.

I hurry down the stairs, grab the box of doughnuts, and rush out the front door.

"Kendall!" Shane calls from inside the house.

"Going to see Vicky!" I yell back.

Shane pokes her head out the front door. "I thought you'd at least have breakfast first."

"I did." I hold up the box of doughnuts, then continue on my way.

"That's not much of a breakfast!"

"I'm fine, Shane."

"Okay, sweetie, have fun. Tell Vicky we're glad she's home." Shane flashes a giant, genuine smile.

"I will, and don't worry. I'll eat vegetables at lunch."

Shane nods, and the warmth of her loving stare travels the yards between us.

Jimmy and I beat Vicky to the tennis center.

She strolls up five minutes late with a notebook under her arm, looking skinny and pale. "This boy better be worth getting up at an ungodly hour." Her huge grin and wide eyes contradict her complaining. She throws her arms around us. "I missed you guys."

After a few seconds, I pull out of the huddle. "We missed you too. I know it's early. His match started at eight. I brought doughnuts." The box of doughnuts sits in Jimmy's lap. Half of them are eaten.

Vicky scowls at him.

"I saved the Boston creams just for you." Jimmy opens the box for her to take one.

With a mouthful of custard, she asks, "Where is he?"

"He's on court five. He'll come see us after his match," I say.

We sit down in an area with a decent view of the court. Vicky sets her notebook on the table.

"What's that?" I ask.

Her eyes darken and fall to the book. She drags it closer. "We'll get to this soon. First, tell me what I've missed around here."

Jimmy and I share a glance.

She adds, with the fervor of a bloodhound, "Tell me about Ryan."

Jimmy waves his hand, giving me the floor.

I seek Ryan out on the court. He's rummaging through his bag for a new racket. The old one leans against the bench with a broken string. I turn back to my friends and say, "Well, I've had my first and second and … lots of kisses."

"This is huge." Vicky slams her hands on the table. "Is he a good kisser?"

Ryan hits the ball, and it sails out. I wince, then return to the conversation. "Yes. Of course, I have no one to compare him to, but his tongue is like velvet. I get goose bumps just thinking about it. And when he kisses behind my ear … "

"Stop right there. Kens and Ryan are boyfriend and girlfriend. Moving on." Jimmy fidgets uncomfortably.

"Let me remind you I've been locked up with no *Cosmo* magazines or reality TV for weeks." Vicky eyeballs Jimmy with disappointment. She turns to me. "We'll talk later."

"Okay."

"What else?" she asks.

"I had an episode—"

"What? When? Because of him!" Vicky's mama bear is showing, and I love her for it.

"No. Long story, but he saw the worst of me, and he's cool with it." I nod.

She sits back and scans me with her eyes, then wags her finger diva-ishly. "Do I know you? Cool with your anxiety? Kissing behind ears?"

A rush of relief or happiness or maybe confidence fills me. It could be pride.

Jimmy folds his arms, and amusement fills his hazel eyes. "Our little

Ken-doll has been up to a lot of new and exciting adventures since you've been gone, including trespassing and stealing."

"Wow. Tell me everything, and I want details." Vicky leans in, and her leopard-print frames maximize the fierceness of her stare.

I give her the play-by-play from the vandalism to the sale of Dragon to the night Ryan and I found Rascal. "And yesterday I skipped school and went to Mr. Turnberry's house."

"Why? Alone?" Jimmy interrogates me.

They both ogle me like I'm a stranger.

Jimmy shakes his head in disappointment, which infuriates me.

"What, Jimmy? Am I supposed to just accept that Dragon is with those people?"

"Yes, Kens. That's exactly what you're supposed to do. Let the police do their job."

"I just wanted to make sure Dragon was okay." I frown, knowing there's more to it than that. My desire to get him back hasn't lessened over time. In fact, it's gotten stronger.

"And was he?" Jimmy asks.

I swallow his bitter words. "Yes, and guess who I saw?"

They both shrug.

"Cruz."

Jimmy takes in a long breath and exhales, rumbling, "Huh."

I hesitate, then admit, "Mr. Turnberry threatened to get a restraining order against me if I didn't leave." My fingers dig into the table, bracing for the repercussions of my confession.

"So you got caught. You're lucky he didn't call the cops right then." Jimmy grunts.

Vicky slides her notebook toward me. "I was really hoping this kid was full of shit, but from what you just told me, I'm scared." She opens the journal, flips to the dog-eared page, and reviews her notes. "His name's Marty, and he's bad, like sociopath bad. He left BTR a week before I did, and right before, this kid gave him money. I knew something was up. You're not allowed to have cash. I overheard the kid ask Marty to place a bet on Ralph. I figured Ralph's a fighter, but then, he said 'dog.' Ralph's a pit bull. When I heard this, I listened harder to get all the info so I could tell you as soon as I saw you." She pauses and looks back down at the page. "He mentioned

Mike's Garage and said the fight was the Saturday night of Memorial Day weekend."

My mouth hangs open. Dread flies in, leaving my tongue dry and my head dizzy. I swallow and breathe deeply. "It's true."

Someone yells. It's Ryan's opponent. I've barely seen any points of his match, but I can't think about that right now.

Jimmy's hand falls on my forearm. "This is awesome. Now Fred can get these guys."

I shake my head. "No. We can't tell Fred."

"What are you talking about? Let the police handle this, Kens." The Wicked Witch green in his hazels explodes.

"No! Absolutely not. I've already blown a chance at catching these jerks. If Fred goes sniffing around all the Mike's Garages in town, someone will get suspicious and start hiding the evidence or move the location. Then we're screwed. Again! There won't be any fights, which means no proof, no arrest. These creeps will continue torturing dogs."

"Maybe Fred and the police will do undercover work," Vicky says.

"For a bunch of dogs?" I tsk.

"Why not?" she protests.

"Money! Fred is always complaining there's no money. And it takes him weeks to do anything, which gives the criminals plenty of time to cover their trail," I say.

"So what's *your* plan?" Vicky asks. The wheels turn behind her brown eyes. "Do we have a mission?"

A mischievous grin plays across her face as a little color brightens her cheeks. She's never been this excited about a mission before. It's awesome having my partner in crime back. Her enthusiasm sparks mine. "First," I say, "we have to find the right Mike's Garage. Second, film it. So we have proof."

"Film a dogfight." Jimmy cringes. The richness of his skin dulls.

Vicky's enthusiasm ices over. "Let a dog get killed?"

I bite my lip and think.

"We have to tell the police," Jimmy repeats.

"Yes, after we have some film coverage. That's the only way. I know it sounds gruesome, but we only need a couple of minutes of the actual fight. Then we'll call the cops. They'll dispatch immediately because it'll be a 911 call involving kids." I pause, thinking this plan out. "We'll get the hell out of there with our proof. The cops will arrest the people and take the dogs to shelters."

"Sounds like a solid plan." Vicky nods.

"Sounds risky. I doubt Ryan'll let you do this." Jimmy looks over at the match.

Vicky's head snaps around to face him. "*Let* her?"

"I don't need anyone's permission." I sneer.

"Back off, sista sista." Jimmy rolls backward.

"Ryan'll *want* to help." My gut drops. "But I haven't told him about yesterday."

"Why not?" There's a triumphant edge in Jimmy's voice that I don't appreciate.

"I'm not scared to tell him. He gets stressed before matches. I couldn't add to that stress by telling him Mr. Turnberry threatened me." I glance over at Ryan. The court's empty. I stand and look around in time to catch him heading toward our table.

I turn a feral glare on my friends. "Don't mention any of this to him. We'll tell him after his next match. Got it."

They nod.

"Nice beat down, brother." Jimmy fist-bumps Ryan.

A small twinkle flashes in Vicky's eyes as she admires Jimmy and Ryan's friendship. Happiness blooms, and there's no room for annoyance anymore.

"Yeah, I kinda felt bad. He got bageled." Ryan frowns.

Jimmy gives him a look that says, *Don't be weak, man.*

"Kinda, but not really." Ryan's lip curls breathtakingly. They continue with their sports bromance. Then he turns to face Vicky and extends his hand. "Hi, Vicky, we finally meet. I've heard so much about you."

She takes his hand. "Likewise."

"When's your next match?" Jimmy asks.

"Not until two thirty." Ryan sits next to me.

His hair slicks back from sweat, and his shirt drips.

"Ryan!" his coach calls.

"Sorry, gotta go." Ryan quickly kisses me, then stands to leave. "Nice to meet you," he repeats to Vicky.

"You too." Vicky waves like the wicked princess she is, and I nudge her. "What?" she whispers. I just giggle.

"See ya, Jimmy." Ryan slaps him on the shoulder before setting off.

"See ya."

Ryan's swoon-worthy body jogs off. There's a small scar on his left calf that I'd never noticed before. It's like finding gold among pretty, shiny rocks. The urge to inspect every inch of him overtakes me, then I turn to see Vicky giving *the look*. "What?"

"Oh my God, you're in love with a Saint Paul Boy."

"No! No. He's homeschooled."

"I know," Vicky scoffs. "You know what I mean."

I return her you're-not-fooling-me look but admit nothing.

"I'm just kidding. I like him." Vicky squeezes my arm and smiles.

"Well, what do we do until two thirty?" Jimmy asks.

"Do we have to watch another match?" Vicky whines, gathering her dark, bushy hair into a ponytail, then winding it into a messy bun.

I glare at her. "You didn't even watch this one."

She shrugs. "Sorry, it's humid. Look at my hair, and my glasses are sliding off my face."

I notice her thinness and paleness again. Her complexion has always been two shades lighter than her mother's South American bronze, but now she looks ghostly.

"Didn't you eat for weeks?" I ask.

"Not really. The food was disgusting." She sticks out her tongue. "Actually, I got a bad stomach bug. They said it was the stomach flu. I said it was food poisoning and threatened to sue their ass. And you wouldn't believe how uncomfortable the beds were. I have permanent spine damage. I'm sure of it. And my roommate looked like that evil guy in *Star Wars*. The one with the inked-up face."

I laugh out loud.

"No fricking joke. Terrifying tattoos on her face. I didn't sleep the first week. I thought she'd go all *Divergent* on me and stab my eye out in the middle of the night. But she ended up being okay to live with. She was quiet. I never found out what she was in for, but I wouldn't mess with her."

Two girls enter the empty court.

"Isn't that Jennifer?" Jimmy asks.

I glance over and meet Jennifer's death glower. I hold it, then look away. "Aah! Time to go. Caffeine?"

We sit outside under the shade provided by a green umbrella, sipping our Venti Frappuccinos, but I'm still shaken from Jennifer's stare down.

Vicky licks whipped cream off the top of her drink. "So this Jennifer girl is Ryan's ex?"

"Yep." I gulp down mocha heaven. It helps ease the angst.

"And she took your wolf? But you took her man?"

"Yep." I nod with pride.

"Well, it's obvious Jennifer wanted to hurt you." One dark eyebrow lifts, rising sinisterly above the leopard frames.

"Thank you!" I turn to Jimmy. "See, I'm not overreacting."

Vicky nods. "Uh-huh."

"She wouldn't even touch Dragon before. She looked completely grossed out."

"Gotta give her props. That's a classic bitch move." Vicky's lips thin.

"Are girls really that sadistic?" Jimmy's entire face widens in shock, spreading the patch of nine freckles on his cheek into a miniature solar system.

"*Some* girls." Vicky laps the last of her whipped cream.

I scuff my chair closer to the table and lean in. "Enough about Cruella de Vil. We've got a mission to plot."

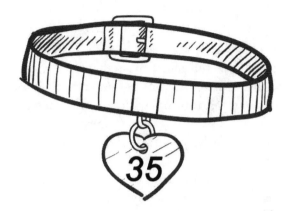

Fred's car is parked in our lot. My heart thunders. He's found something. He's caught the a-holes. I rush up the ramp and swing open the door, but the mood is anything but happy. Eight unfriendly eyes bore into me.

"What's going on?" I ask.

"Fred has a restraining order. Any guess who it's for?" Mom's tone is calm but sharp as knives.

My head drops.

"This is serious." Fred frowns.

My head bobs droopily.

Mom simmers under her skin, Shane struggles not to hug me, and Fred sighs deeply with concern, but it's Rock's sympathetic eyes that tear me to shreds. There's no raging bull today, just a giant teddy bear, and I've ripped out his stuffing.

"Tell us what happened, sweetie." Shane's arms reach toward me, then fall by her sides.

"I just wanted to see Dragon. That's all!" The tears spring forth. I swipe them away. Everyone in this room will never trust me again.

"According to this"—Mom waves the document viciously—"you're stalking Mr. Turnberry's daughter!"

"What? No!" The tears burn away from the fire of my rage.

"How could you be so stupid, Kendall?" Mom's words slap me across the face.

"Because no one is doing anything! Because you sold Dragon. For money! Dad never would've." I slap her right back.

"Are you fucking serious? You think I'm—we're—not doing anything?" Mom sighs, shakes her head, and paces. It's the trifecta of pissed off. "I'm doing everything the law will allow me to do. Every gash, bullet, bruise, I've documented. I've traveled half of goddamn Florida with other agents trying to figure this out, put this miserable son of a bitch behind bars. Fred's working his ass off, and he's not even in our jurisdiction. He's doing this on his own time. And now you've just made it worse for all of us."

"I'm sorry," I say.

"You're sorry? You were chased at three in the morning by criminals, and now you've managed to make an enemy out of the richest man in Delray!" Mom's anger builds with each syllable. "You're sorry!"

"Cat." Rock puts a hand on her shoulder. His touch smoothers the furious embers.

"I wasn't stalking Jennifer. You know that, right? That's a lie!" I plead. They have to see the truth. "Fred, can you correct that? It's fine that he has it on record that I was trespassing but not stalking."

You'll be the biggest freak of Atlantic High and all of South Florida if it gets out you were stalking Jennifer! Just imagine the tweets. She's brilliant! Jennifer is a master manipulator, and you were the idiot to fall straight into her trap. Peter claps his eight legs inside his vivarium, happy to have a voice again. *Bravo, Jen!*

My neck reddens. The itch burns and begs, but as soon as I start scratching, I won't be able to stop the bleeding.

"I'll see what I can do, kid," Fred says.

"Please tell me you're close to catching these guys. What have you got on the dogfighting ring?" I ponder giving up my intel from Vicky but wait to hear his response.

"We have some leads. We'll get them unless I have to keep bailing you out," Fred says.

"What? What leads? Tell me what you've got." My words push through the tense air, beating answers out of Fred.

"I'm not at liberty to say right now. But you'll be the first to know."

I nod. He's either got nothing or he won't tell me because of my priors. "What have you got, Mom?"

"You're grounded," she answers.

"Why?" I try to be stalwart and ask without whining.

"You have to ask? You're a danger to yourself and the rest of us. You think the barn fire was an accident?"

Fred interrupts, "Cat, you know we have nothing to link the fire to the dogs."

"Come on, Fred. The evidence points to arson." Mom's entire body flexes. The ink lines thicken as her biceps bulge. Even her tattoos look irate.

She doesn't say anything more, but I can tell she has more to say. I wonder what. Just what has Mom been up to? Maybe she and Rock have their spy missions just like I do. Perhaps we're working against each other, hiding pertinent information like the CIA versus the FBI. What I do know is that Mom is not only angry, she's worried, and so is Shane. Shane's too quiet, too reserved. She's let Mom curse and explode without a comment.

"Two weeks, Kendall. Straight here." Mom points her finger so hard downward that I swear the floor dents. "Here, after school. No biking off. No going to Ryan's. School and work, and that's it. And I will be checking up on you. In fact, I'll be driving you."

Two weeks. I count the days in my head and conclude, "Memorial Day weekend."

"There'll be no Memorial Day weekend for you this year. I'm punishing you for all fourteen days of those two weeks." Her chest heaves as she spits out the words.

I want to argue, to complain, to build another refuge mountain in my room, but none of that will help now. Mom's furious, and I need to wait it out, bide my time. Hope she caves before the fourteenth day. Be exceptionally law-abiding and get out on good behavior. They've never before grounded me for the entire sentence, but I've never before done anything this reckless either. What sucks is I won't be able to help Vicky and Jimmy research the local Mike's Garages. I've royally messed up this time.

For the fourth day in a row, I sit on my bed, completely helpless. Four days of being grounded. Four days of no Ryan. No dimples. No husky laughter in my hair, kisses on my neck. No cherry lips to taste. It hurts to be separated—severed. I had no idea this kind of pain was even possible. He's like an addiction.

Mom and Shane haven't budged from their stance. I've tried every teenage-girl conniving trick in the book, and they remain a united, impenetrable wall. My one consolation and link to the outside world is my phone, which is glued to my ear as Ryan gives me the play-by-play.

"Two more miles," he says.

So far that's all he's given me—mileage. He's abnormally quiet, and since I can't see his facial expressions, I don't press him. Jimmy advised me that he wouldn't want to talk about his loss, so I fall back onto my pillow and listen to him breathe while he drives our mission without me.

"I played awful," he finally says. "Couldn't make a volley to save my life. Served like shit. I could've beaten that kid this morning."

Ryan doesn't stop talking about the loss and how bad he played for several minutes. I guess Jimmy was wrong, or Ryan feels comfortable talking to me about his shortcomings. Whatever it is, I let him vent, throwing in a couple of "ohs," and "uh-huhs," just to let him know I care. And I do. I care more and more about him every day, but I don't know what to say to make him feel better.

It's been so lonely these past few days not seeing him. His smell lingers in the hoodie I'm wrapped in. His touch that always comes at just the right moment phantoms on my skin. Our lead stretches so tautly that it's going to rebound once we are in the same room together.

"Well, I'm here. It's in a strip center. This is definitely not it," he assures me.

I can hear him shaking his head. "Take a picture." It's not that I don't trust his judgment. I just need proof. Ugh! That sounds exactly like I don't trust him. I add softly, "Please. I believe you. I just want to see it. I'm so bored."

He snaps the photo without acknowledging my babbling and shoots it over to my phone. The image pops up on the screen, and my shoulders slump. Sure enough, it's a tiny beige store wedged between a nail salon and a dojo.

"This is an auto supply store, not a mechanic shop," Ryan says.

"I see that." I'm annoyed. This is the fifth shop my spy minions have gone to and reported back to me about. Sighing loudly, I say, "Another one to cross off the list."

"I know you want to do this—"

"Don't."

"Kendall."

"I'm doing this." There's no room for doubt in my voice.

We remain in uneasy silence miles apart. I can hear the sounds of air conditioning blowing and his fingers rustling something. He's probably getting one of his cherry candies.

"This place is sketchy. I'll call you later."

"Okay. Bye. Thanks."

"Of course."

For a minute I'm calm, then his words stir. Why does everyone tell me to chill, to lay off the chase? I punch the wall and then my chest of drawers. My hand smarts, and for a second, the physical pain replaces the emotional chaos.

As I pace my room, my brain overflows with rapid injections of thought—Trax's rescue, constant drama, Dragon's absence, Mom's betrayal, Dad's death. I collapse onto the bed and drown a scream in my pillow, then curl up in a ball. My only consolation: Peter is not here. Maybe this is my new normal. Misery has replaced anxiety.

At some point I dozed off, because I wake to a strange ticking noise. It's coming from my window. Ryan is tapping his fingernail on the glass. His face and chest are an abstract image pressed on the glass as he leans into my second-story window.

How is this possible?

I rush to slide the window open, then halt. Is there an alarm sensor on it? I look for the little white box. None. Good! I unlock it and whip it open. He's propped a ladder against the house. Luckily, my window faces the backyard full of trees, but I survey it anyway. No one's around.

"Are you crazy?" I help him crawl through the window.

He laughs, and it's like heaven rumbling. "Haven't I already proved to you that I'm crazy? I'm tracking down criminals at the risk of being pummeled by a very huge man and scary woman."

I laugh too, and it feels easy. He slides an arm around my lower back and pulls me into him. Our lips lock. My arms fold around his neck. I melt into the vast plain of his chest. The feel of his body on mine takes all the misery away, relieves the tautness of our lead. Beach Boy has done it again. His best superpower ever. Transformation. He's turned me into a gleeful, carefree girl.

"I had to see you," he says.

"I'm glad."

We both jump at the sound of the front door slamming.

"Get in the closet," I order.

He looks around.

"There." I point, forgetting he's never been in my room before. Well, just that one time.

He runs to the closet as I shut the curtains to hide the ladder. Shane knocks on the door.

"Come in," I holler from my bed, where I lounge, casually reading my science book.

"Hi, sweetie." Shane crosses the room and sits at the end of my bed.

"Hey."

"I was thinking. Since Cat's not going to be home for dinner, why don't we order pizza and watch a movie."

"Where's Mom?"

"She's doing that training class. The one in Palm Beach. Filling in for the woman that just had her baby."

"Oh yeah. Sure. Pizza and a movie would be great."

"Good. Give me about an hour." She stands and looks down at me. "I have a few things to enter in the computer. I need Ryan. He's such a help. When's he coming back?"

I shrug, then almost choke when Ryan's big blueberry eyeball peeks out from the slats in the closet door. "I think he lost today so he's out of the tournament. Bad for him. Good for you. Now let me finish my homework so we can watch that movie."

As Shane shuts the bedroom door, Ryan opens the closet. I leap to the lock, fearing Shane may turn around and want to tell me something else.

Ryan grins.

"Oh my God, your ego."

"So this is your room without Mount Kendall." He takes extra-long steps around the room like he's waltzing, but in a cool way.

"Shut up." I look down. I'm so far from that place right now.

"Looks bigger. It's nice." His face is a domino effect—first the grin, then the dimple, then the eye twinkle, and lastly the cocked eyebrow.

At this moment he could ask anything of me, and I'd say yes. God, I'm whipped. But of course, he asks for nothing but my time. We slide onto my bed. He props up against the wall, and I curve around him. His fingers lightly strum my back as mine twirl around his forearm.

Minutes pass. He's been here too long. We're pushing our luck. He needs to leave, but my hand won't let go of his. I rub the rough spots on his palm. My head nuzzles into the crook of his neck as he stares at the opposite wall.

"You need a poster. Right there." He points.

I observe the bareness of my walls. "I had some. I should get more."

"Uh-huh."

"I guess I'm never in here, or I never used to be in here."

He shifts his hips, and I feel his mood shift too. He's about to lay into me about not telling Fred about the Mike's Garages. Tell me he doesn't want me to get hurt. The last thing I want is an argument. Shane might hear us and come upstairs. I'd get another week of grounding for sure, and Ryan would no longer be the golden boy. Funny that I used to hate how much my moms adored him. Now it's my salvation. I start to sit up, to make him go home, when he speaks.

"Driving up I-95 reminded me of my brother. I searched up and down

211

the beaches for Reagan. I pounded on the doors of all his druggie friends until I finally got the name of his dealer. I beat the shit out of him. Little greasy kid." His lips scowl more savagely than I've ever seen. "I didn't know I could reach that level of violence. Rage is a powerful thing."

He turns to look at me, and I'm speechless. This is not the argument I was expecting. I was ready with all my counterpoints. Ready to tell him how positive I am that we'll take down the dogfighting ring, but this, his brother's story, there are no words.

He continues, "But none of it did any good. The amount of money my parents put into private investigators, I could've updated the rescue center ten times over. It would've gone to better use. And I hate him for it." He muddles a chuckle that's sensitive and breakable. "I've never said that before. I didn't know you could love someone to the point of hate." He wipes his nose with the back of his hand. He's hardly holding himself together.

This would be a good time to say something comforting, but the words elude me. I know exactly how he feels. I've felt it all, the entire grief spectrum, but nothing anyone says helps. "Life screwed you over," I finally offer softly.

"I guess." He laughs robustly, regaining his composure. "Most people wouldn't say that."

"Most people don't know the real you."

"Yeah." He squirms down the wall and wraps me in both arms. "But you do."

"I want to know more."

His chest expands, then falls, exhaling a jagged breath. "My brother disappeared two years ago—today."

"Today! No wonder you lost." I can't see his face, but I suffer the peaks and valleys of his breathing lungs.

"I was playing *this* tournament. He promised he'd come watch, and I kept looking for him. He never showed. I won. Beat Jerry Rienbech. Jerry was ranked way better than me, and I'd never beaten him before. Couldn't wait to tell Reagan. I found his empty room." He squeezes me tighter, so I can't pull away, can't see his tears, but his heart thunders against my cheeks.

I hate that I wasn't there in the stands cheering him on. Just another reason to despise the Turnberrys. I should tell him it's okay to cry, to let it out, but I can't. If I talk, I'll cry. And honestly, I have no idea if that's good advice or not.

He swallows and seems to regain control. "At least your dad wanted to stay with you."

"I don't know what to say. But you know he's an addict. It's not you." Jimmy told me the story, but I'd never asked Ryan about his brother, and he'd never brought him up. "Tell me about him."

Ryan tilts his head back and, with one long exhale, relaxes a little. "He was my best friend. I had a big brother that actually wanted to be with his annoying little brother. He was über-competitive. Ten times worse than me. When he played, I was in awe. He was that good. I think he was addicted to the high of winning, being in the zone. I don't know when it happened, but at some point, it wasn't good enough. He needed another high. I just can't understand. We all drink. I've gotten high; my friends still get high. I never thought it was a big deal. I'm fine. But Reagan. It's different. I just don't get it."

He props up on his elbow to face me, his adorable dimples gone, his clear complexion blotched, his mouth soft but straight with anger. He searches past my eyes as if I've hidden the answer.

"Two years. I thought I'd moved on, but after shanking a thousand balls today, I realize I'm not over it. And I'm pissed off at him." His head falls back onto my pillow.

Now we're both staring at the ceiling as if it has all the answers. Believe me, it doesn't.

"And he was always in trouble, always giving my parents a hard time. I got robbed out of good parents because he stole all their time and energy. I guess that's why I hang out at your house so much. God knows I don't need any more community service hours."

"Yeah, I think you hit your quota weeks ago."

An awkwardly refreshing laugh erupts between us.

"And this quest we're on, it's dangerous, and if anything happens to you." There's no more laughter.

"It won't."

He ignores me and continues to talk to the ceiling. "I'll never forgive myself, because I can end this. Tell Cat and Fred. I *can* stop you."

I turn onto my side and whisper, "But you won't."

He smiles. "You're right."

"You'll be with me. You and me. Me and you. Isn't that a song?"

"Yeah, a dumb song."

"Hey." I shove him, but he barely moves.

He laughs. "Weakling. How are you going to fend off dogfighting lowlifes?"

I sit up. "Okay, you can leave now."

He tickles my waist. "Sorry."

"Stop."

"Can I stay?" He continues tickling.

"Yes, now stop."

He stops.

"We'll just film about five minutes, then call the cops. That's it. Simple."

"Simple," he repeats. He zones back out and stares at the ceiling again. "And you think you can escape your grounding by next Saturday?"

"Absolutely! Shane's pizza offer is a sign. She's breaking. And technically, the grounding officially ends around five on Saturday. That'd be two weeks."

He sighs but says nothing. We fall back into silence. The digital clock on my nightstand counts the minutes, reminding me that Shane's hour has long passed, that Ryan isn't supposed to be here.

"I need to go downstairs." I don't move.

"Yeah." He doesn't move.

"Yeah." I still don't move.

He finally sits up and smiles, cute dimple resurfacing. "Kendall Marie Shepherd, you amaze me."

The fragile threads holding me together come undone. The most good-looking, kind, and generous guy has just said *I* amaze *him*. His irresistible fragrance lures me to him, melting me into nothingness. I have to kiss him. I crawl on top of him and tug at his shirt, almost ripping it, to get my body as close to his as possible. No millimeter of air can come between us. Not one molecule. If we were famous, they'd write books about this kiss. This kiss blows away every kiss I've ever seen on TV or read in novels. Because before Ryan that's all I knew of mind-blowing kisses. This is most certainly a top-rated, mind-blowing kiss! Five stars!

Shane knocks on the door. "Ready for pizza?"

"Sure. Give me a sec." My voice cracks as I smother a scream, or maybe it's a laugh. Whatever it is, my heart races from almost being busted.

"Okay." Shane's footsteps pad away and back down the stairs.

Ryan's head flops back on the pillow. "Her timing sucks," he says between heavy gasps, his arms still pulling me into him.

I suppress another giggle.

Eventually, Ryan tiptoes back into the closet.

"Stay here," I whisper.

"Here?" His eyes widen.

"Yes, spend the night with me."

He shakes his head.

I give him one last kiss before closing the closet door and sealing him into my room. If I could, I'd dead bolt it. Trap him. Force him to stay. Tie him up, maybe. There's rope in the barn. I take a second to rid myself of psycho love-sick-girl thoughts and recoup my composure. I fix my face into a facade of misery, and as I stumble down the stairs, I drag out my question in a monotone. "What movie?"

"Something funny. I need a laugh."

"Fine." Good! A drippy romance would suck right now, all things considered.

Halfway through the movie, there's a crashing sound outside.

"What was that?" Shane jumps.

"What?" I play it off.

"You didn't hear that loud bang?"

"Nope."

"Oh." She settles back onto the couch.

I'm thankful she didn't go outside to check. I hope he's okay. Covertly, I text him.

> Me: U ok?
> Ryan: Yes. Sort of. Not as easy climbing down. C u tomorrow.
> Me: k bye sorry

The ache in my heart overrides the humor of the movie. I force fake laughs when Shane glances in my direction. Did he take the ladder? Where'd he get the ladder? Did he stop at a hardware store? Would he do that for me?

I smile at the effort. If only he'd stayed. Waking up all tangled together like the night in the barn would've been magic. But that's stupid. Very stupid.

Mom would find out for sure, and then she'd sentence me to two more weeks of grounding and ban Ryan from the house. She'd slap an alarm box on that window for sure.

Shane laughs hard, snapping me back to the movie. She looks over, and I join in laughing, hoping it sounds genuine.

A few scenes later, my thoughts drift back to Ryan. Alone. In his house. On this day. *The* day! My heart sinks, tugging the tether.

Me: Are your parents home?

They better be home. They wouldn't leave him on this day. Would they?

Painful, swirly thoughts tornado inside me. His confessions. He'd shared so much of himself tonight. I'm happy, no, more than happy. Honored.

Ryan: Yes

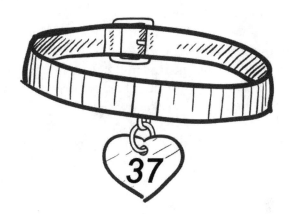

Ryan, Vicky, and I sit on my bed with the printouts of all the Mike's Garages, Mike's Mechanics, Mike's Auto Body Shops, Mike's Detailing, anything Mike and car related. It seems that Mike is a popular name in the auto world. Giant red Xs strike through the ones we've already ruled out.

The ladder leans next to my window, and Jimmy keeps guard down below.

Ryan has mastered the art of sneaking into my room. He knows the range of the security cameras and how to avoid getting caught. He parks his car at the vet hospital, then sneaks down the pathway, hopping into the woods if he sees anyone.

"So we're down to eight possibilities, from Fort Lauderdale to West Palm Beach," Ryan says.

"Can we go south today?" Vicky asks.

"Sure. Why?" I ask.

"I want to hit that crepe house in Lauderdale. It's been too long since I had a good crepe."

"Oh, that place is legendary." Ryan organizes the papers into an orderly pile and stuffs them into a folder for safekeeping.

"We have two shops heading south, and one in Lauderdale, so let's move. I can't be gone long." I shoot to my feet with excitement. This room has become a claustrophobic prison.

"You should stay here. We'll report back just like we've been doing," Vicky says.

I stare blankly at her, wondering where my partner in crime went.

"I agree. Why risk it?" Ryan nods.

I scowl at both of them. "Shut up! I'm going." *Case closed.* No more discussion. Jeez, I sound like Mom.

We clumsily escape down the ladder, then pile into Ryan's Range Rover and hold on to the grab bars for dear life, preparing for impact as Ryan merges into traffic. No impact. A collective sigh of relief fills the car.

After a thrilling drive down I-95, and two wrong turns, we find the street we're looking for. Ryan cruises slowly as we all scan the signs and addresses.

"That's it." I thrust my hand across Ryan's chest as if that's going to stop the Rover.

"I see it," he says.

"Find a place to park," Vicky says.

"Did the yellow truck out front have dog cages in it?" Jimmy asks.

I smile. "I saw that too. Thought I was just crazy again."

"I'd say that's a red flag." Vicky adjusts her glasses. They're new and don't seem to fit correctly.

"I saw the Bentley," Ryan says.

Vicky scoffs. "God, is that all you think about—nice cars."

"No, Mr. Turnberry has a Bentley." Ryan swings into a pawnshop and parks facing the garage.

"Oh." Vicky smiles, still tweaking the frames.

"Yeah, *Mean Girl* Lohan," Jimmy rebukes.

"Thanks, man." Ryan clucks his tongue.

"Got your back, bro."

"Whatever." Vicky dismisses them with a playful flip of her hand.

"Yeah, but this isn't good. If he sees my car, he'll recognize it."

"We're pretty far away; plus, your tints are dark. Take a picture with this fancy camera you brought." I take the camera out of the case and hand it to him.

Ryan zooms in and snaps a photo of the truck with dog cages. A man begins to unload the cages, and Ryan gets video footage of it. "I can't get the license plate of the Bentley from this angle."

Vicky perks up. "He doesn't know who I am. I'm going to walk by and get a photo of the plate. Be right back."

I protest, but she's already slammed the door shut.

We all watch her strut across the street and down the sidewalk. She holds her phone like she's taking a selfie, gets the shot, then keeps walking.

"Why is she walking away from us?" I ask.

Mr. Turnberry strolls out of the shop with his daughter. A lead weight drops on my chest.

"Wow. I never would've thought she'd—" Ryan shakes his head.

"I did. Never doubt my evil–ex-girlfriend detector again." My laser eyes burn Ryan.

Jimmy asks, "Do you think Jennifer saw Vicky?"

No one answers. We're focusing on the scene playing out. Vicky's already two blocks down the street before Jennifer looks up from her phone, so I doubt she saw her.

"Drive! We have to go get her." Panic rises at the thought of Jennifer recognizing my best friend from the tournament. Mr. Turnberry could make her life hell. I glance around, and my heart sinks. Everyone in this car could suffer if this plan doesn't go right.

"No," Jimmy says. "We have to wait for Mr. Turnberry to leave first."

"What's he doing?" I twitch and squirm as the seconds pass, and he hasn't even backed up from his parking slot. It's not safe here and not just because of Jennifer and her dad. Vicky's curvy little body will draw attention from the wrong kinds of people on these kinds of streets.

The gold Bentley carefully backs up, then moves forward onto the street and drives away.

"Finally!" I sigh.

Ryan whips the Rover out of the pawnshop and drives up to Vicky. She's attracted a greasy man that's muttering something about cash and drugs. He looks aggrieved when she steps into the Rover, and we speed away.

"Well, that was fun. I made a new friend." Her eyes roll as she laughs. "I hope one of you got a picture of Jennifer and her dad?"

"I did," I say.

"That has to be it, but it doesn't look big enough to hold a lot of people or dogs," Jimmy says.

"It's plenty big. There's a warehouse and yard in the back," Vicky says.

"Turn around and drive by slow again. I want to get a better look so we know what we're doing next Saturday night." I white-knuckle the grab bar as he about-faces the car.

"See there." Vicky points to a side alley that connects the area where the dog cages were unloaded to the back warehouse and a wooden fence.

I click some photos as Ryan creeps past.

"Looks plenty big," Ryan says.

"Not many cars for a supposed auto garage," Jimmy says.

"Scumbags," I mutter.

"Can we get Nutella crepes now? I think I've earned it."

"You can even have whipped cream." Ryan smiles, glancing back at Vicky through the rearview mirror.

"Thank you." Vicky's eyebrows bounce.

"Show me the picture." I turn to Vicky in the back seat. She hands over her phone. The photo of the license plate is vividly clear, and so is the garage it's parked at. "Perfect."

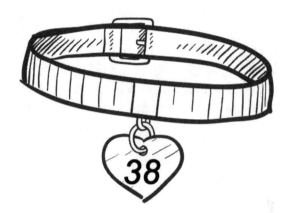

Ryan sends a tennis ball soaring through the air for Duke to retrieve. All four paws leave the ground. He flies six feet in the air, makes the perfect catch with his jaws, then lands gracefully and saunters back to us to do it all over again.

Ryan hits another yellow ball, then looks at me. "You ready for tomorrow night?"

No, I want to scream. "Sure, I guess." School sucked so horribly that I can't even think of an adjective to describe just how bad it was.

"What's wrong?" he asks.

"School sucked to the millionth degree."

"Oh. Tell me about it."

"Mr. Young." I sigh. " He treats my Twitter like it's a Shakespearean tragedy. He thought he could fill the virtual world with positivity." I wiggle my fingers in the air as if conjuring up magic fairy dust. "It didn't work. No one in the virtual universe cares about happiness. It's a ruse. It's all filtered or covered up by stupid puppy dog ears and flower halos. I received more nasty tweets than before."

Ryan slams another tennis ball harder than usual.

"Then he tried to complicate it with graphs and charts, injecting variables like the fire and the rumor that I stalked Jennifer. That was so awkward. I wish he'd just shut up about it."

"Maybe you should tell him how you feel."

Another loud sigh escapes me. "Yeah, I might."

He hands me the racket. "Hit a ball. Get your frustration out. Pretend it's Jennifer's face." He grins.

"Okay." Smack. I still feel like crap.

Ryan takes the racket and continues to play with Duke.

During class, I read a tweet from Jennifer. I knew I shouldn't, but it pulsated and drew my attention as if cartoon bubbles appeared saying, *Read me! Read me!* So like an idiot, I read it, and from that moment on, the past burned into my conscious. My mind revisited the day I caught her leaving Ryan's hotel room. A snake of jealousy slithered into my heart, wrapped its length around the chambers, and hasn't left. The rational part of my brain knows there's nothing to be jealous about, but it seems the two halves aren't communicating.

Of course, if I mention any of this to Ryan, it'll just ruin everything. He doesn't need to know I'm overthinking our relationship. It just sucks because I'd been on a high. My moms were softening and hinting at ending my punishment tonight or early tomorrow. We had found the accurate Mike's Garage and had a good plan of action. The grounding had only brought Ryan and me closer. Something about forbidden love was a huge turn on. But the royal suckiness of today shoved all that goodness down the drain. All the possible problems with our mission flew to the forefront of my mind, as did the fact that my friends could get hurt.

"Did it help?"

Ryan's question draws me out of my head, and I respond, "Sort of."

He hands me back the racket and another tennis ball. "Try another one." *Smack!* I feel a little better.

"I think our plan is solid," Ryan says.

"I don't know."

"What don't you know?" He runs a hand through his fauxhawk.

"It's risky." I touch the pieces of his hair that are too long to stand up.

His head tilts in the same direction that his hair flops and nests in the cup of my palm. "Of course it is, but you and I went over all the possible scenarios."

"Did we? How can we imagine them all?" My eyelids close with the weight of the day.

"It'll work. Jimmy'll be the lookout, and Vicky's the getaway driver. We'll text them to call 911 once we've got the crime on record, and then we'll leave. The police will arrive and bust it up."

I nod but say nothing. That's the plan we've set up and worked on for days now like we're some sort of covert CIA spies. Teenage undercover cops or something. But we're not. And it sounds ridiculous.

Ryan drops the tennis racket to his side.

Duke's butt and head sag with disappointment.

Ryan asks, "You're having second thoughts?"

I nod. "We'll be attending a criminal affair, we'll be interfering in a police investigation, and we'll be face-to-face with very bad people. I'm worried."

His hands grab mine. "Don't worry."

His words fly out of his perfect lips and swirl around my heart, actually making me feel miserable. I love him so much for being reliable and loyal. How can I put his scholarship—or worse, his health—in danger?

My Corolla's been fixed for two days now, and I haven't told anyone. Mom and Shane won't let me use it until after my two weeks are up. They've been driving me to and from the school like I'm a flight risk. However, I do have the keys. I could sneak the car and do this mission all by myself. If the plan goes south, I'd be the only one in trouble.

"You can't do this, Ryan." As I say this, I feel the color leach from my cheeks.

"I'll be fine."

"*You* have a future, a scholarship. *I* have an inner demon named Peter." The confession flies out of my mouth, then floats between us.

His eyes squint, then close. "What?"

Every drop of energy drains from my blood. "Yeah," is all I say.

"I don't get it."

"Of course not."

"That's not fair, Kendall. What are you saying?"

The truth builds. It pushes against every organ, squeezing out the words. "I'm saying I'm inherently unpredictable. My anxiety actually has a personification. It started as a coping mechanism but grew to a second personality. I'm mean, sort of."

His face tightens.

I sigh. "I'm not schizophrenic."

He doesn't talk or move.

It hurts, and I try to swallow the fear away. "I know I probably won't have an anxiety attack, but I can't rule out the possibility. If I freak out, we get caught. We could get in serious trouble with the law."

Finally, he runs a hand through his hair. It's reassuring. He's not gonna run away and never look back. But does he get it? The severity.

"Or what if you get hurt? So hurt that you can't play tennis anymore. You said it yourself; these guys are criminals that won't think twice about shooting us."

"You're right. I was worried. But you were so determined and sure."

It's true. I was sure. Kendall the Superhero, the girl more powerful than a locomotive, had kidnapped my senses. Tricked me into believing it was a brilliant idea.

I slouch and sigh and try to come clean. "I know I was, but now that it's here … I can't bring you down with me."

"Bring me down?"

"Yeah … to my level."

"There are no levels, Kendall."

"Yes, there are. There's the golden-scholarship-future level, and then there's not. And that's okay. It's not a judgment. It's a fact. A fact that you should be proud of, and I'm proud of you for it." The tears sting but don't spill. "Please. For me. Don't help me with this."

He steps back. "No! If I don't go, then neither do you. If this is how you feel, then we tell Fred. Let's go. We'll call him right now."

Sparks of panic skim the surface. If I remain still and quiet, it may go away without exploding.

"Come on." He reaches for my hand.

I take a few deep breaths. "No. Not yet."

His feet shuffle toward me, then away several times. I'm making him nervous by screwing everything up at the last minute.

"I'll sleep on it. Okay?"

He nods. "You've just had a bad day. Tomorrow morning you'll feel better. Trust me. This plan will work. Your anxiety … " His gaze drops. "Peter … won't mess this up."

He can't even look at me.

At breakfast Mom gives me the good news. She's decided to let me off my grounding one day early to enjoy the Memorial Day weekend, the hints she'd been dropping realized over pancakes and coffee. She and Shane shower me with praise. They think I've suffered the last two weeks and wanted to reward me for my good behavior.

Deception festers in my gut. The only thing keeping me from admitting what a rotten and deviant daughter I've been is the tears caught in my throat.

When I woke up, I'd decided that telling Fred was a bad idea. That Ryan was right, and I would trust him. But now doubt and shame bubble and roll through my blood, threatening to allow Peter to escape for the first time in weeks.

I clear my throat and prepare to tell them everything, enlist their help. It's the smart and mature thing to do. "I have a confession to make."

It's harder than I expect with Mom and Shane focusing all of their attention on me.

"I—"

The phone rings. My fragile courage evaporates.

"Hold on." Mom grabs the phone and listens intently. She nods and squints and concentrates. Evidently, another dog needs rescuing. "A puppy's fallen down a well or a pipe. Apparently, it's a very long and narrow space. Let's go." She looks at me.

I hesitate. It's Saturday. *The* Saturday. I've got courage flip-flopping and nerves sparking and panic rising. Not so sure I should go. Or maybe this is just the thing to take my mind off getting my friends in trouble or hurt or killed.

"Do you want me to call Rock?" Mom asks.

Shane answers for me. "No. No. He's planned that nice family picnic. His cousins are in town. Why don't I go? Let's let Kendall enjoy her first day off." Shane gathers the plates.

The unease multiplies, and my heart plunges.

"Fine. Doesn't matter, but we need to go now." Mom's already grabbed the keys to the truck.

The adrenaline from my guilt and the thrill of the phone call swoop me to my feet. I gather the plates and silverware from Shane. "I'll do this. Go get ready."

Shane rushes upstairs to get dressed. They leave moments later.

My phone chimes, and I jump. God! I'm a firecracker next to a flame.

    Ryan: Hi

He hadn't called all night, and neither had I. I wanted to. It was torture, but I'd spent the night on the phone with Vicky. She assured me I did the right thing by telling him the truth about Peter. And she convinced me, just as Ryan had, that it would all go as planned.

    Me: Hi

He responds immediately.

    Ryan: All good?
    Me: yes! You?
    Ryan: Yes. I've got practice. Pick up
    at 9
    Me: Ok C u at 9

The day and evening pass slowly. The puppy rescue has proved to be a problematic all-day ordeal. The idea of involving my parents in tonight's mission fades with the sun, but the determination to keep my friends safe rises with the moon. The only constant all day has been my will to save those dogs. A dogfighting ring will not exist under my watch in my town.

It's eight o'clock at night. I hold the Corolla key in one hand and the lug wrench in the other.

T he Toyota Corolla zips down I-95. My hands grip the wheel so tightly
that they've gone numb. I take one hand off to shake it out, then the
other. Ryan has probably already discovered his missing tire. The last thing
he'd ever assume was that I could change a tire, but owning a run-down car
has its advantages.

Last year when I got stranded on the side of the road, Rock came to my
rescue but made me change the tire on my own. Said I needed to learn and
be self-sufficient, so naturally I put my skills toward a life of crime. I glance
back at the high-quality tire in the back seat and snicker.

The note I left behind begged him not to tell anyone until ten thirty.
That'd give me half an hour to get inside and film. Then I told him to call the
cops and tell Mom. I hope he understands. He's too good to be a criminal.
As for Vicky, she's going to kill me for sure. I laugh, envisioning the temper
tantrum she's throwing right about now after finding out I bagged her from
a mission. I drive faster.

I won't jeopardize the future of the only boy that ever looked past the
weirdness and dog dirt to get to know me. And I refuse to set up my best
friend to be a repeat offender. What happens to juveniles that break the law
twice, even when it's standing up for what's right? It's not a tea party with the
governor. And Jimmy, my shining bright star, I couldn't risk dragging his good
name through the mud. Let's be honest, he doesn't let that wheelchair hinder
him in any way, but he'd be at an unfair disadvantage. Yes, he was supposed

to stay in the car and be the lookout, but missions never go as planned. Never! My life has never once gone as planned. I can't risk contaminating them with my bad luck. They mean too much to me.

Plus, I'm unstable. If Peter erupts again, God only knows how bad this adventure will go. I feel good now, in control, but that could change. That's why, tonight, it has to be me. And it feels good to be alone with nobody to worry about.

But I'm not really alone. Dad's photo lies in the passenger seat. "Let's do this, Dad." I wink at him.

It's early. The street is quiet. I have my pick of businesses to park at, as they have all closed for the night. I steer the Corolla into a wholesale bakery shop. The store has an easy entry and exit to make a clean getaway.

Ten minutes pass, then a couple, dressed in clothes more suited for a night at a posh restaurant than a dogfight, emerge from a red sports car.

Click. Got their photo.

Here comes the kind of people I'd associate with this establishment. Four sleazy men sporting T-shirts with images of women in erotic positions and knives dripping blood onto roses strut into the garage. One is swigging a bottle of Jack Daniels, and the others drink from beer cans.

Click. On the record.

For the next half an hour, I snap over a dozen photos of people. The strange thing is that they are either dressed for a business meeting or dressed for the back of a Harley Davidson. Is there a VIP section? Shivers of contempt flutter up my spine.

It's time to do this. I mentally prepare for the gruesomeness. I don dark jeans, a black T-shirt, and Ryan's black hoodie, nothing that stands out in a crowd but something that can protect me in a fight. It's the invisible look—straight hair, little makeup, drab clothes. So I can get in and get out.

One more glance at Dad. "Wish me luck."

My car door flies open, scaring the shit out of me.

"You bitch!" Vicky yanks me out of the driver's seat.

"Shut up," I whisper loudly.

"I can't believe you did this to me." Her serrated whisper cuts deep.

"You can't get in trouble again, V."

"Let me be the judge of that!"

Ryan stands behind her in silence, which is more hurtful than her tirade.

"Sorry." The panic rises. A spider leg unfurls. "You guys make me nervous."

"Well, too bad! Just deal with it," Vicky says.

She knows *dealing* with it is tricky, but there's no time to argue.

"It's almost ten," Ryan whispers. No smile. Just words. He doesn't even glance in my direction. His eyes look over and around me.

"Fine, but don't blame me when everything goes wrong," I whisper.

Vicky pins me with her stare. "Back to the original plan. I'll be in the Rover with Jimmy. You two inside."

Neither of us moves.

"Hurry!" Vicky could run an army.

Ryan and I enter separately. It's crowded. My elbows nudge lots of people I'd rather not have any contact with. Ryan and I stay close to each other but act as if we're not together. It's not difficult, considering how furious he is with me. He's dressed in a well-tailored dress shirt and designer slacks and looks maximum handsome. He's working the Mr.-Turnberry's-guest-list angle, assuming there is one.

I discreetly snap a bunch of photos, but nothing has begun, so I still have no proof of criminal activity. This place smells of filthy sweat, dirty people, and garbage rotted by the heat. A lady's perfume diffuses the air, but it can't cover the rancid stench of corruption. I really want to leave.

A man wearing a too-small shirt over a too-large potbelly speaks into a microphone. He's announcing the dogs' names as if they're heavyweight champions. There's fear and rage in the dogs' eyes as they're paraded around. Someone has bred this evil into them. Someone has made these dogs vicious. Someone has trained madness into their blood. Probably that same someone that secured Trax to the railroad and tightly knotted the rope. Any of these people could be that someone.

Vomit pools in my throat, but I steel my nerves, and the strength builds. I want to hurt these someones, all these faceless cowards.

The dogs are let loose. It's more sickening than I'd imagined in my nightmares. This horror I couldn't fathom. I wince at the first bite. There's blood everywhere. My eyes drop and never leave the ground as I point the phone in the direction of the brutal sounds. People shove me, pushing and nudging my position. I try to hold the camera still as I'm inched away from Ryan.

Hatred lives throughout this place. It's an unavoidable pulse that beats through everything, including me. Now I despise myself for not telling Fred, for not stopping this. I can't bear it any longer. Even though I focus on my feet, the suffering of the dog that's not winning is unmistakable. I must stop the killing. I have to blow our cover and save that dog!

Dad's voice comes through loud and clear. *These dogs need you to be strong. Film the fight and the faces of the guilty. You can do it, Tweety. Get the evidence and put an end to these jerks.*

It's my gut-wrenching job to make all these despicable humans pay for participating in this barbarism. Just a few more seconds of video footage. A few more. That's enough. I look up. Cruz! He's only ten feet away. Shit! I tilt my head down and slide on the hood. I sneak another peek, and our eyes meet.

Have his eyes always been so beady and sinister? He looks like a vulture. A short, hunched, filthy rat with wings.

Something in me snaps. I plow through the crowd, the infectious hate surging through me, like a burning current producing superhuman energy, speed, and rage. The entire arena falls away from my reality, and I tunnel vision a path directly to the rodent.

He turns and scurries his way toward the back, toward the darkness, away from the crowd.

I follow. The people have their backs toward me. The lights face the other direction. The bodies cast shadows, deepening the darkness. It's a dead end. I've cornered him. We're alone.

"What are you doing here?" Cruz asks in a strained whisper.

"I'm bringing you and your boss down."

He sneers and seems to grow taller. "You're dead."

The words are precise and undaunted, but my anger is some sort of force field that ricochets the fear away.

"You're busted." I lift my phone and snap his picture.

Something glints in the small beam of light that seeps through the gaps in the crowd like a wink. It's a blade. He jabs it at me. I slide to the left. The shiny edge passes next to my waist. I think it punctures the sweatshirt. I think there's blood. I retreat. He's got the momentum, and my bravery fades.

Kendall, what have you done? You're not Black Widow!

Another quick jab comes at me, and again I slide. My ankle rolls. I crash to the ground. The impact thrusts the phone from my grip and explodes my bones. Cruz squats over me. The knife plunges down, aimed at my abdomen. My eyes smash shut, but there's no pain. He's not there. He's been knocked to the ground by a couple, obviously drunk and looking for a dark corner to hook up.

I jump to my feet, but he tackles me to the ground. My back tenses in pain, paralyzing me for a second. We spiral down a slope. I'm shoved against the fence. The knife rises again, but before it comes down, I donkey-kick the fence, propelling my body forward. The force is powerful enough to knock him over. His head smacks the rocky ground. He's dazed. Now I've got the advantage.

"It's her. Dog Girl," he yells.

I panic and land a solid punch to his temple. His head flops, dizzying him some more. I punch him again to make sure he's out. Hyperventilating breaths attack my lungs. I frantically glance around, but no one's paying any attention to the scuffle that just occurred in the corner. It's too dark and loud, and these people are accustomed to fights. I stand and let the tremble leave my legs before attempting to walk away. But there's a shadow of a man. He's skinny and young.

I muster a stare so threatening it could rival Jennifer's daggers. Dad's strength and determination materialize in my eyes. My voice lowers. "He thought he could steal my wolf."

The kid doesn't look the slightest bit surprised. "I bet on the wolf too." His voice is an emotionless rebound.

"You what?" My voice spikes, but my eyes remain steady.

He's leaning against the fence I was just pinned against, picking dirt out of his nails. He was just going to lean there while I got stabbed to death. And the dogs' lives mean one thing to him—payday.

He says, "Yeah, the wolf's gonna take this entire event. No way a dog can kill a wolf."

Kill a wolf? Dragon!

The blood drains from my limbs, and I wobble away from the sociopath. I don't get far before running into Ryan. By the hollow of his cheeks, he's gathered the same information.

"I found the dogs." He grabs my arm and leads me toward the front.

Mr. Turnberry waltzes in.

We pivot and run the other way, deeper into the evil arena. I tighten my hood, but Ryan doesn't have one. His head lowers while his eyes dart around, looking for another way. We're trapped. Everywhere we step leads back to the fight. We want out.

The sound of a shovel scraping the concrete assaults my ears. Someone's cleaning up. Vomit fills my mouth. I swallow it down.

My phone!

"I dropped my phone," I whisper to Ryan.

"Where?"

"Over there." I point. We're not that far away. We've gotten pushed back into the nightmare to avoid Mr. Turnberry.

The creepy kid holds my phone. Contention brews in his multicolored eyes, but he gives me the phone. As I take it, his other hand wraps around my wrist. "It'll cost you."

"Let her go," Ryan's voice shoots over my shoulder. Four crisp one-hundred-dollar bills thrust forward. "You'll never get this much at a pawnshop."

The creep drops me for the money.

The phone is black and won't turn on. I tuck it into my pocket. Cruz still lies on the ground. A bracelet of hair-raising sensations circles my wrist as if the creep still had a hold on it. Ryan leads me away.

By now our path is clear. Mr. Turnberry's gone. Ryan pulls me through a door and into a dark, damp room. It's like a carnival's haunted house, but right now I'm numb to everything. The Devil himself could be conjured up, and I wouldn't be surprised. I definitely feel the hardening of my soul, and I'll never be the same again. Maybe Satan is real. He was in Cruz's eyes tonight. That surely wasn't the same man I had worked with at the rescue.

Ryan's arm slips around my waist. He whips it back. "You're wet." He touches my side some more. "It's blood." He pulls up the hoodie and turns his cell phone flashlight on me. "It's shallow." His shoulders sag as the breath leaves his lungs. He pulls me into his arms.

The abhorrent cheering and heart-wrenching cries penetrate the walls.

"Where are the dogs?" I ask.

The light breaks up the shadows, revealing useful objects.

"Get that." I point to the tire iron.

He picks it up. "This way."

I grab box cutters and follow.

We make our way through the blackness to find the holding room, but a guard stands between the cages and us.

"Stay back, I have an idea," Ryan says.

I put my hand on his shoulder. He glances back. His face flattens in seriousness, but mine reflexively smiles. I want to say a million things, but all that comes out is, "I trust you."

He nods, but there's no reflex smile, just a grim expression. He hands his phone over. "Text Jimmy to call the police now!" He holds the tire iron behind his back and waltzes into the room.

I remain behind under cover of shadows, and text.

Me: Call 911!

Jimmy responds with a thumbs-up emoji.

The door is slightly ajar, and I watch Ryan. He's poised and looks as if he has all the confidence in the world. He says in an adamant tone, "What are you doing?"

The guard stutters, "A ... huh?"

"Mr. Turnberry specifically told you to keep the wolf separate. That's not the cage we sent over!" Ryan continues to speak in a powerful voice.

"That's the only cage I seen," the guard replies, but his voice hitches, and even though I can't see his face, I get the impression that his eyes flit around in desperation, trying to locate the appropriate cage.

Then Ryan backhands the tire iron, and the guard's body falls to the floor with a thud. I rush into the room and freeze. I look at Ryan. He looks at me. We both look at the man on the floor. This lasts probably a second but feels like ten minutes. I snap out of it and cut open all the dog cages, including Dragon's. Chaos breaks out. Mr. Turnberry steps into the room, followed by two dangerous looking men.

"What's going on?" Mr. Turnberry asks.

Ryan pushes over a bench. Tools clatter and glass breaks, creating a hazardous maze. We crawl behind cages. The loose dogs turn on one another. They turn on us. I shield us from vicious, hungry teeth with the box cutters. Snarls and growls and blood fill the room. An angry pit circles us like prey. Dragon pounces it. Men shuffle through the dogs, debris, and cages. I glance around the room, searching for a way to escape. It's not a room. It's a garage.

The large garage door spreads across the back wall. If I could open it?

I elbow Ryan and point to the garage door. "Where's the remote control?"

We both scan the area. There's a control mounted on the wall about ten feet away. Ryan lunges and hits the button. The grumble of the door opening distracts Dragon from his fight. Mr. Turnberry and his men turn to find the source of the noise. It's a long enough distraction for us to slide under the door as it slowly opens.

The dogs have already slipped under the door and scattered down the street, their senses far keener and faster.

I grab a fistful of Dragon's hair before he gets away and bolt to the Range Rover. I cross the street, but Ryan's not beside me. When I reach the Rover, the engine is running.

Good! V's on it.

I coax Dragon into the back seat, throwing his hind legs in with the Herculean strength that comes from a tidal wave of adrenaline. He's in the car for a second, then leaps out. I reach for him, but he's too quick. He's running away.

"No!" I yell to him, but it's no use. He isn't turning around. All energy drains from me as he disappears into the night.

Across the street, two men attack Ryan.

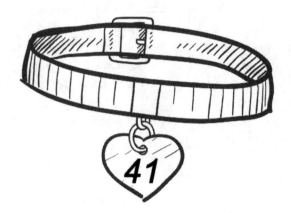

"Drive!" I slam the car door and run back to Ryan.

"I'm not leaving you, K," Vicky yells.

I turn and glare at her. "Go after Dragon!"

Three top-of-the-line blacked-out wheels and one ugly spare spin wildly as she speeds away.

The crowd remains in the backyard, anticipating more repulsive fun, utterly unaware of the commotion in the front. Ryan fends off the two thugs with his tire iron, but he's not doing a good job at it. He's been hit, blood gushes from his nose, and he's stumbling.

There's no time to plan, so I shout, and the men turn. This second gives Ryan a chance to utilize his weapon to its fullest effect. He knocks out one guy with a forehand swing, but the larger one turns and lunges, scoring a direct hit to Ryan's side and a kick that sends him to the ground, writhing in pain. The tire iron clinks as it skids across the pavement. The man reaches for something inside his pants. I scream, but the man is determined. He points a gun at Ryan.

I charge at the man and thrust my head into the side of his rib cage, a football tackle maneuver I've seen but never physically done. It's as if my head plows into the solid mass of a bull. My neck crunches, and my cut skin rips farther, stinging like madness. But he's off-balance and stumbles. The gun goes off. The noise deafens me, and all the pain from the fight vanishes. I'm flung into survival mode, and life accelerates around me.

Headlights blind us all. The bull man stumbles some more, then runs away. I rush to Ryan and help him to his feet. I pick up the tire iron for self-defense, but his attacker runs away. Blue police lights flash, and sirens blare. Complete chaos breaks out as people scramble to escape.

Vicky pulls up. "Get in!"

We dive into the back seat.

Vicky slams the gas pedal to the floor, and we're on I-95 in a flash, heading north. The cars on the highway whiz past in a blur, just as all the night's events are. My brain struggles to organize the details, but the slime of savagery fades my recollection like a gory night terror disappears with daylight.

"Where's Dragon?" I cry.

"Sorry, K. I tried." Vicky's knuckles whiten as she grips the wheel and concentrates on the road.

The inside paneling of the car closes in on me. I'm stuck in a stifling bubble of sticky, hot air, fighting to regain my senses. My blood-slickened fingers open the air-conditioning vent. Soothing cold air blows on my face. Soon, Ryan's voice is no longer a muffled, distant sound. Slowly, his words become intelligible. He's recounting all the particulars to Vicky and Jimmy. I hear the pain in his voice, both emotional and physical.

My hands roam over his body.

He looks at me, bewildered.

"You're not shot."

"No," he says.

"Are you okay?" My voice shakes.

"I'll be okay."

"I'm so sorry." I rub my hands on my thighs, ridding them of dirt and blood.

"Me too. It's going to work out. The police came." His eyes fall. He doesn't have the heart to give me false hope.

I choke out the truth. "Dragon's gone."

Next thing, we're inside my house. Mom and Shane yell at us with tears streaming down their faces. Vicky plops on the couch, and Jimmy parks by the table. I'm still holding on to Ryan. He leans into me for support while cradling his ribs. Greenish-purple bruises halo Ryan's eye. His nose is bloodstained, and fresh red oozes from an eyebrow cut.

He could've died.

I support his weight. "You saved my life. You swung that tire iron like a tennis racket."

"Killer forehand," he jokes, but can't laugh without agony.

Mom yells, "What's wrong with you all? Did you even think!"

Shane barks, "You could've been killed!"

I release Ryan to pull off the hoodie. The T-shirt underneath lifts, revealing the gash.

"You're bleeding!" Mom shouts.

Shane rushes over.

"It's fine," I say, but my body catches up to the pain. The cut starts to ache more and more.

"It's not fine!" Shane storms off to the medicine cabinet.

Abruptly, Rock and Fred barge into the packed living room. Rock engulfs me in his arms, then casts rage-filled eyes at all of us. His embrace tortures my injured side.

"Peanut, you're gonna kill me," Rock roars.

"I'm sorry," I say.

"Tell me everything." Fred stands feet apart, hands on hips, and eyes ablaze like a cartoon cop. It should be funny, but it's not.

We obey. My phone takes a long time to turn on, so Ryan shows him his photos and footage first. I'm worried that psycho kid erased my data somehow. He was definitely going to chuck it for money. Thankfully it powers up. I show him all of the photos and video I shot tonight, as well as last Saturday.

Shane lifts my shirt and gasps. Blood weeps from my laceration. "This needs stitches." Her head shakes the entire time she pats me with peroxide and covers me in Steri-Strips. She does the same for Ryan's face. His chest is clear of blood, but a bruise blooms from within.

"Cruz was there." I don't mention that he could've knifed me to death, or that I came face-to-face with a sociopath.

Fred's phone rings. He answers it, retreats outside, and paces while talking. He comes back inside. "They've arrested Cruz and about fifteen people, and there's plenty of evidence to secure convictions." Fred's expression sours, making his face slide downward.

My heart shatters. What kind of grim evidence was found?

"They've also picked up two of the dogs you let loose. The others have run away." Fred's eyes drop. "No wolf. Sorry, kiddo."

My broken heart barely pumps enough energy to speak. "What about Mr. Turnberry?"

"They didn't find him." Fred pinches the bridge of his nose.

"Aren't you going to arrest that piece of scum?" Vicky asks.

"Wish I could, and maybe something will emerge, but he's not on the videos from tonight," Fred says. "I have Kendall and Ryan's testimony, but no hard evidence."

"What about the photos from last Saturday or that he hired Cruz?" I argue.

"Unless Cruz has hard evidence, it's all circumstantial," Fred says. "But we'll present it all and do what we can."

"He's going to get away with it." A lump drifts up to my throat.

"Nobody's getting away with anything. I guarantee these men will be thrown in jail for a long time," Fred says staunchly. "We've confiscated guns and might be able to match the ballistics to the bullet that was lodged in Trax. ... Maybe." He gives us a strange nod.

I think he's trying to say *we done good*, but obviously he can't say that, all things considered.

"Thanks, Uncle Fred." I swallow, but the lump sticks.

He punches my shoulder and shakes his head. "Is this it? Are you done being stupid now?"

I shake my head. "Now that I've seen what I've seen, I'm gonna fight harder, advocate louder. This shouldn't happen anywhere, ever."

"I understand, but you're lucky. If Cruz had seen you—" he looks at me and Ryan "—who knows what would've happened."

Ryan and I exchange a glance. Ryan's eyes soften, and I know he'll keep my secret, but I decide to tell the truth. "Cruz is the one that sliced me down the side."

The room stills, then everyone comments with grunts and sighs. I think the floor shakes from Rock's rage.

Fred's face stiffens. His throat widens as he swallows, attempting to cool off his temper. "He'll talk. I'll make sure of it. I'll use your statements and try to keep some of your foolish actions out of the incident report, but I don't know." He shakes his head and walks to the front door. "I gotta go do damage control. You two should see a doctor." He refers to Ryan and me. "Vicky and Jimmy, go home and get some rest," he orders. "I may need more statements tomorrow." We nod. "Sis, lock up, set that alarm. Got it?"

"Got it," Shane says.

"Cat." Fred nods to Mom.

"Fred." She nods back. They exchange an unspoken understanding.

The door slams behind him, and a haze of remorse mixed with relief clouds the room and all our emotions.

Ryan stands to leave but wavers and sits back down.

"Cat, we need to get him to the ER," Shane says.

Mom and Shane step into action, escorting Ryan to the truck. Vicky rushes to my side as I follow them. Her elbow wraps around mine. Somehow, her tiny body bears my weight and guides me into the back seat.

"He's going to be fine." Her steady voice and tenacious stare give me the needed courage to remain level-headed and strong for Ryan.

I smile in thanks to my best friend. Jimmy's behind her, my ever-present sunshine.

Rock says, "I'll drive Vicky and Jimmy home, then come back to tend to the dogs."

"Keep an eye out for Dragon." The words drip desperation. My eyes search wide across the field, down the pathway to the vet, through the barn. I hope to see glowing eyes on the horizon, but I don't see anything, just blackness.

"I will, Peanut. I'll walk the perimeter. He'll come back. Don't worry."

But all I can do is worry. Fear and angst pack my blood, flowing down my limbs and pumping through what's left of my heart.

"Alright." Mom waves a quick goodbye and drives to the hospital at full speed.

Ryan's hand is cold. I squeeze it and don't let go, even as we exit the truck. Eventually, the nurse separates us, and I'm forced to release my grip. My hand is frozen. I gaze into the empty palm. I'm scared. What have I done?

Ryan glances back and smiles. Then he's out of sight, but the ghost of his dimples haunts me. The icy room freezes my bones, making me curl into myself. I want to fold and fold and fold until I disappear. Peter's vivarium is vacant. I'm hollow. What I wouldn't give to hear the hiss of his cynical, loathsome comments in my head. But I'm on my own.

Shane and Mom talk, but I don't listen. It's just white noise in the background. They should be a comfort, but they're not, because Ryan's tennis career could be ruined. And Dragon's out there where he could get hit by a car or picked up by the wrong kinds of people. People like that psychopath.

We've been here for an hour. I've been stitched up, and now we wait. I'm balled up in the small chair, hugging my knees. I've been frozen in fear, too scared to cry, blink, or even think. The appearance of the nurse breaks the numbness, and all my senses react at once. My tears spill. My breaths quicken. My brain bursts. I hide it all. Suck it in.

The nurse escorts us to Ryan's bed. He's dressed in a mint-green hospital gown. His wan skin and dried lips break my resolve, and the tears spill again. I swipe away the evidence.

"My nose isn't broken, but my ribs are bruised; one's fractured, but I'm fine. I can go home," he says with a crooked smile.

Thankfully, he looks worse than he is.

"I guess this young man is going home with you all," the doctor states.

"Yes, his parents are out of town." The edge to Mom's voice reminds me that we're still in big trouble.

"Okay. He's technically an adult, so he can sign his paperwork. I've given him ibuprofen for the pain and inflammation. It seems to be working. He has a prescription for Co-codamol if he needs something stronger."

"I don't want it," Ryan interrupts.

"It's just a prescription. You don't have to fill it," the doctor says.

"No." Ryan's blues adamantly harden.

"Okay." The doctor nods. "No tennis for six weeks. He has no lung obstruction, but should he have trouble breathing, have him looked at by his primary. These types of injuries normally heal fine on their own with lots of rest."

While the doctor speaks to my moms, Ryan strokes my hand and smirks. He whispers, "You were worried about me?"

"Of course I was." My frantic tears have been replaced with a severe case of the giggles because Ryan wiggles his eyebrows and flashes his irresistible, boyish grin. He fought off a criminal with a gun, risked his life, and fractured his rib—and he's making googly-eyes to make me laugh. "I'm sorry you can't play tennis for a while."

"No biggie."

It is a big deal, but he's being considerate. "I tried to keep you safe."

"Uh, yeah, my tire?"

Chuckling, I say, "It's in the back of my car, parked at the bakery."

"I'm just glad it was me and not you."

"So chivalrous." I peel away the bandage to show him my stitches.

"I guess you're stronger than you look."

I lean over and kiss my wounded Prince Charming.

Shane clears her throat, and Mom throws poisoned darts from her eyes at us.

"Let's go," Mom says.

Once we're home, I drill Rock about Dragon. There's no sign of him anywhere. Mom refuses my request to search the grounds.

She collects four of our largest dogs and Rascal from the barn. Next, she locks the door and sets the alarm. "You'll sleep down here with the dogs," Mom growls at Ryan.

"Okay. Thank you, Cat."

She glares at him, but her soft, caring eyes deceive her, and it's apparent she's happy he's here safe.

"Good night, Mom." I give her a hug and a kiss.

"Night, honey." She kisses me too, then pulls me in for an embrace. Her back shudders. She holds on longer than usual. I barely hear her whisper, "I love you."

"I love you too, Mom."

Shane brings Ryan loads of pillows and blankets to make the old sofa more comfortable. "Are you sure you'll be okay on this lumpy couch?"

"Yes, thanks, Shane. I've got more than enough pillows should I need them."

"Okay, but don't hesitate to get me if you need anything."

He nods.

"Don't be afraid to wake me up." Shane pats his back.

"But don't wake *me* up," Mom growls.

"Don't listen to her." Shane swats the air, dismissing Mom's threat.

"Okay." Ryan smiles.

"Well, good night, you two. I'm so glad you're safe. Don't ever … " But she can't finish the sentence. She gives me her good-night hug and kisses, which I return times ten.

After they retreat upstairs, I turn to glance at Ryan. "You can sneak into my room later."

He cocks an eyebrow.

"If the couch is uncomfortable. I'm just looking out for your health."

"Sure you are."

"Of course."

"I'll risk the couch over Cat. She'd break my ribs for sure."

The living room becomes an ocean between us. He sits on the couch, while I stand at the foot of the stairs, ready to climb up. Only I can't leave him. The slack of our binding rope slowly tightens, diminishing the ocean to a lake to a harbor to a stream.

"We make good crime fighters," he says.

"We do." The joke stings, because the reality of the seriousness of our night sets in. "We really don't. It could've been so much worse. You could've been shot."

"Yeah, and you could've been stabbed."

My fingers brush the bandages stuck to my side. "I was stabbed."

"Come here," he says in a gentle voice.

I'm conscious of every step taken, of the space between us lessening. And when I finally reach him, I'm heavy and fall onto the couch next to him. He tucks a strand of my hair behind my ear and smiles. I don't know how he does it, but his half smile, his eyes—they melt me. I'm like a blob of Jell-O with a revved-up libido.

"There's our cupid." He gestures to Rascal, who is sprawled out on his back, exposing his underbelly, his pink tongue flopped out. "That day I saw you with Rascal was hilarious."

I laugh and cringe at the memory. "That dog has caused me a lot of trouble."

"The way you were just yourself with dirt on your face. You were so confident."

"Me?" I'm astounded. That isn't an accurate interpretation of that day.

"You." He nods.

"Not quite how I remember it." As I recall, it was a sequence of humiliating events.

"Well, that's the day I knew I had to get to know you. So we're keeping him. And we're keeping Lucy and Dragon." His voice drifts away.

My breath skips.

"He'll come back."

My eyes sag as they look into his. There's no conviction in either of us, only grave hope.

"Trust me." His gentle lips steal a kiss on my cheek.

"I do." My eyes close, letting the sensation of his kiss heal me.

He inches closer. "You intrigue me."

My eyes open. His lips curl into that lopsided smile I love so much. Those dimples. Butterflies fill my stomach. Their wings beat hard against my insides. It's like I'm stuffed with actual alive butterflies.

"I've had the best spring of my life."

I laugh. "You enjoy having a gun pointed at your head?"

"I'm never bored or alone, and I'm always amazed by your beauty ... honesty ... courage ... "

"Stupidity!"

"I love you, Kendall."

That's it. My arms wrap around him. I nip his neck and whisper, "I love you too."

His mouth finds mine, and we kiss with a forceful passion more meaningful than before. Hunger surges and controls me, and I thrust him down and crawl on top of him. He moans, but not in a good way, in a painful way.

"Oh, sorry." I pull back. My stitches throb. "God, that was a disaster. I suck at this."

"No, you don't."

He lifts my shirt and softly circles my wound with his fingertips.

I throw the shirt off. It's filthy anyway.

His warm blues rove over my bare skin. He caresses a scar below my left breast half-hidden under the band of my sports bra. "What's that from?"

"I got between a rottie and her food when I was eight. If Rock hadn't been there, I'd probably be dead."

He continues to devour my body with his eyes.

Slowly, I bend forward, taking care not to put any pressure on his ribs. My hair falls, curtaining our faces. Even with a swollen nose, he is a relief sculpture. Shadows slope and circle his angles. I delicately kiss each shadow. His fingers trail up and down my back, awakening everything inside me, releasing the thousands of butterflies. They're free. I'm free.

I feel heavy and light. My hands hold the armrest behind his head to brace myself. Our bodies rock rhythmically. It's decadent and dangerous.

I don't know how many minutes pass; all I know is I don't want to stop. Then the one thing no lusty teenage girl wants to hear—Mom's voice.

"It's time for Ryan to go to sleep … alone!" Mom's words fly like arrows, rushing down the stairs from her bedroom, targeting us.

I push myself away as he clings to my arms. We both giggle. He grimaces with each intake of air. He shouldn't be alone when he's injured.

He says, "You better go." But he holds tight to my hands.

He finally releases them.

I begrudgingly lumber up the stairs and into my room, where I stare out my window. Scanning. Searching. Finding no glowing eyes.

At sunrise I rush to the window. No Dragon. It was a dream. I'd seen him in the field. His presence felt real.

Ryan shuffles into the kitchen, half-asleep and moving carefully. His hands fumble around and knock over the coffeepot. The glass carafe nearly tumbles onto the floor, but he catches it.

In a groggy, full-of-sleep voice, he asks, "How do you work this thing?"

"Just press the button. Shane sets it every night." I laugh. He has a complicated self-grinding espresso machine at his house, but my cheap Mr. Coffee is a mystery. "How'd you sleep on the couch last night?"

He gives me an exhausted look.

"I get it. I feel like I've been run over by the Science Diet truck."

"Let's just say, the extra pillows were necessary, and the dogs snore. And Rascal farts."

I howl. "I know. His farts are the worst. The only dog usually allowed to sleep in the house is Lucy. I guess Mom wanted them in here for protection."

"I'd bet my scholarship Rascal was a strategic move."

"Could be." My eyebrows rise.

Mom waltzes down the stairs, overly awake, with a giant grin confirming Ryan's suspicions. We burst into giggles and snorts, Ryan cradling his ribs in pain.

"What are you two laughing about?" She heads straight to pour herself a cup of coffee.

"Nothing," I say.

She huffs. "Fred just called."

"What'd he say?" Ryan and I both ask.

"He's almost here. And it's all linked. The dogfight, the hate mail, that nasty vandalism, and the arson," she says.

"I knew it. How?" I ask.

"Before you'd even rescued Trax, I started making some phone calls. Gary over at Palm Beach Animal Control and Sue down in Miami had a few concerning incidents too. I tagged along with the agents to investigate, but we couldn't make any connections." Mom swigs her coffee.

"You were always gone." I'm the last to get coffee.

Mom nods. "They were concerned too, but we weren't thinking about dogfighting. Thought we had some sicko on our hands, might end up finding little girls' bodies next. That type." Mom takes another gulp.

"God, Mom!"

"Yeah, well, it happens. I must've hit too close to home, and the guys running this dogfighting ring didn't like it. They had a good thing going with Cruz, right here under my nose. I basically offered the lambs up for slaughter."

"You couldn't have known, Mom." I wrap my arm around her and try to absorb some of the guilt she's harboring.

"They used the graffiti and the fire to scare me, and it worked. Keeping you safe became my top priority. You're still grounded, by the way."

I ignore that last sentence. "I'm sorry, Mom. You've had so much to deal with."

She pats my hand and shrugs off my admiration like every astounding thing she does for our family is no big deal. "The repairs kept me so busy I barely had time to help the other agents investigate. But the bastards didn't count on you." She winks at me. "And you proved more relentless than me."

Fred knocks. Ryan opens the front door for him. Mom's already poured him a cup of coffee before he sets foot inside.

"Here, Fred." Mom hands him the cup.

"Thanks. I need this." He gulps down half the cup.

We all stare at him in silence.

"That Cruz is a real dirty crosser. Trying to pull one over on me. Keeps saying he planted Trax to shed light. Says he wanted the dogfighting ring to be discovered, but he feared for his life, so he had to keep working for them. Bullshit." Fred walks into the kitchen and pours more coffee.

I follow on his heels, my mind reeling with rage. "Cruz tied Trax to the railroad tracks!"

"Yep. And he thinks somehow he can swindle a deal. I'm telling you, I got a lot of guys that want any excuse to beat his ass. I gotta restrain them. An innocent dog." Fred throws up one arm and grunts.

"But it's bullshit?" Ryan asks.

Fred nods. "Yes. From what I've gathered from the others, Cruz wanted the publicity. Probably didn't expect it to be quite so widespread and out of control, but he wanted the higher-ups to sweat it out. Plant the bomb, then be the one to defuse it and look like the hero. None of these types are irreplaceable, and they know that, so they gotta find a way to be valuable." He takes another gulp and sighs. "A couple days in jail with guys scarier than him, and I have no doubt Cruz will give up the real story."

"Has he ratted out Mr. Turnberry?" The disgust in my voice bellows.

"Unfortunately, not yet. He said he didn't know anything about Dragon's involvement. I know he's lying. I guess he'd rather throw the dogfighters under the bus than Lucas Turnberry. Remember that." He looks at me. His final words are an unmistakable warning.

"If Dragon doesn't survive this, if he vanishes without a trace, Mr. Turnberry has to pay for it." I pace the room.

Ryan says, "He will. Right, Fred?"

Fred lets out a long, gruff sigh. "Look, we'll find the wolf eventually, and Lucas won't be allowed anywhere near him. That I *can* guarantee."

"Okay." I nod, but my hopes knock down a notch knowing Mr. Turnberry is probably lawyering up right now.

Fred grabs a coffee to go and heads back to work.

Soon, the kitchen smells of bacon and eggs. After we eat and clean up, I notice Ryan's at the front window, his eyes fixed on something.

"Dragon?" I rush to look too.

He shakes his head. "The media. Channels ten and eight and the UCF documentary team."

My heart lifts, knowing I'll see Adam and Marie.

"And here comes Animal Planet and the YouTube girl."

"Johanna?"

"I guess it's true news does travel fast." Ryan's hand rests comfortably on my back.

Shane rushes over to peer out the window.

Mom curses under her breath.

Shane sighs. "Here we go again."

The four of us stand and gawk as the crowd gathers.

"You better go handle this." Ryan smirks.

I match his grin. "I better."

His eyes light from within.

Mom and Shane both say in worried voices, "Are you sure?"

"Yeah, I know exactly what I want to tell them."

With my head held high, Ryan and my moms beside me, I walk out the front door and down the wheelchair ramp to the flashes of cameras and chatter of reporters bombarding me with questions. I stop, square my shoulders, and let them all lean in with anticipation. I'm no longer scared of them. Peter isn't filling my head with the hiss of harsh commentary and insecurities. My thoughts are my own.

I tell the story of how Dog Girl and Beach Boy—no, Tennis Boy, with his killer forehand—took down the bad guys of dogfighting with the help of their two sidekicks, Black Racer and Juvie Chick.

The words spill effortlessly. No fear or anxiety. And I'm proud to say I helped to destroy the dogfighting ring, save the rescue center from foreclosure, and keep Dad's dream alive. I had a part in all of that. And here comes my future strutting toward me.

"Miss Shepherd." A woman wearing an Animal Planet T-shirt weaves her way through the gathered crowd.

I shake her extended hand.

"Can we talk?" she asks.

"Absolutely." I grin. Perhaps, if I make wise decisions now, my future influence might be more significant than the Mr. Turnberrys of the world.

"Looks like you're a popular girl." The lady from Animal Planet gestures to the growing gathering.

I gaze out over the crowd. Vicky and Jimmy lead a large group of kids and teachers from school, even Chloe and her boyfriend. Rock's bald head shines in the distance. Everyone I love is here to support me.

"Move out of my way, bitches." Johanna plows her way through.

I expect to get a camera shoved in my face. Instead, her arms wrap tightly around me. My eyes widen and land on Ryan, who shrugs.

Before I know it, Rock is making his way through the crowd too. People part to let him pass. They're terrified to get in his way.

No. That's not what awes them.

I blink and do a double take. Rock's holding a leash. It's connected to a collar that circles the neck of a wolf covered in dirt.

"Dragon!"

Rock lets the lead go.

Dragon runs straight into my arms.

#DirtyWolfGirlandProud2B

Acknowledgements

There are so many people I need to acknowledge. This book wouldn't be here if not for my incredible agent, Sharon Belcastro. She sent my manuscript back to me several times before I'd even signed with her. It wasn't ready yet. And she was right. I am forever grateful for her sharp eye and constant assistance. She wasn't the only agent to read and assist this story, but she's the only one that wanted to see it after I'd made the changes. Because my rejection letters were so intensely detailed and thoughtful—they'd actually read the story—I knew I had a hit. I also knew I had to work harder. Thank you to all those wonderful agents who took the time to offer much needed advice.

A huge hug to Georgia McBride and Swoon Romance for taking a chance on *Dog Girl*, for seeing the wonder in this story, and the value it'll have in the marketplace. Thank you for believing in me.

All of the Tampa Writers Association has my gratitude, but there are a few I want to personally acknowledge because they served as beta readers. Annette, your expertise in animal care was much appreciated, as was your constant support and encouragement not to mention your detailed critiques. Alycea, you have a knack for finding my bad habits. Thank you for pointing them out and helping me learn and improve. Cassie and Allison, my mom and daughter duo detectives that saw the good and bad in my early manuscripts. Thanks for loving my characters and rooting for them. Lisa, you took so much time and care beta reading and offered invaluable advice, thank you. And to the FWA conferences crew, Marggie, Kim, Sarah, Diane, Cassie, Bob, Anne, Annette, and Alycea, that provided loads of laughs and alcohol making the terrifying interviews and thought provoking sessions doable.

A big thank you to Madi, Mia, and Malia. You're teen perspectives truly helped. You kept me honest and up to date. Thank you for being fans of

Kendall and Ryan. I know you'll see a lot of changes since you last read it. I hope you like them.

Thanks to my friend, APRN, and beta reader, Jen, who loved the story and encouraged my commitment to it. Sorry the antagonist is named Jennifer.

To my beta reader, Priyanka, thank you for all of your input, especially regarding Kendall's anxiety. You helped so much.

I really hope I didn't forget anyone. A giant hug to all the readers.

To my editors: Tasha Vincent, who was there in the very beginning. Tremendous thanks for wading through the rough drafts. I'm so glad we met in the mall selling books. I treasure your critiques, kind words, and guidance. To my online friend and editor, Heather Cashman, your keen eye caught so many things to be improved on. Yes, I may have thrown the paper across the floor in angry refusal before realizing you were correct. You truly made Kendall's journey a better one. Lastly, to Jackie Dever my editor who put the magnificent final touches on *Dog Girl* and made it shine. Your critiques and suggestions were spot on and when you liked something, your comments always made my heart smile.

And always to my children who provide constant inspiration. Of course, tennis plays a role in this story and I thank my oldest son for finding the love of the game. He was the first child to enter the teenage realm and fill my world with excitement. I was with my daughter when inspiration struck. Not sure if the birth of this story would have happened without our trip to Puerto Rico. The middle child, the one that read *Dog Girl* with enthusiasm even though she would rather have been watching Grey's Anatomy. Then there's my youngest son who is continuing the tennis tournament journey and suffering my endless hugs and kisses because he's the last skin baby in the house. The last child doomed to suffer his crazy mom's writing chaos, but always patient, well almost always.

A giant thank you to Jason for understanding and picking up the slack when the house chores or meal prep went undone because my nose was buried in my laptop. He's the best steak griller around and probably loves dogs more than I do.

And to my parents that have never let me down. I couldn't do all that I do without your help. My furry babies are so thankful to have had you feed them and play with them when I left before the sun came up or got home after it had gone down.

Lastly, I acknowledge all the animals in my life. They loved me uncondi-
tionally and shaped the furry characters of this book.

Mama Cat
Tiger
Ginger
Cricket
Ralph
Kahlua aka Clyde because my dad decided that suited him better
Nikki
Gizmo
Bear
Samson
Frankie aka Nana from *Peter Pan*
Duke aka Duke from *Dog Girl*
Juicy
Kwan Tai
Dallas
Taz aka Rascal from *Dog Girl*
Shadow
Charlie
Luna
Tank

Gabi Justice

Gabi Justice is the mother of three children and numerous animals. Her time is spent writing, reading, taking care of her animals, and hanging out with her family. She loves traveling and tennis and has traveled to several countries for her children's tennis tournaments. Living in Florida, she's spent many vacations at Disney World or Universal Studios and relishes a thrilling roller coaster and make-believe world. A graduate from the University of South Florida, she earned a BA in English Literature and enjoyed an eclectic college career in many creative arts – theater, art, film/TV, dance, creative writing.

CONNECT WITH US

Find more books like this at http://www.myswoonromance.com

Facebook: https://www.Facebook.com/swoonromance
Instagram: http://www.instagram.com/swoonromance
Twitter: https://twitter.com/SwoonRomance
Tumblr: http://swoonromance.tumblr.com/
Georgia McBride Media Group: www.georgiamcbride.com

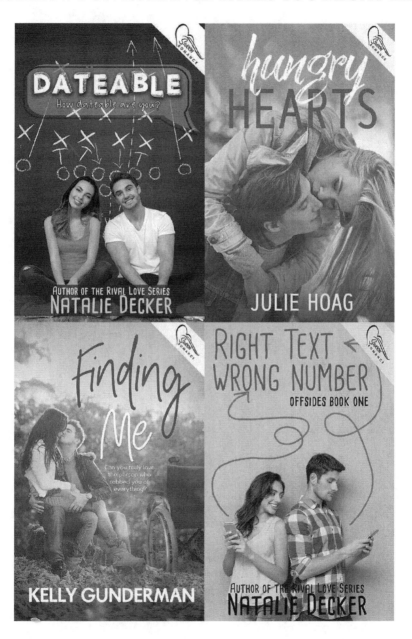